ε for *The Escapement*

A *Publishers Weekly* Top-Ten SF/Fantasy/Horror for Fall 2021

"Lavie Tidhar is a voice to be reckoned with. With *The Escapement*, he fearlessly crests the wave of the New New-Weird with a wild, decadent hybrid of *The Dark Tower* and *Carnivale*. A vivid beach read, if the beach was made of greasepaint and gunpowder."
—Catherynne M. Valente, author of *Deathless*

"To say *The Escapement* is unique sells it way short. It's part weird western and part quest; half dream and half epic adventure tale set in a memorable Daliesque landscape. Tidhar lets his imagination run wild in this vivid book, all told in spare, beautiful prose."
—Richard Kadrey, bestselling author of the Sandman Slim series

"Can we just all admit now that Lavie Tidhar's a genius? He's written another brilliant book—a beautiful fever dream that somehow manages to be laugh-out-loud funny, psychedelically weird, and deeply moving."
—Daryl Gregory, award-winning author of *Spoonbenders*

"*The Escapement* is absorbing, bizarre, haunting, and compelling. Lavie Tidhar continues to shatter the boundaries of literary and genre fiction with a novel that is equal parts horrifying dreamscape and an affecting meditation on parental love. There are a lot of books out there, but this is an experience."
—David Liss, author of *The Peculiarities*

On *Unholy Land*

Best Books of the Year
NPR Books • *Library Journal* • *Publishers Weekly*
UK Guardian • *Crime Time*

"Lavie Tidhar does it again. A jewelled little box of miracles. Magnificent."
—Warren Ellis, author of *Gun Machine*

"Thoughtfulness, suspense, imagery, and beautiful prose. Highly recommended."
—*Fantasy Literature*

★"Incredible twists on multiple realities and homecoming. This latest from Campbell and World Fantasy Award winner Tidhar (*Central Station*) is fascinating and powerful."
—*Library Journal*, starred review

On *The Violent Century*

"A tour de force."
—James Ellroy, bestselling author of *L.A. Confidential*

"A stunning masterpiece."
—*The Independent*

"Unforgettable."
—*The Jewish Standard*

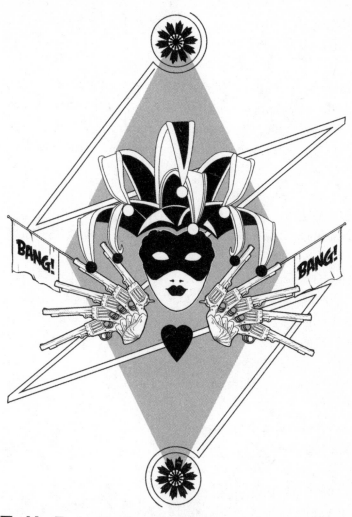

THE ESCAPEMENT
LAVIE TIDHAR

TACHYON · SAN FRANCISCO

The Escapement
Copyright © 2021 by Lavie Tidhar

Cover design by Elizabeth Story
Interior design and map by Elizabeth Story
Author photo by Kevin Nixon; copyright © 2013 by Future Publishing

Tachyon Publications LLC
1459 18th Street #139
San Francisco, CA 94107
415.285.5615
www.tachyonpublications.com
tachyon@tachyonpublications.com

Series Editor: Jacob Weisman
Editor: Jill Roberts

Print ISBN: 978-1-61696-327-9
Digital ISBN: 978-1-61696-328-6

First Edition: 2021
9 8 7 6 5 4 3 2 1

Selected Books by Lavie Tidhar

The Bookman (2010)
Osama (2011)
The Violent Century (2013)
A Man Lies Dreaming (2014)
Central Station (2016)
Unholy Land (2018)

"Tiny forms in huge empty spaces"
—JOAN MIRÓ

Think, Lord, a jester's life is sad,
Change not "he has" into "he had,"—
Grant me my son.
—FROM THE CLOWN'S PRAYER

ONE:
THE RED FLOWER

THE BOY WAS VERY STILL in the small white bed.

The man held the book and he tried to keep reading from it but his voice wouldn't work and after a moment he let it drop by his side.

The boy's breathing was shallow but regular, and his eyes were closed. The man thought of a day in spring, not that long ago, when he'd first taken the boy to see the circus. They'd walked hand in hand through the Midway, past candyfloss and popcorn stands and the flashing lights of carousels and hay-rides. They saw the clowns. He bought the boy a balloon and gave it to him to hold, but the boy let it go and the balloon floated far high into the sky, until it vanished. The boy had burst into tears and the man picked him up and held him close in a hug he wished would never end, and after but a moment the boy smiled and held the man's face in his hands and looked at him with such trust and love that it would have broken the man's heart had he let it. Dad, he said. Dad.

He looked at the boy so still and so small in the bed.

I can't, he said. I can't.

The machines around the boy beeped and chirped.

He staggered out. Down, down to the ground floor.

Out of the doors into the night.

A vehicle went past flashing blue and white light.

It rained.

A small red flower bloomed by the side of the hospital gates.

A small red flower bloomed by the side of the road. The Stranger paused, following the trail of red drops down the slope. Pine needles crunched underfoot. The broken moon hung in the sky, as deformed and grotesque as a clown mask. The Stranger had been travelling for a long time, searching for the Flower of Heartbeat, and he was destined to travel for a long time more. He shifted the long rifle on his back and then drew it, cautiously. He proceeded down the slope.

The night sky was clear and in the distance he could see the first signs of a coming storm. Loose ankhs flashed on the horizon, and glowing ichthys fish burst briefly in vibrant blues and reds. The storm was coming, but it was still a long way off. The air smelled fresh and sharp. The Stranger discerned pine resin, gunpowder, blood. The pine trees were not tall and the needles brushed against his face as he passed through the trees.

When he reached the clearing he stopped, and then he put the rifle back over his shoulder. He stood stock still, looking at the bodies.

The massacre must have taken place only a few hours earlier. There were eleven bodies, and some had been shot in the back and some from the front but either way they were all dead. Some had tried to flee their attackers and were gunned down, and some had stood stoically and awaited their death. The Stranger smelled greasepaint, candyfloss, gunmetal oil. The tattered remains of a yellow balloon lay on the ground.

The Stranger examined the scene of the massacre. He had been witness to such scenes before, in other places, far away from there, but he never grew indifferent to such a sight.

Eleven clowns lay on the ground.

Unusually, while five were Augustes, four were Whitefaces and two were Hobo braves. The two Hobos had stood up to their attackers, and the Stranger noted the remnants of the custard pies they had thrown.

He took everything in methodically, though he was furious inside. The Stranger could not abide an unkindness to clowns.

Each of the clowns had been scalped, and the Whitefaces' red ears had been sliced off, as were some of the Augustes' red noses. The Stranger knew it was the habit of bounty hunters to do this, to create a brace of the ears and noses for easy transport and to display; and that they would be aiming to collect a bounty for this, the massacre. Clowns were—as much as anyone could tell—indigenous to the Escapement, while people were not. And there was just something about clowns that people inherently hated. Now they killed them for their sport.

The Stranger also noted that not all ears and noses had been taken. Perhaps they had been interrupted, or were spooked, as they were collecting their trophies. He glanced around him a little more uneasily. The symbol storm was still distant but it could herald the coming of other forces, though sometimes it did and sometimes it didn't.

None of this was, strictly speaking, his business, but he determined nevertheless to make it his. He, perhaps alone in all the strange travellers upon the face of the Escapement, felt that clowns brought joy. And somewhere, elsewhere, in that other place, there lay a boy who had loved clowns.

Perhaps that was enough.

The Stranger went back up the slope and retrieved his horse. He spurred it down, but around the copse of trees, and he noted the hoofprints of the horses and the direction they went.

The riders went in a hurry. Something *had* spooked them, he decided. The hooves had scattered pebbles and dust as they ran at full gallop from the scene of the massacre. The Stranger noted five sets of hoof prints on the ground. He spurred his own horse to a light trot. He did not bury the clowns. Golden spirals and tetractys flashed briefly overhead on the horizon. The Stranger rode away into the distance, following the scalp hunters.

He rode from sunrise to sundown without encountering a living soul. Only once was he startled, when the sun began to dip in the sky and the air grew cooler. He had looked west, where the storm had passed, and for just a moment, it seemed to him that a shape appeared there, immense against the sky: an immovable stone statue, as tall as a mountain, sat in a carved throne; and the sun shone over its head like a crown.

At the sight of this apparition the Stranger spurred his horse into a canter, and when he next looked the giant figure had disappeared as though it were never there.

That night, when he camped in a dry riverbed, the Stranger

heard the distant sound of fighting: booming, maniacal laughter that echoed magnified across the Escapement, part-sob and part-screech, and the thump thump thump of giant feet, trodding on the ground, and the terrible ticking of clocks, and this was accompanied, or perhaps accentuated by, irregular bubbles of sudden, and somehow awful, silence, a sort of negative sound which had the horse whinnying, but in a sort of quiet desperation.

The Stranger listened to the sound and unsound of battle as it raged on for hours, until at last it grew faint and passed on, the two unseen armies skirmishing to the west.

By noon the next day he came to a small crystalline brook flowing in between two green hills. The horse drank greedily and the Stranger drank sparingly and filled up his skins.

The land had changed over the past few miles and in the air he could smell distant smoke, hints of custard, and fresh horse shit. By the side of the brook he found a circle of stones engulfing another dead fire, and in this one the coals felt still warm. The Stranger, thoughtfully, checked his rifle and his revolvers.

He had turned to check on the horse next, which was feeding on the grass by the bank, when he saw the child.

The face that stared at the Stranger from the bushes on the other side of the brook was pale white and startled. The child's eyes were large and solemn, the mouth an exaggerated stroke of red, the nose a conical red protrusion. The child looked into the Stranger's eyes, with that strangely melancholic expression that is unique to clowns.

The Stranger put his finger to his lips. Never taking his eyes off the child, he walked back to the horse and mounted.

The child watched him as he rode away.

The horse walked at a steady pace, and it was only when they had turned round a bend in the stream, and the child disappeared from sight, that the Stranger spurred the horse into a full gallop.

He was concerned that the boy had managed to sneak up on him so, but clowns had that ability, sometimes: to move in deathly silence, to go unseen, to pass upon the flesh of the world without leaving a scar. The Stranger rode fast and furious now, not in impatience but with an urgency he did not feel before.

This was clown country.

He heard the outlaws even before he saw the smoke of their campsite, for they seemed to feel themselves secure, and they did not bother to hide their fire or lower their voices, and, moreover, seemed to him drunk. The Stranger tied his horse to a tree and proceeded alone, his rifle in his hands.

The outlaws' voices echoed weirdly in between the hills, and the Stranger navigated carefully, listening to the voices as they seemed to vanish and reappear elsewhere without warning; and he realised then why they must have felt so safe.

For this part of the Escapement must have been a maze or, rather, a broken part of one. He navigated slowly, treading from one hill to the slopes of another, across a brook and past a conifer which he marked carefully with a knife.

And yet when he proceeded he found himself traversing the

same patch of ground, or encountering a tree identical or near as made no difference; and the distance to the assassins' hideaway never varied. Their voices echoed queerly from one end of the maze to the other, but within the transference of voices he thought he began to discern a pattern.

The Stranger knew that all mazes are ultimately solvable. There was the random mouse approach, and there was wall following, there was the Pledge and the Trémaux.

But mazes on the Escapement were not always *static*, and the unwary traveller using one such method could find that the maze itself would shift unexpectedly around them.

The Stranger, instead, listened for the absences of sound, and it was into their gaps that he directed his steps, ignoring the geography, until the voices coalesced into clearer coherence around him, and their wild seesawing slowed and became recognisable speech, and he was through at last into the heart of the maze.

A small mill house of weathered white stone stood on the bank of a gently rolling stream. There were cracks in the stone and moss grew in between the cracks. The wheel of the mill had long since broken into several pieces, which lay sunk in green grass and mud.

The Stranger took shelter behind a rock as he watched the hideout.

A small fire burned by the side of the old mill house, and five men were seated around it, their horses grazing in the nearby grass.

The men were laughing. They passed a bottle around between them.

They were as ordinary denizens of the Escapement as you could find. Two were veterans, or perhaps simple victims, of the war. One had half of a melted clock fused into his abdo-men, a black minute hand protruding from his naked flesh like a cockroach's antenna. The other had living bees trapped in a glass globe embedded in his thigh, and the bees beat angrily against the glass.

The man, with a long-practiced motion, would occasionally tap sharply on the glass with the end of his fingernail, momen-tarily silencing the creatures, who would soon start up again.

He seemed comfortable enough in his lot.

The other three were unaffected with materiel.

Altogether, they were an ill-kempt, ramshackle group. The Stranger noted that the bottle they drank from was clear, and that the liquid inside was a pearly white colour, and he knew that the assassins must have found substance, and had mixed it up with water to create this drink, which was called Sticks.

The men, he knew, would be comatose in minutes. They must have felt confident in the security of the broken maze, enough not to even leave a guard.

The Stranger squatted behind the rock and waited.

The men fell one by one, noiselessly.

They lay on their backs, their mouths masticating without sound, their eyes staring unseeing at the sky, their limbs twitch-ing occasionally. The bees were silent in the veteran's thigh.

The Stranger was about to rise when someone beat him to it. He saw a shadow detach itself from a hiding place on the opposite hill and begin to journey down.

It was a woman, wearing two low-slung pistols on her hips, a wide-brimmed hat which shaded her face, and a large, curved, nasty-looking knife on her thigh, which she unhooked smoothly and held as she descended.

She crossed the stream with long, easy strides. On the other side of the bank her head turned, for just a moment, and in the light he saw her face. She wore a black patch over one eye and her other was a deep, calm blue.

She approached the men who were unmoving on the ground.

The Stranger watched the woman rummage unhurriedly through their stuff, upending their bags until she found the brace of clown scalps and this she held for a moment as though considering its worth before she put it back on the ground.

Next she went to the nearest of the lying men and knelt beside him with the knife in her hand.

She cut the man's throat with one quick, clean motion.

The Stranger watched. The man spasmed on the ground, and his legs kicked as though by their own accord, and then he went still. The woman had cut through his carotid artery, with a skill the Stranger could almost admire.

There was not much blood.

The woman next went to the veteran with the bees, who beat against the walls in their glass prison, but the woman ignored them. She killed the man with the same easy motion. When he died, the materiel in his thigh did not change but the bees with a soft sigh sank to the floor of their cage and expired.

The third man was different.

Perhaps he had imbibed less than the others, or perhaps what horrors he saw of that other world, with its traffic-choked streets and its electric lights, the call of sirens, with its accountants, banks and accruements, the ring of phones, the smell of grease and diesel, had pushed him back to the Escapement.

As the one-eyed woman brought her knife to his throat, the man's hand flew up and grasped her wrist, taking her by surprise. With a scream, the man, small and wiry, leaped at the one-eyed woman, pushing her off balance. As she fell the man reached for his gun and the woman desperately tried to reach for hers.

A shot rang out.

The sound filled the air before it was snatched away at the edges of the maze, and there it echoed queerly, carried from one path to another. For a moment the two adversaries seemed frozen, as though not sure which of them had been shot. Then the man, slowly, toppled to the ground, half his head missing from the rifle shot.

The woman stood up. Her hands and her face were covered in gore from the killings, but she did not seem to mind. She let go of the knife and her hands rested on the butts of her pistols, but she did not draw.

She watched for where the shot had come from.

The Stranger came out from behind his rock. He was holding the rifle. He was not quite aiming it at the woman, but he wasn't not aiming it, either.

The woman watched him. Her single eye was very blue. She did not yet draw her own guns, but the Stranger assumed she could draw them very quickly if she wanted to.

He took a few steps down to the camp. He saw that some of the dead man's brain had sprayed the wall of the old mill house. The woman watched him calmly. She did not take her gaze off him as he approached.

"They're mine," she said.

The Stranger approached. He nodded. He pointed the rifle low, and shot the nearest of the two still-living men. He then went and stood over the other of the two veterans, the one with half a clock embedded in his abdomen.

"Bounty?"

"They're mine," the woman repeated.

The Stranger pulled the trigger and shot the man who was fused with materiel. It was a head shot, like the other.

Now all five men were dead, and he was left alone with the woman.

"Why a knife?" he said.

She shrugged. "Why waste a bullet."

"How did you get through the maze?"

Her gaze was icy. "I've been here before."

"They killed eleven clowns, three days' ride from here."

"They killed many more than that," she said. "You just shot two of the Thurston Brothers."

"They were brothers?"

"Only the gimp leg and the first guy you shot. But that's what they all called themselves, as a gang."

"It isn't much of a name."

"They're worth two hundred ducats each," the woman said. "Paid by the Central Bank of Jericho."

"For killing clowns?" the Stranger said, surprised, for the hunting and murder of clowns was often encouraged by the rough settlers of the Escapement.

"For bank robbery," she said.

"Ah."

The Stranger looked at the corpses. "Two hundred ducats each? That's a lot," he said. "They don't look worth shit to me."

"They're mine," she said, again, patiently, as though explaining a complex problem to a child. "I've been following their trail for a while, you know. Since outside of Marxtown, where they hijacked a shipment of substance bound for the rail terminal there. I lost them in a symbol storm somewhere in the Doinklands, and by the time I got out they'd gained a lead on me. . . . I finally tracked them here, but by then they'd gone off on a scalping raid. I breached the maze . . . and waited. The only thing I wasn't counting on was you."

The Stranger nodded.

"That's fine," he said. "I wasn't after them for the money."

"Prospector?"

"Sometimes."

"I'm Temperanza," she said. She said it a little expectantly, as though he should know the name.

"You're a bounty hunter?"

"Aha. Do you mind . . . ?"

He shrugged. Temperanza removed her hands from the butts of the pistols and picked her knife up again. The Stranger watched her. She worked efficiently, with quiet confidence, until she had taken the scalps of all five men, or what was left of their scalps.

"I really would have preferred if you hadn't shot them," she said.

"Are you complaining?"

"I didn't need your help, stranger. Don't flatter yourself." She sawed off ears where the scalps were too damaged to collect.

The Stranger picked up the bottle of Sticks. Only a tiny bit of dirty-white residue remained at the bottom of the bottle. He tossed it at the mill house wall, where it shattered.

Something moved behind the walls of the mill.

"What was that?"

The Stranger held his rifle, and Temperanza had drawn a gun before he'd even noticed.

That sound behind the walls came again, louder.

The Stranger and Temperanza exchanged glances, wordlessly, and then they moved in tandem, circling the mill.

The Stranger saw that an old wagon was hidden behind the walls of the mill. A faded yet garishly painted sign on the side of the wagon said PROFESSOR FEDERICO, THE MAGNIFICENT.

A door was set into the side of the mill and the dirt had been recently swept, and someone had put a Welcome mat on the ground. A few balloons and bits of broken mirrors, and strings of flags and paper streamers hung from the door.

"*Streamers?*" Temperanza said.

The Stranger said nothing and he stepped over the threshold with the rifle in his hand.

"You there!" a voice said. "You killed my men and they were ever so helpful. That wasn't very nice of you, you know."

An elderly man in a white lab coat and white whiskers and moustache materialised out of the harsh bright lights. "They brought me clowns," he said; and somehow the words brought a chill to the Stranger's heart.

The old man carried no weapons. He rubbed his hands together as though cold.

"Well, never mind, never mind," he said. "They drank too much and cussed *awfully*, you know."

"What the fuck?" Temperanza said.

The Stranger held on to his rifle.

But the old man seemed not to register their weapons in the least and, after a moment, he brightened up. "Well, come on in, come on in!" he said. "I get so few visitors out there. It's partly why I chose this place, of course. Just on the edge of the Doinklands and away from people and their judgement. I am so busy, so busy you see. It's quite fascinating."

"What's fascinating?" Temperanza said.

"Clowns!" the old man said. "Oh, I am so sorry, I did not even introduce myself. I am Professor Federico, the M—"

"Magnificent?"

The old professor beamed. "You have heard of me?" he said.

"Lucky guess," Temperanza said.

"Can I offer you anything? Water? I make my own, from re-cycled urine."

". . . No, thank you."

"What is it you *do* here, exactly, Professor?" Temperanza said.

She had not taken her finger off the trigger.

"Come, come, see for yourselves!"

The man vanished deeper inside. The Stranger paused. It smelled bad in there. It smelled of chlorine and ammonia, and they in turned merely overlaid a deeper smell, of piss and blood and fear. . . . It smelled like a hospital in there, he thought.

He looked to Temperanza. She just shrugged.

They followed the old man deeper within.

They came to a makeshift room where a large steel table sat in the centre. Bright lights rigged to some sort of prim-itive generator chased away all shadows. The Stranger saw pieces of materiel lying about, the strange ethereal debris left after some storms: a fur-covered saucer, cup and spoon; a half-melted clock; a miniature tree growing earrings.

His eyes were drawn away from the horror on the steel table.

He saw the specimens collected behind glass: the giant femur bone of a boss clown. The grinning skull of an elderly Hobo. An entire petit Pierrot floating in murky formaldehyde.

Temperanza stared aghast. The Stranger wanted to throw up but didn't.

He looked at the table.

A dead clown lay on the smooth metal surface. He had been stripped naked and dissected with some care. Skin flapped open, a ribcage exposed.

"What . . . have you *done?*" the Stranger said.

"Oh, this? My research, man! My life's work. I will title it, *On the Nature of Clowns.* You see," Professor Federico said earnestly, "we must try to *understand* clowns! Are they alone a species native to the Escapement? What is the taxonomy of clowns? What is the role of the Big Boss Clown in the social hierarchy of their society? Why is it that they so rarely speak? How come they slip on banana skins so often? And why aren't they *funny?*"

"Nobody likes clowns," Temperanza said. "The Bank has a standard bounty on them. But this . . . You are insane."

"Why aren't they funny!" the professor said, ignoring her. "I cut, and cut, trying to find the answer. This one's a White-face. Note the large red nose, the elongated feet bones. The genus, of course, is *Homo farceur.* The large feet may suggest an evolutionary need to run from predators. I have so much work to do, still. So much work. You see," he said, peering keenly into the Stranger's face as though sensing in him somehow a fellow aficionado, "we know they're clowns, but what *kind* of clowns?"

Which was when Temperanza shot him.

♦ ♠ ♦

In the back of the old mill the Stranger found a cage with iron bars, and behind the bars he found a shudder of clowns.

The prisoners stared at him as he opened the door of their cage.

They emerged one by one out of that tiny enclosed space, too many of them than seemed possible. They tripped and slipped and collided and fell. They never spoke.

The last, an elderly Hobo, carried a small red flower on his breast. He motioned for the Stranger to smell it.

The Stranger leaned over, and the flower squirted him with water in the face.

The Stranger laughed.

The Stranger and Temperanza rode away together. They torched the mill on their way out. They made sure it burned, that it burned well, so that the horrors inside would never be found. There were some questions one should never ask, the Stranger felt. Some people wanted an answer to everything, every detail of the world explained, every corner mapped and named. The Stranger had been travelling for a long time, searching for the Flower of Heartbeat, and he was destined to travel for a long time more. He knew that some mysteries just were.

And that one should never be unkind to clowns.

TWO:
TINKERERS

THE MAN WALKED ON. At a corner store he bought a fifth of bourbon. He drank it furtively, his walk aimless, through streets and neighbourhoods teeming with unsaid words. The very nature of the light was furtive, he thought.

He passed a baker shop with a beggar in rags sitting under the awnings. All he could see were bright brittle eyes under a hood, the face swaddled in shadow.

A woman accosted him. She wore fingerless black gloves. Her breath smelled of sweet liquor, coconut and rum. She gripped him by the shoulders. She only had one eye. She leaned close to him and whispered in his ear, urgently, telling him not all was lost, telling him about a place beyond the Mountains of Darkness, and of a flower that grew only there. She let him go and he walked on, deep into the night, until he heard footsteps, running, and someone shouting his name. His keys dangled in his hand. He let them help him through the door and he sat on the couch and waited for them to leave, politely, but frozen, until he heard the door shut close.

Then he lay down on the sofa, with his head on the boy's stuffed toy clown, and it was only then, finally, that he started to cry.

A painter's brush smeared strokes of yellow paint over the horizon, and the sky gradually turned a light blue. The clouds in the sky resembled clowns' balloons, and the Stranger, on his horse, looked up over the Escapement. The landscape stretched away from him in all directions, with not a town or a hamlet in sight. They were two days' ride away from the broken maze and clown country, and at least another day, he calculated, from a small outpost town called Kellysburg. Clumps of scorpion weed and five-needle prickly leaf lit up the parched earth with vivid blue and yellow colours.

"What is it that you are looking for, Stranger?" Temperanza said.

She drew on her cigarillo, and blew out two perfect rings. The rings floated in the air until they linked with each other, and slowly dissolved in the breeze.

"A flower," the Stranger said.

Temperanza gestured at the land around them. "There are plenty of flowers here," she said.

"It is called the Ur-shanabi, and it lies beyond the Mountains of Darkness."

At this Temperanza's face grew troubled and she smoked for a few moments without comment. Thick drops of ash blew away on the breeze. Then she said, "I am not familiar with that flower, nor with that particular geographic region."

"But you have heard of it?"

She shrugged. "Stories. Stories are all we have, really, in this world or the other."

"What sort of stories?"

"I don't know," she said. "Don't ask me."

"I must," he said. "I need to know. I have been searching for an awfully long time."

"Time means nothing, here."

"Please," the Stranger said. He knew that she was not quite what she seemed. Temperanza's frown deepened. She blew out three smoke rings in quick succession. The rings interlocked above the brook and seemed suspended there.

She said, "Long ago, I was on a wagon travelling in the north. It snowed, and the sun went down faster than we expected. The horses were scared, you could smell their fear, and their breath turned to fog in the air. Our breaths, too. A storm was coming over the mountains, an ordinary one at first but then we began to catch flashes, pilcrows and octothorpes and trefoil knots . . . The horses whinnied and ran faster, the wagon jostling from side to side. It was then that we began to hear the sound of giant footsteps, of vast and ancient stone pounding the frozen earth."

"The Titanomachy."

"It was only a skirmish, I think now. We never saw the Colossi, only heard them. One of the horses turned into a crow and flew away. My companion's ear melted like wax. It dripped on the seat. As for my eye—" She touched the eye-patch, gently. "Well."

After a moment she continued.

"We came to a stop. Another of the horses had gone so mad with fear that I had to shoot it, out of mercy. We waited out the storm, infinities bursting around us. Then it was all over, and the storm had passed and the battle, it seemed, simply moved away. We'd survived. When the sun rose up we saw that the road was littered with materiel, a giant, melted trumpet, a dead lizard with a tiny tree trunk for a tail, bowler hats, a sunflower with a baby's face. We left the wagon, unhooked the horses and rode on. Shortly after we came to what remained of a farmhouse. There was a well outside, and the skeleton of a donkey beside it. We sought shelter inside the house, from the elements. It was there that we discovered the soldier.

"He wasn't, by then, much of one. One of his legs had been blown clean off, and the remaining one had turned into a string instrument of some sort, long and delicate, with silver inlays, but it had no strings. The man was drunk on Sticks. He went in and out of lucidity. I think he knew he did not have long for this world, or the next.

"He spoke of many things. It was hard to understand him, and harder enough to care. We grew resentful of his constant babbling. We wished him to die but still he held on. He was a camp follower of sorts. He followed the Titanomachy where it went. And yes. He spoke of one place, with huge figures standing motionless in the sand, and dark mountains, so dark it was as though they sucked the light and made it vanish. But they were far in the distance, I think. These mountains. He was not very clear. Colossi, and some sort of guards at the mouth of a tunnel at the end of the world. I don't know of any flower." She jerked her cigarillo into the brook. It hissed when it touched the water.

"No. I lie. He said he wished to smell one, and he used a name. The one, I think, you used. It seemed important to him, as though, if only he could smell it, all would be well. Then he died."

She shrugged. "It wasn't a meaningful or noble death, you understand. He passed from here. Whether he lives still in that other place or not I do not know. We didn't bury him. The next morning, as soon as the snow had stopped, we continued on our way. Now I avoid the cold, and when a storm comes, I take shelter."

She was silent then. The Stranger mulled over her words.

"Thank you," he said at last.

They rode on, in companionable silence, accompanied only by the horses' farts and occasional whinnies, with the horses chomping at the wildflowers or bits of grass whenever they could find them, and the Stranger gnawing, from time to time, on a chunk of dried beef. The Escapement here was flat for miles, the sky serene, and there was no sign of the war.

As the miles passed by, the Stranger rocked in his saddle, lulled by the unchanging landscape.

He was brought sharply awake, however, at the sound of a pistol shot.

The sound was somewhat muffled, and yet it carried across the open air of this part of the Escapement. When the Stranger scanned the horizon he saw, snaking across the plains, what seemed to him the remnants of a white road and, coming in from the west, a plume of slowly rolling dust, which might have been a wagon.

The Stranger made to head that way.

"No," Temperanza said.

"No?"

She shook her head, simply. "No."

"But I want to see—"

"Do you know the old saying?" Temperanza said. "Shadow battles stone. The lizard scuttles—"

"From the glare of the sun, yes," the Stranger said. "What of it?"

Temperanza shaded her eyes and looked out, to that distant plume of dust that was slowly approaching along the white road.

"Beware of shadows, Stranger," she said. "I'll see you in Kellysburg, I guess."

Then she rode away, and took her share of the outlaws' horses with her; and the Stranger marvelled, for he knew then what she was; and one did not often see a member of the Major Arcana ride out into the world.

The Stranger, whose curiosity had led him down all kinds of twists and turns in the maze of the Escapement and his quest, did not heed her advice but rode on, and he directed his horse at the road, at a point ahead of where the wagon would eventually arrive.

The other horses followed him obediently enough.

They crossed the distance, passing through isolated patches of flowering cactuses and fever trees, stopping only for the horses to drink at a shallow pool of muddy groundwater. All this while the small plume of dust continued to roll sedately enough along the white road, and as it came closer the Stranger could see that it was indeed a wagon, and it was pulled by two dirty, piebald donkeys.

When the Stranger at last came to the road he stopped, and the horses milled nearby. Such roads could be found, from time to time, in the farther reaches of the Escapement, and who, if anyone, had built them, or for what purpose, the Stranger didn't know. They led from nowhere to nowhere, seldom in a straight line but rather in a crazy curlicue of a twisting and looping arabesque, like secret inscribed messages in the landscape. In the Thickening, that part of the Escapement that had been partly subdued, or perhaps suborned, by the relative thickness of population, there were no ghost roads, and the settlers had constructed new railway lines. And yet even those would often find themselves subject to the external forces of vastation and revel, and loop upon themselves or terminate, abruptly, in a place where no terminal was.

The Stranger waited, his hands resting on the butts of his revolvers, and watched the road. The solitary wagon traversed along its path, never straying, and as it came closer the Stranger could see that it was a small, wooden wagon, once brightly painted, but the paint had faded and flaked, the wooden wheels creaked, and it was only when it pulled to a halt, at the sight of him, that he saw the legend along the side of the wagon, which read TINKERERS.

Two small figures sat up front in the wagon driver's seat. They were both bundled in rags, as though to defend themselves, vigorously, against a cold snap, which could, they seemed to silently suggest, strike at any moment. One was male and the other was female, though it was hard to tell them apart. They were both watching the Stranger and neither said anything, nor did they appear to hold a weapon, and the Stranger did not draw his own guns.

The male tinkerer at last pulled out a long-stemmed pipe and stuck the bit between his teeth. He next reached for a small cloth bag, from which he extracted tobacco, which he proceeded to stuff into the bowl. Having done that he struck a match, and a fragrant, cherry-flavoured smoke rose into the air and turned it blue.

"How goes it, stranger?" he called. His voice was surprisingly youthful and high, and not unpleasant. "I am, uh, going to assume you are not a highwayman or a horse thief"—his tone suggested that he was far from convinced on that score but for lack of a better choice, was willing to give the Stranger the benefit of the doubt—"and anyway, as you can see, we are but, uh, poor tinkerers, with nothing worth stealing." He made a desultory gesture at their wagon.

"I heard gunshot," the Stranger said. "Some distance back."

"Nothing to do with, uh, us, I'm sure," the tinkerer said.

"I can't think where else it could have come from."

The tinkerer shrugged. The woman beside him cupped her hands and whispered into his ear. He nodded. "Ah, yes," he said. "We ran into some problems a while back. That's right. A wild, uh, snake. My, uh, sister had to shoot the creature. A shame, really. We value all life."

The woman measured out a span with her hands.

"A big one," the tinkerer added, unnecessarily.

"A snake."

"It is, uh, so."

"What happened to it?"

The woman whispered again. The man said, "We left it behind. I was, uh, asleep at the time. I sleep heavily, you see."

It was none of the Stranger's business, and he did not press the point just then.

"Why do you travel on the road?" he asked instead, with curiosity. "Would it not be quicker to follow a straight route to your destination?"

"Ah," the tinkerer said. "You would, uh, think so, wouldn't you. But the straight route is seldom the quickest, on the Escapement. And there is an old saying, uh, it is the journey that matters, stranger, not the destination."

The Stranger nodded politely. The man puffed on his pipe. In the wagon behind them, something banged sharply, and for a moment the wagon rocked from side to side. The woman ducked under the canvas and disappeared, and the Stranger heard a sharp crack, followed by silence. The woman re-emerged and took her seat. She smiled at the Stranger and her teeth were white and even.

"Rats," she said.

"I'm, uh, Fledermaus," the man said. "This is Titania."

"Howdy, stranger," Titania said. "And which way are you travelling, if you don't mind my asking?"

"Kellysburg," the Stranger said. "I have horses to sell."

"You won't get much for them there," she said.

The Stranger shrugged. "I'll take what I get."

"Won't we all," she said, and laughed, a surprisingly coarse sound. "As it happens, we're on our way there ourselves. Not by choice, you understand, but it's the nearest habitation for miles, and bad trade is better than none, in my opinion."

"You're, uh, welcome to travel with us," Fledermaus said. "The road doesn't go to the town but it passes nearby, or, uh, more correctly it fades as it nears the outpost. Or so it was the last time we've come this way."

The Stranger considered the two of them. At last he nodded, and the woman, Titania, took the reins and cracked them, and the two piebald donkeys began to pull the wagon without complaining, slow and sedate, as though they had all the time in the world. Fledermaus continued to draw on his pipe, and Titania hummed the same few bars of some wordless tune the Stranger didn't recognise. He spurred his own horse, walking alongside them, and the other horses followed behind—though he noticed they gave the wagon itself a wide berth, and walked some distance from it by the side of the road, on which they seemed reluctant to step at all.

Overhead, the sky's hues deepened by degree, from azure to ultramarine; as the sun traversed the sky, the travellers cast sfumato shadows, which lengthened as they trailed their originators like furtive ghosts. The road itself changed with the light, growing in turns ivory and snow, ghost-white and smoky, until the Stranger found it easier to not look directly at the road at all, but ahead.

"You came from out west?" he said.

"That we did," Titania said.

"I saw signs of a battle there, six, seven days back, on the horizon."

"That is, uh, true," Fledermaus said. "Yes. Yes. We think. We were still some distance away and when we saw the coming storm we sought shelter."

"We reached the place a day and a night later," Titania said. "After the battle had moved on. But we are not scavengers, stranger. We didn't dally there."

"You found nothing of value?"

He saw them exchange a glance, though what it meant, if anything, he didn't know.

"What is of value to some is of no value to, uh, others," Fledermaus said.

"We do not trade in substance or materiel," his sister said.

The sun had dipped low in the sky when they caught sight of a dwelling in the distance. As they came closer, they saw it was an abandoned chapel. The weathered stone was dirty with dust, and the broken windows gaped open like empty eye sockets. Over the steeple, only, there remained a stylized balloon painted a vivid red, and it swallowed the reflected light of the sun. The travellers, by unspoken consent, halted there, near the old church.

"A strange place for a mission," the Stranger said.

When people had first come to the Escapement, one could still see the Wild Harlequinade pass by on the prairies, and even Harlequin itself was sometimes seen. Some of these new arrivals fell under the spell of clowns, long before ever the first strongman and the first bearded lady married and brought into being the great circus houses of Boreal and Mercator.

And they believed.

There were still preachers, here and there, though you had to wish you'd never meet one; and here and there upon the body of the Escapement there were still the missions, built in years past, when people still found magic in a pratfall of clowns.

The tinkerers did not offer a reply to the Stranger's comment. The woman, Titania, disappeared again under the canvas, and could be heard moving around inside the wagon. The man, Fledermaus, climbed down from the bench and stretched, though it was hard to make him out under his layers of clothing. He looked like a short, fat mushroom.

"It will do, stranger," he said. "It will do."

That night, the travellers built a small fire and sat beside it. The horses grazed in a patch of grass nearby. Earlier, Titania had disappeared into the Escapement, and when she returned there was a bloodied hare in her hands. The Stranger had heard no gunshots. The woman skinned the creature and her brother set a pot to boil over the fire, the two of them working in wordless unison. From within the wagon they fetched two shrivelled onions and several lumpy potatoes, dirt-encrusted and hard. They added the vegetables to the pot and Titania flavoured the soup with salt, and dried herbs the nature of which the Stranger didn't know. The smell of the soup as it cooked made the Stranger's stomach grumble. It had been weeks since he'd had a hot meal. Fledermaus relit his pipe and sat there content, puffing out clouds of smoke that more often than not resembled balloon animals. His sister sat warming her hands by the fire, and she hummed the same few bars of that song the Stranger didn't know. Her mostly tuneless humming had a soporific effect on him, so that he found his thoughts kept wandering, trailing off and returning, and every now and then he'd startle himself awake, and stare around him as though he were seeing the place and his companions for the very first time.

No sound came from within the wagon now. If there were rats indeed there, or something else entire, it was silent now, but the horses still did not approach the wagon or come close to it. The swishing of their tails merged with the crackling of the wood in the fire and with the whisper of the soup in the pot and with Titania's humming. The smell of the cooking meat overwhelmed the Stranger's senses.

"It is kind of you," he said, "to share your food."

"You look like you could use it," Fledermaus said, and chortled. "If you don't, uh, mind me saying so, there's less meat on your bones than even on that, uh, hare in the pot."

They ate out of wooden bowls, the meat tender and the potatoes soft and full of flavour. The liquid was subtly spiced, and it filled the Stranger's body with warmth. When they had finished eating, the brother and sister both lapsed into silence, staring at the flickering flames. The Stranger found that his own limbs felt loose and heavy, and that a certain light-head-edness threatened to overpower him. He excused himself, and rose with some effort from the warmth of the fire.

Standing, he found it hard to balance. All felt peaceful and serene, and in the night sky the star constellations shone brightly, moving and changing with a slow majesty. The Stranger felt dwarfed by the night sky, in which the stars crowded the vast blackness from horizon to distant horizon, and in their light he felt small, and insignificant, and so he sought refuge at last inside the old chapel.

It was warm and dry there. The air hung undisturbed. Deflated whoopee cushions sat forlorn on the empty pews. The Stranger walked down the aisle. Under the open windows, shards of multicoloured glass collected on the floor. The Stranger halted at the altar. It had sustained some damage in an earlier time, the wood chipped and bent and the stylised balloon icon violently broken. He walked round the dais and discovered there, hidden in the chancel, a window of stained glass that somehow remained unbroken, perhaps, he saw, because it didn't look out over anything. The Stranger swayed gently on his feet as he studied the artwork, muted now as no light coursed through it. It was boarded up on the other side, and though the glass was dark the colours had remained vibrant.

The picture portrayed the Harlequin, a creature perhaps male, perhaps female, with a sensual, almost cruel mouth. It wore a chequered costume made of triangular patches of varying colours, and on its head it wore a three-pointed hat. In its hand it held a bright red balloon.

The Stranger studied the painting, and the creature bound within the bits of coloured glass, or perhaps defined by them,

seemed to him to sway and move, as though capering or dancing. The world around the Stranger grew fuzzy, then opaque.
There was a saccharine taste in his mouth. The Stranger
swallowed but his lips and tongue were dry. He touched the
glass, from which the Harlequin had disappeared, and wiped it,
and it was like wiping fog off a glass. Beyond, he now saw, was
that other place. It was like looking through a clear glass window, onto a modest living room in an apartment, somewhere
in the city. There were a couple of paintings on the walls, in
rather lurid colours, like the magnified covers of pulp paper-
backs, and a shelf full of books crammed onto it untidily, and
a potted plant, wilted, in one corner, and a couch and a coffee
table and a television.

There was an ashtray and a bottle on the coffee table, and
an unlit and half-melted candle. There was some old picture
showing on the television, the images flickering rapidly. On the
sofa, a man was lying down. He looked like he'd been crying.

The Stranger violently wiped the glass, and the image,
mercifully, faded. He breathed deep and filled his lungs with
air and staggered out of the silent church and into the night,
where the constellations chased each other across the sky in a
sort of fluid dance. The Stranger saw that the fire had burned
down to embers, and they glowed faintly in the night. The two
tinkerers were ensconced on the ground. Covered in their
multiple garments, he could not even make out their faces.

Something moved inside the wagon.

The Stranger froze. The sound came again, as though something heavy moved inside and hit the floor. It made metal pots
and pans clang within. The two tinkerers hadn't moved from
their place by the fire. The Stranger drew his revolver. He
edged towards the rear of the wagon.

The broken moon hung in the sky. The Stranger hesitated, his finger on the trigger of his gun. The heavy thump from inside the wagon came again, and the wagon rattled on its wheels. Something fell off the wall and hit the floor with a bang. The Stranger reached for the thick cloth curtain that blocked the inside of the wagon. He parted the curtain and for a long time he stared.

"What do you think you're doing?"

The curtain snapped shut. The woman, Titania, stood in the moonlight, a nasty little sawed-off shotgun in her hands. She was without her heavy coverings, in nothing much more than a slip, and in the moonlight he saw that she was both younger and older than he'd thought, for she had a young woman's body but an old woman's hands. Her voice, however, and the simple fact of her finger on the trigger of the sawed-off, said she meant business.

"I heard a noise," the Stranger said.

"So? And you can put your gun back in the holster. Slowly."

The Stranger did as she said.

"You put substance in the soup," he said.

"I know," she said. "It flavours the meat. What are you getting at?"

"Nothing," the Stranger said. "This isn't my business."

"You're damn right it isn't." She gestured with the sawed-off. The Stranger took a step back from the wagon, and another, and his shadow hastened to match his steps.

He looked at Titania. Her own shadow billowed behind her, a huge, undulating mass that swallowed starlight in its wake. The Stranger took another step back and his shadow hid behind him.

"There was no offence meant," he said.

"Good."

Abruptly, she released her hold on the sawed-off, and with that she was gone. The Stranger took another breath and emptied his lungs slowly. When he returned to the fire he saw that both of the tinkerers were fast asleep, entwined in each other's arms under their heavy coverings. He lay down himself, on his back, and stared at the distant stars.

He had got a good look into the glum interior of the wagon, before Titania caught him. He saw the hanging iron pots and pans, old and bent and blackened by countless fires. He saw the bags of nails, the hammered horseshoes, the beaten copper bowls, the kettles and coal irons, the heaps of badges and buckles, and the spurs with their rowel and chap guards.

It was, then, just as described, a tinkerer's travelling emporium, cramped and dark, smelling of rust and the road, filled with the debris of everyday life and its mundane demands. Nothing more, nothing out of the extraordinary.

On the floor, in the centre of all that cramped space, a vast object lay partially covered in dirty blankets. From time to time it struggled feebly against the bonds that held it down, and its vast, black-and-gold head would hit the floor with a powerful thump that shook the ironmongery all about it. It had two glass eyes and a mouth with many jagged teeth. It was about the size of a tuna. Its scales, even in that quick half glimpse of the Stranger's, with the cloth flap only momentarily raised, and but little light coming in, nevertheless shone a bright gold, and its intricate mechanism rattled and whirred as it flopped there on the floor. Behind the glass eyes, a look almost human had stared out at the Stranger in supplication. On the fish's forehead, above the eyes, there was a nasty-looking dent, perhaps from a recent gunshot.

No more sound came now from the wagon. The giant piece of materiel that he had witnessed moved no further within. The Stranger lay on his back and his limbs grew heavy. The embers whispered with dying fire. The stars streaked across the sky, forming sentences in a language he wanted to but couldn't read. He felt himself dropping into sleep.

The two impish figures that stood in the moonlight had shed off their protective clothes, and in the broken light the Stranger saw them for what they really were, thin and delicate, with wide, clown-like mouths, mischievous eyes, and near translucent skin, under which their skeletons appeared as though composed of fragile fish bones. In the moonlight, too, the old abandoned chapel and the road both seemed to glow a bright ivory white, while the wagon seemed bigger, near palatial.

The Escapement spread outwards from them in all directions, and the sky seemed never to end over the lit landscape. The road snaked in loops and curves across the land, and far in the distance the Stranger felt, more than saw, the movement of ghostly yet durable troops, marching. The male who had called himself Fledermaus stood there watching the Stranger with the curve of a smile, and his shadow, like his sister's, grew behind him, immense and cephalopodian. It was as though the shadows were the real body, and the tiny human figures were merely the mouthpieces for the darkness beyond.

And then the Stranger knew them then for two of the pupae umbrarum.

In her hand, Titania held a small, dandelion-like flower. She blew on it, gently, and the tiny florets, startled by her breath, detached from their anchorage and took flight, one by one, until they dispersed to all corners and Titania remained holding only the bald stem of the flower.

"Do not seek the Ur-shanabi," she said, in a voice melodious and clear. "For the Plant of Heartbeat brings only heartache when it flowers."

"I need to find it," the Stranger said. "I have to."

"Then find a fucking cartographer," the thing that was Fledermaus said.

The vast shadows behind them coalesced, and bellowed in an invisible gale.

Somewhere, there was the sound of wind chimes.

When the Stranger woke, he found himself alone by the side of the old white road. The sound of the horses raised him from his stupor, their neighing and farting and the patient sound of cloven hooves stamping on earth, of tails swishing, of grass being ripped from the ground and chewed. The fire in its circle of stones was dead, and had been so for some time. He stood up groggily. The day was overcast and the sun was wreathed in mist. Of the tinkerers and their wagon there remained no sign. The Stranger relieved himself and washed sparingly. When he went inside the old clown chapel he saw that only his boot prints were in the thick layer of dust on the floor. And yet when he reached the place behind the dais he saw that the stained glass window with the Harlequin's visage had been violently broken and the pieces scattered on the floor.

Tucked on the wooden board, behind where the window had been, was a small and naked dandelion.

The Stranger rode out that day along the twisting road, the horses following patiently behind him. By mid-afternoon the road had begun to grow faint at the edges, and soon it had faded away entirely, and when he looked back he could not see a sign that it had ever been there. He rode on and soon he saw the small outpost town of Kellysburg in the distance, its dismal single-storey buildings with their chimneys churning black smoke into the air, and in the distance like a series of hash signs was the railway line.

The Stranger spurred on his horse and rode into town.

THREE:
THE LONG DROP

THE TOWN OF KELLYSBURG looked like an ugly spider bite when the Stranger approached it at dusk. An ill-omened wind blew from the east and it stirred the stunted shrubs and sent a brightly coloured scorpion into shelter in the shadow of an upturned rock in the shape of a severed fist. The train of horses, patient, followed behind the Stranger. The town was lit with thieves' lights, crude torches soaked in diluted substance, casting off a flare-bright glow, and they hissed and fizzed sporadically. In their light, the Stranger could see the ramshackle, lean-to houses, hastily erected constructions built with dark mud, bad wood, rusted nails and spit. But the storms had left their mark on the town, and the Stranger saw a circular staircase rising high into the sky, with no walls around it, until it stopped abruptly in mid-air; and he saw the houses that grew on stalks, and disturbingly reminded him of watching eyes; and he saw the bridges that connected nowhere to nothing and looked like the tentacles of some giant beast. The air was so thick with substance that even the horses began to seem ghostly and translucent, and the Stranger's senses were assailed with the noises of that other place, the honk of car horns and the sound of engines and a telephone ringing, somewhere nearby, over and over, and a television whispering of things to buy.

This was prospecting country. There was so much substance they were using it for light. As he came closer he saw that a small cemetery had sprouted near the entrance to the town, rows and rows of graves denoted with the slash of a clown smile, and a solitary gravedigger at his work. The Stranger passed by and stopped, contemplating the stooped, skinny man with the worm-white skin who was digging a fresh grave in the hard cracked earth.

He said, "Who's that for?"

The gravedigger straightened and wiped his face with the back of his hand and shrugged. "Night's yet young," he said. "Throw the dice and take your pick, stranger."

"I don't play dice."

The gravedigger grimaced and tilted his head. The ghostly outline of a late-model Ford rose towards them in the darkness, its twin headlights shining as it passed through the gravestones and disappeared back into that other place.

"I hate this fucking town," the gravedigger said. He stared at the Stranger and the Stranger saw he had one blue eye and that the other was a milky white and made of glass. "You ever miss it, stranger? You ever want to go back?"

"I can't," the Stranger said. "I am looking for something. Something precious."

"I must have been looking for something, too, once," the gravedigger said. "Now I just dig holes in the ground. Watch your steps tonight, stranger. There's a bad wind coming in from the Doldrums, and the fresh graves never stay empty for long."

"I'll be sure to bear that in mind," the Stranger said, touching the brim of his hat. He saw that the gravedigger had one bare foot, and the skin on his hands was coarse and rough. The sound of the spade hitting the hard ground came regular as the ticking of a clock now. Then the gravedigger stopped, but the ticking continued, and the Stranger saw that he had unearthed half of a melted clock, with the second hand still ticking, blindly, stuck in the same spot.

"Is it always like this here?" the Stranger said.

"I hate this fucking town," the gravedigger said again. He pulled the clock out savagely, like a weed, and tossed it aside on a heap which already included the bent front wheel of a penny farthing, the upper half of a storefront mannequin with too many arms and three eyes like tears down one side of its smooth, blandly handsome face, and a typewriter on which all the keys were small round mirrors. The Stranger shook his head and spurred on his horse, leaving the cemetery and its gravedigger behind.

As he approached the town proper he saw a crude wooden sign planted in the ground, and on it, in chalked letters, the legend No Gunfights No Ordnance No Clowns.

Along Main Street the shadows from the thieves' lights fell at all angles. Furtive figures skulked between the buildings and some lay flat on their backs with their eyes open and unseeing, drunk on Sticks or raw substance. Ghostly figures moved through shop walls and several times headlights once again appeared and disappeared, but the Stranger avoided the ghostly apparitions of that other place until they faded to nothing more than a nuisance at the edge of vision. But the town itself set him on edge.

The street was unpaved and the ground dry and cracked.

Horses were tied up along the shopfronts and their dung had been left to steam on the dry ground. At the end of Main Street he could just make out the train terminal and the railroad line running off into the distance, deeper into the Thickening. The wind really did carry a bad smell, of rotten eggs and curdled custard, and the Stranger saw that many of the residents walked with hands ready on their weapons, and looked about them as though spooked by something they could not yet see. Most of the people he saw were prospectors, and he saw them line up before an apothecary shop where two men wearing dirty smocks and double-lens glasses were measuring out the raw deposits and exchanging them for ducats as armed guards watched with shotguns cradled in their arms. This must have been why the railway line extended this far, to this remote outpost on the edge of the Thickening: a chondrite impact that left a rich seam of substance for the prospectors to exploit. The Stranger saw several bars, an ordinary smithy, and a laundry that seemed permanently shut. He saw no church or balloonery but had expected neither. There was also a gaol, and a rotten-looking gallows with not enough height on it for the long drop.

The many coloured lights burned unevenly and cast the town in an oily sheen of smog in which the shadows seemed separate from their sources. The Stranger found the quietest of the bars and, once inside, spoke quietly to the owner, and in short order the horses he had captured from the dead scalp hunters were exchanged for hard ducats, room and board. The owner, a short and muscled woman native to the Escapement, seemed oblivious to the substance fog or to any ghostly apparitions from that other place, and more than happy to acquire good horses cheaply. The Stranger sat down at the bar and ordered moonshine, which was the only other drink they served beside Sticks. He had the feeling that something bad was coming, but he did not know what.

The Kid said, "I see your Magician and I raise you Death."

The Stranger had the Emperor but not the Empress or the Wheel of Fortune, and though he retaliated with the Moon it was no good and the Kid swept the money to his side of the table with one scrawny arm. There was an old piano in the corner, and a one-eyed woman tickled the ivories, playing a Dibdin piece. She'd flashed the Stranger a grin when he'd come in earlier.

"So you've met the Lovers and lived," she said.

The Stranger inched his head in reply. Then Temperanza went back to her playing. She looked like she was waiting for something; though she was probably just waiting for the train.

"I'm going to take a piss," the Kid announced, and he strutted across the floor, his spurs making a rasping sound across the scuffed wood. The Kid had been drinking moonshine steadily throughout the game, but he was still beating the Stranger at cards.

The Stranger watched him go. The Kid wore his pistols low-slung on his hips and his hat at a cocky angle, but for all that he just looked like a kid playing at dressing up.

They were almost the only people at the bar. It was not a place that invited confidences or offered comfort. The tables were rough-hewn wood, and tallow candles burned with oily smoke but offered little light. In one corner sat a small man cowled in shadow and now that the Kid had gone to the outhouse the man got up and sauntered over to their table and sat down without being asked.

"New in town, stranger?"

He had an ordinary face and hard black button eyes and his nails and his hair were both cut short. The Stranger looked, but he couldn't see if there was a dagger hidden up the man's sleeve, though he rather suspected so all the same. He said, "What's it to you?"

"Just making conversation."

The Stranger shrugged. "It's no secret," he allowed.

"You rode in from the Doinklands?" The black button eyes turned shrewd. "You didn't happen to've come across the Thurston Brothers, did you? Scalp hunters, there's a reward out for them. Good money, too."

"I think that bounty's claimed," the Stranger said, and over by the piano Temperanza smirked without breaking melody.

The other man nodded.

"Is that so, is that so. Well, never mind, I'm sure. The world's a better place for it and so on."

"Professional interest?" the Stranger said. The other man shrugged.

"Listen," he said. "Out there, did you see any sign of the war?"

The Stranger nodded. "The Titanomachy rages on. I saw a battle in the distance, but I didn't go close, and who won it, if any, I don't know. Why?"

"No reason, no reason," the other man said. "Only, there's rumours, see? I am looking for something, yes, yes, there could be a handsome reward in it for a man such as you. A piece of materiel, rumour says. Some sort of weapon. Yes. What it does, no one knows for certain. Something big, though."

The Stranger thought uneasily about the tinkerers; and about the vast slab of mechanical fish he had caught sight of, for just a moment, hidden under blankets in the back of their wagon. But he shook his head, slowly. It could have been anything.

"You're a Pilkington?" he said. The other man shrugged.

"We all got a job to do, ain't we?" he said.

"Bit far from base," the Stranger said.

"Pilkingtons go wherever they must," the other man said. At that moment the Kid came sauntering back into the room and sat down, glaring at the Pilkington.

"I thought I told you to keep out of my business, Clem," he said.

"This ain't your business, kid."

"Fucking Pilkingtons," the Kid said. The other man glared at him but said nothing.

At that moment, the Stranger felt the wind change. The tinkle of wind chimes began to sound ethereally in the air, and the smell of rotten eggs and custard intensified. Faint on the breeze, the Stranger thought he could hear a demonic laughter, like a distorted echo of the sounds one heard when one came upon the Colossi walking the Escapement. But this was not the inhuman sound of the Colossi but a terrifying, yet very human, sound. He heard two gunshots go off outside, one after the other in rapid succession, coming from two different places.

The three men moved independently but almost in unison. Temperanza alone, unconcerned, remained at the piano, and the music she played was haunting and sad.

The Kid held his pistol and the Pilkington, Clem, had a sawed-off shotgun that seemed to just appear out of nowhere, and the Stranger had the uneasy feeling it had been taped to the underside of the table.

He himself held his revolver. They had all moved to the window, guns drawn, and the Stranger peered out onto Main Street. He saw the shops were rapidly closing, their internal lights extinguished, and the people outside were running for shelter, and in mere moments the street was deserted. Behind them, he heard the owner of the bar loudly pump a shotgun.

"He's coming," she said.

"Who?" the Kid said.

But then they heard it. The cries, faint at first, but growing in volume, from one side of Main Street to the other.

"Pogo!"

"Pogo's coming!"

"Pogo's *coming!*"

The Stranger and the Kid exchanged bewildered looks; but Clem, the Pilkington, grinned in savage satisfaction. The Stranger stared out. The burning multicoloured lights cast the street in a non-linear chiaroscuro. Even those prospectors passed out on the side of the road from Sticks were gone now, dragged away by their comrades to safety.

Then he saw it.

The figure materialised at the end of Main Street, near the railway terminal, and began to progress in an easy saunter down the road. It seemed Goliath-like in size, as the light behind sent its shadow sprawling until it touched the fronts of shops like a rising tide. But as it came closer, the Stranger saw that it was a figure of medium size, almost slight, and for one terrible moment he thought that it was a clown.

"Pogo!"

"Pogo's coming!"

The face was deathly pale and a jagged, bloodied red mouth had been painted over it. The eyes were jagged triangles. Pogo wore a red hat and a striped suit and his hands were empty. He carried a suitcase in one hand. The Stranger saw a hanging rope and a machete on his hips.

"A clown . . . ," the Kid whispered.

"He's not a clown," the Stranger said. "He's just a thing painted to resemble one."

"He comes out when the winds blow heavy out of the Doldrums," the bar owner said. She had her shotgun pointed steadily at the door. "Every time he claims his fill of victims and disappears again. Three times we hired hunters to go after him, but none came back, and each reprisal inflicted on the town was worse than the last. Now we just hide, and hope it's not our turn."

"He's not a clown," the Stranger said again. "He's a grotesque mockery of one."

"Nobody cares, stranger," the Pilkington said, and licked his lips. "What are you, some clown lover?"

Watching, the Stranger saw Pogo stop outside the shut apothecary shop. The clown-impostor laughed again then, and the sound was very human and very chilling, and it was the only sound in the whole town. Then he bounded at the windows and smashed them as easily as a child playing with toys, and he leaped inside, and then there were screams. When Pogo emerged, he was dragging one of the white-smock-wearing apothecary men by the scruff of the neck and he threw him on the ground and lifted his machete. The smile painted on his face never reached his lips or his eyes. He sniffed over his victim, lovingly, as though scenting a meal.

Someone—someone bold, or stupid, or still high on Sticks—

stepped out of the shadows then with a gun raised and he fired at Pogo. The thing in the clown costume lifted the apothecary man one-handed and the bullets landed in the soft flesh of this human shield, and Pogo laughed and threw the machete at his attacker. He dragged the apothecary man with him and reached his attacker and the Stranger saw the machete was buried in the man's chest and his blood stained the dry ground. Pogo laughed and pulled out his machete and raised it high in the air and screamed out in rage or defiance or joy, and then he brought it down and chopped off the man's head with one strike, and he began to march down Main Street again using the head for a kicking ball. The head rolled ahead of him and the air smelled of cupcakes as the wind blew harder through the town.

"Will no one stop him?" the Stranger said, and the bar owner said, "No one dares," and the Kid said, "Then I will."

The Kid and the Stranger looked at each other and they were in agreement, and they made to move to the door.

"Hold up," the Pilkington man, Clem, said. He turned to the bar owner. "Is there a reward?"

"The mayor offered one, before he was taken," the woman said. "That was back when we still had hope. Now there are only the empty graves in the cemetery, waiting."

"What was the last reward?" the Pilkington man said.

The bar owner named a figure, and Clem whistled, then laughed. "Triple it, and I'm in."

"You can claim anything in this town, if you kill him," the bar owner said.

Clem shrugged. "Not much of a town," he said. He pumped his shotgun and joined the other two. "But I was getting restless anyway."

The Kid and the Stranger exchanged glances again, and the Stranger nodded.

He looked to the piano, where Temperanza sat.

"You coming?" he said.

She sent a trail of notes his way and shrugged.

"I'll mop up the mess if you can't finish," she said. "Have fun playing Dead Man's Bluff."

She kept playing.

"Come on!" the Kid said. He pushed the door open and the three men stepped outside, guns drawn. Pogo was still up-road from them. He had captured a victim outside of one of the bars and the man was convoluting in his arms as he died. The three men began to march, wordlessly. They fanned out, with the Stranger in the middle and the other two flanking him, a little behind, on either side of the street.

"I see you!" the Stranger called, and he said a name. It was the name of a murderer who once lived in that other place. "I know what you are!"

Pogo turned his head sharply. He dropped his victim on the ground with a careless shove and stepped over him as the man died. His face filled with an animalistic fury that only seemed to animate his painted grin.

"I . . . am . . . Pogo!" he bellowed.

The Stranger fired a shot in the air. "You died once," he said. "Now you're just a bad dream, Gacy."

"I . . . am . . . Pogo!" the thing howled in rage, and the Kid muttered, "All my dreams are gonna be bad dreams after this."

The three men progressed, Clem and the Kid in the shadows, the Stranger right in the middle of the street. The faux clown stood facing them now. He looked from side to side, as though not quite believing anyone would dare come after him.

"Fire," the Stranger said.

The three men shot at the faux clown. The Kid squeezed out a round of shots and methodically reloaded. The Stranger fired more sparingly, alternating his two revolvers as he let off shots. The Pilkington man, Clem, fired steady bursts of shotgun explosions. The air filled with the smell of gunpowder and smoke and, still present, that smell of rancid custard.

It was hard to see through the smoke. The Stranger advanced, but now he withheld his fire. The other men's shots halted too, as both advanced and reloaded. As the smoke cleared there was no sign of the faux clown.

The Stranger whirled around, but it was almost too late. Pogo stood behind them, his entire face leering and his eyes dead as he raised his machete to strike. It came down just as the Stranger slid to the ground and it missed his head by a hairbreadth. Pogo roared then, in hatred and frustration, and his oversized red boot stomped down hard on the prone Stranger. The Stranger raised his hands protectively and managed to fend off the worst of the blow, but his gun fell away and a thrum of pain vibrated through him like the chime of a struck bell. Just then the blast of a shotgun filled the air and he saw Pogo thrown back, but the faux clown soon gained his footing again and he screamed in an awful mockery of laughter, and reached into his pocket. When his hand emerged it held a small glass canister, and with a sharp movement, he threw it on the ground between him and the three men.

The glass shattered against the hard ground.

The shotgun fired again and the Kid's gun went off but it was accompanied by a scream of pain as Pogo's machete cut into his side with savage force. The air filled with hexagrams, crosses, and obeli, and the Stranger fought to rise but there was so much substance in the air that it was hard to hold on and he found himself slipping once again into that other place.

Somewhere a telephone was ringing and had been ringing for a long long time, but the man didn't get up to answer it and it finally went quiet. The darkness outside gradually turned to light, and the man could hear the sounds of early morning, the garbage trucks outside and a police siren in the distance and shop shutters opening, and then someone was knocking on the door, saying, Are you in there, let me in, over and over. The man didn't want to rise and he held on to the child's stuffed toy and he said, You don't understand, I have to find it, I have to find the Ur-shanabi, it flowers only beyond the Mountains of Darkness. But the person knocking wouldn't go away and at last the man rose to answer them.

"Come on, stranger!"

He staggered to his feet. The Kid was bleeding from his side and the Pilkington man was binding the wound. Pogo, leaping and somersaulting, was getting away from them, down Main Street, towards the railway terminal. The Stranger retrieved his gun.

"Can you walk, kid?" he said.

"I can shoot," the Kid said, grimly. The makeshift bandage stemmed the flow of blood. "I've been hit worse."

"If you say so . . . ," Clem said. He checked his shotgun and nodded to himself. "So, do we go after him?"

"You want that reward money, don't you?" the Stranger said.

The Pilkington man grinned, then spat on the ground. "Right now," he said, "all I want to do is fill this fucking clown with holes."

"He's not a clown!" the Stranger said, exasperated.

They tracked Pogo down Main Street; past doors hammered

shut from the inside, with eyes that tracked them behind heavy blinds and offered no help. Pogo had slowed down. He kept turning his head, staring back after them. There was something hungry and cunning about his face. He reminded the Stranger of a wild, captive animal, of something that had been locked up inside its own head for so long that it had gone mad with it long ago, and all that it wanted to do now was hurt and maim and kill. Pain was his only joy.

Pogo led, and the three men followed. Outside the railway terminal, heavy bags were placed in orderly rows, waiting for loading. Powdery substance spilled at their edges. Beyond lay only the Escapement, and the railway tracks disappeared into the distance. The broken moon hung in the sky. The stars shimmered and danced in the black night ceiling of the world. Pogo stood on the wooden platform and raised his arms in the air, glaring down on them. The Stranger raised his gun and the others followed suit. It had the air of a well-ordered execution.

The men opened fire.

The faux clown's body danced like a marionette on invisible strings. The gunshots tore off his striped clown suit and blew away his jaunty cap and shredded his wig but still he stood glaring down on them in defiance. Behind him there opened a great blackness and the Stranger knew it was the substance in the air, showing him that other place, but Pogo no longer existed there, and the bullets seemed to offer him no harm.

Pogo had disappeared from view as though he'd dropped underground, and a rope whispered through the air and looped around Clem's neck and tightened. Clem could not cry out and he was dragged out with inhuman force, and he disappeared down the hole. The Stranger and the Kid exchanged weary glances and the Kid shrugged and his face twisted in pain from his wound. The Stranger said, "Stay up here and cover me."

The Kid nodded. They approached the hole and the Kid trained his guns on the entrance and the Stranger dropped down into the ground. The fall was shorter than he expected. He could see seams of white substance in the walls, faintly glowing in the dark.

Something crunched underfoot when he landed. When he looked down he saw part of a human femur, a caved-in rib cage, delicate frond-like finger bones. He followed the tunnel ahead. Human skulls looked up at him from the floor, their empty eye sockets beseeching him without words.

As he went deeper he began to see more recent victims, body parts rotting, and he covered his mouth and nose with a cloth. Drag marks on the ground marked where Pogo had taken the Pilkington man.

The tunnels twisted and branched, but he followed the drag marks and the sporadic patches of blood, and just when he thought he was lost he found Clem.

The Pilkington man was sitting bound to a chair that stood in the middle of a circular opening in the rock. His mouth was gagged with a bright red ball. His nose was bloodied and his eyes stared with unholy horror at the Stranger.

The eyes moved. The Stranger followed their gaze. He stepped through as the false clown's machete swung at him. The Stranger grabbed hold of Pogo's wrist and it was like holding an iron bar. The false clown bared his teeth at him. With his costume shredded and his makeup running he was something feral and sick. There was nothing in his eyes the Stranger could understand. He kicked, hitting Pogo between the legs, and stepped around him as the false clown howled in pain and rage. He twisted Pogo's arm behind his back and *pushed*, hard, until there was the sickening sound of breaking bone, and Pogo cried again.

The Stranger pulled out his gun and put it to the back of Pogo's head, intending to put him down, but he had underestimated the thing. With a howl of rage, Pogo wrenched his broken arm free and with the other he shoved the Stranger, with such inhuman force that the Stranger flew off his feet and hit the far wall. His head rang with the pain. Then Pogo was on him, kicking and screaming, and the large red rubber boots hammered against the Stranger's ribs until he felt his own bones break. Desperately he reached for the knife strapped to his leg and he pushed the blade up, burying it with the last of his strength in the false clown's belly.

Pogo didn't cry now. Blood trickled out of his mouth and onto the Stranger, and his lips moved without clear speech, but only an inane mumble. He took one step back, and then another. He stared dumbly at the knife buried in his stomach. Then he turned on his feet and half-stumbled, half-ran into one of the dark tunnels.

The Stranger rose, groaning, and he went and untied Clem. The man could not stop shaking. There were meat hooks on the walls and a sort of leather harness, and there was a smell in that cavern that was hard to describe, an old, sweet, awful smell of decay, of butterscotch and rot. Clem licked his lips and then he was sick all over the floor and over his pants and boots.

"Can you walk?" the Stranger said.

Clem wiped his lips with the back of his hand. "I'll manage," he said.

"Here," the Stranger said, and he passed him one of his guns. Together, they followed into the tunnels.

Blood and snot and detached pieces of entrails led them and soon they could hear Pogo's laboured breathing and that mutter again, never ceasing, a mumble of syllables that repeated without rhyme or reason, and the Stranger held tighter to his gun, and wished that it would be enough. The tunnel sloped upwards here and as they burst through into the next cave they saw that it was another shaft, and an old ladder led back up to the surface. Overhead, he heard gunshots, and as he emerged up into the moonlight he saw the Kid coming through with guns blaring. The gibbering thing that was Pogo ran at him and knocked him down, and began pawing at him and trying to bite the Kid's face. It was then that the Stranger saw the lights.

The Kid rolled and he tried to strangle Pogo, his hand round the creature's neck, but Pogo kicked him off and he scampered again. The lights seemed to confuse him. He stood between them and the two men, unsure which way to run. The Stranger felt rather than saw Clem emerge from the shaft and stand beside them.

And now they were three. He cocked his gun.

"Fire."

The hail of bullets decided it, and the half-blind, insane thing turned tail and ran at the oncoming lights of the train. They could hear it now, the slow, unstoppable chug-a-chug of the pistons and the belch of the engine, and for one moment, the man who had called himself Pogo was perfectly framed in the twin headlights, caught like an animal, before the train rushed along the tracks and hit him.

Even then, Pogo didn't quite die.

Somehow, he was still alive, and he glared at them out of one remaining eye, offering crazed hatred to his hunters. On seeing him, Clem was sick again, and the Kid sagged down to the ground, holding the wound in his side.

"Enough," the Stranger said, tiredly. Then he pulled out his gun and shot Pogo in the back of the head.

Pogo's body shuddered and fell and yet even then, in the throes of death, he tried to crawl on, hand by laborious hand, leaving bloodied palm prints on the ground. Just then the Stranger felt the wind change, and the smell of rancid custard which had been in the air all this time was suddenly gone.

Pogo crawled one last, exhausted length, and then he fell. A shadow leaked out of him and vanished into the dark.

In death, he was just a man, the Stranger saw.

The Stranger sank down to the ground to join his comrades, and then he began to laugh: an exhausted, heartfelt, *relieved* belly laugh, a true and clean sound that echoed through the night and cleared away the horror, until the two other men, first the Kid and then, at last, even Clem, began to laugh with him; and that sound, like the peals of old struck bells, was heard that night all across Kellysburg and beyond, and reached Colossi and pupae umbrarum both.

On the other side of town, the gravedigger looked up at the sound of laughter and shook his head, for he disapproved of such frivolities. He hefted his spade and began again to dig, for the world was forever in need of fresh graves, and it was his job to both dig them and fill them.

FOUR:
THE GREAT TRAIN ROBBERY

From the high-above perspective of a flying caique, or other clown bird, the railway line appeared more like a sort of tangled mandala, following not a straight path but the twisting contours of the landscape; and it often doubled back on itself, crossing the former line with a new one, creating a series of curious knots. The terminus point of Kellysburg appeared as a smudged thumbprint in the distance. Ahead, the tiny engine puffed out a steady plume of smoke as it pulled the passenger cars and hoppers behind it. The hopping cars were loaded with sacks of crystalline substance from the pits and quarries of the Kellysburg claims. A couple of cattle cars held horses, including the Stranger's horse, who was munching sedately on hay.

From high above the Escapement, the train was nothing but a toy set, huffing and puffing its slow way along the narrow tracks. A flock of caiques, birds uneasy with flight at the best of times, settled themselves onto the branches of a tree high above the railway, where they chattered animatedly and mimicked the whistle sound of the train to amuse themselves.

The train struggled as the land's elevation rose. They were still only on the edges of the Thickening, where the majority of human settlers lived, and beyond lay the Doinklands and the Doldrums and the great graveyards of the wild elephant herds.

Far in the distance, one could almost imagine they could hear the sound of giant stone feet, treading softly on the earth. . . .

The Stranger watched the view roll past beyond the window. Mountains rose in the distance and their peaks were white with snow. The sky was a calm blue, and the air felt fresh and clear as the wind blew in. The train crawled along the ledge of a high precipice and the Stranger could see the Nikulin River down below, a wide expanse of cerulean blue, and the sunlight caught a leaping fish and reflected off its silvery scales.

"I don't like this," the Kid complained. He kept fidgeting with a pendant that hung from a necklace round his neck. The Stranger had noticed it before. It was a silver thumb-tip, and on it, engraved, was the legend *Vernaculus*: it was an old word, and it meant both clown, and slave.

The Kid saw the Stranger looking at his pendant and put it back under his shirt, out of sight.

"You mean we just sit here?" he said.

"That's how it goes," the Stranger said. He was not in a hurry. He felt content for the time being to simply sit and look out on the ever-changing Escapement and not to think too much. It was soothing. The train was headed to Jericho, a large town deeper in the Thickening and a terminus for several of the rail routes. The Stranger hoped to find a cartographer there.

"Listen," the Kid said. "In your travels, did you ever run into a conjurer?"

"A conjurer?"

"You know. White gloves. Black clothes. Wears a tall black hat. Makes ducats disappear. A fucking conjurer."

There was a sort of pain behind the Kid's eyes. The Stranger said, "I can't think as I have."

"This one wears pistols with silver handles on his belt," the Kid said.

The Stranger shook his head. "I'll keep my eyes open," he said.

"Yeah. Well."

"Where are you from, kid?"

The Kid shrugged. "A small town called Bozoburg, on the Fratellini plains. The sort of place where nothing ever happens."

"A one-clown town."

"Yeah." The Kid reached for his pendant again, absent-mindedly. "What about you?" he said. "You're one of them, aren't you?"

"Excuse me?"

"You're from that other place."

"Ah," the Stranger said. "Well, that's a question, isn't it." He looked out of the window. High above, he noticed a line of Erlandson trees, tall, graceful trunks like vaulting poles and twisting branches shaped into hearts or arms or lightning bolts, and he thought he saw dark shapes dart between the high branches, but if so he could not make them out clearly. Yet they made him uneasy. The train continued to chug gaily parallel to the Nikulin down below. The air grew colder by degrees, and a flurry of snow blew down in a sudden gust of wind, never reaching the ground but bursting overhead in tiny flashes of sunlight and microscopic rainbows. "I mean, do we dream that other world, or does it dream us, do you think?"

The Kid shrugged, indifferent. He had no parallel. Sticks gave him nothing but a sickly hangover. "As much as I enjoy talking metaphysics," he said, "I think I prefer playing cards." When he spread his arms, Tarocchi cards leaped between his fingers. The Stranger caught flashes of wands and swords and rings, of Death, of Temperance, and of the Hermit. He said, "You seem to have a little of the conjurer in you, yourself."

The Kid scowled. He got up smoothly, making the cards disappear. The wound in his side was healing nicely. Only a slight stiffness when he moved betrayed its presence. "I'll be in the dining car," he said, "if you'd like to join me."

"I might, later," the Stranger said.

The Kid grinned. "If only you played cards the way you shoot . . . ," he said, and shook his head in mock sorrow. He disappeared down the corridor. The Stranger turned back to the window. The motion of the train lulled him to sleep and yet he watched uneasily as the river expanded farther ahead, how the mountains loomed, how dark shapes seemed to fleet swiftly between the vines and high branches of the Erlandson trees. The snow had gone as quickly as it had come, and what remained now in the air was merely the ghost or the idea of snow.

In time, the Stranger fell asleep. From high above the Escapement, the flock of caiques watched the little toy train with amused interest, and some of the birds surfed against the tree bark or the wet leaves down below, propelling themselves in play by their beaks, rolling and wrestling with each other. But the caiques were soon disturbed in their frivolity by the larger, fleeting shadows, and their chatter turned nervous and soon they took flight as one, an explosion of feathery colour, yellow and snow-white and green, as they followed the contours of the mountain.

High on the branches of the Erlandson trees, the aerialists halted. They were dressed in simple whites, and their lithe, strong bodies seemed impervious to the altitude and the cold. They paused, perfectly balanced. There were five of them. Their leader, Carl, followed the slender branch of a tree as it bent over the sheer drop above the Nikulin like a fishing rod. He stood with his arms at his sides, watching the train.

"Well?" Loretta asked. She backflipped lazily across her branch and leaped into the air, catching one of the Erlandson tree's rings. She raised herself to a sitting position above the others. "But I don't *want* to rob another train," she said.

Carl ignored her. Carl was tall and handsome with short-cropped blond hair and a thin blond moustache. He'd been loose and charming when Loretta first met him, she had hung on his every word. But he had gradually become more and more like stone, hard and unyielding. She tried to tell herself he simply wasn't himself these days.

Carl's gaze traced the path of the railway line. Ahead were two low mountains, the Petit Philippe and the Grand Philippe, and the train would pass through the saddle to reach the other side. Beyond, the Nikulin snaked under the towering mountain range, until it reached a natural breach in the landscape, a deepening into which both the river and the melting snows drained, forming a wide lake called the Chagrin.

Beyond the Chagrin, the train would take a sharp turn away from the mountains and down to the fertile plains, heading away from the Doinklands and into the Thickening proper, far from the sounds of war and the pratfalls of clowns. But to make its getaway, the train would have to first cross the bridge over the lake. . . .

The troupe of aerialists listened impassively as Carl outlined the plan. Loretta knew not to show any more emotion now, let alone disagreement. Carl tolerated chitchat but any outright disagreement would likely result in terrible punishment. Carl did not tolerate dissent. That, she'd learned the hard way. Carl could be charming, and funny, and wise: he had gathered them to him from across the sad places of the Escapement, helpless, hopeless, friendless, aimless—and he gave them help, and hope, and friends, and purpose. He made them a part of a *family*.

His family.

It was only later that Loretta realised what he really was, and what he was capable of doing.

Carl was finished. He looked at each of them in turn. Then they once again took to the air, leaping from vine to hoop, from stilt to swing, traversing the curious trees that grew all along this side of the mountain, and only the little caiques watched them pass.

The knocks on the door kept repeating until, at last, the man had no choice but to get up off the couch and fumble with the door. She stood there glaring at him before pushing past him. What have you been *doing* with yourself, she said. She began to move around, tidying up. She emptied the ashtray with a sound of disgust and she turned off the television set and opened the blinds. Sunlight streamed into the room, making his eyes hurt.

You don't understand, he told her, speaking thickly, I am not really here, this is just the effect of substance, I am looking for the Plant of Heartbeat—

She touched his cheek. Her touch was so light and yet it burned through him and he turned his face away. As she tidied up she picked a book from where it must have fallen behind the sofa. It was *The Fabulous Flying Banditti*, he must have been reading it to the boy the last time—

The Stranger was jolted awake as the train took a sharp turn and passed back on itself and looped in a knot in the rail. It was a sort of ankh-shaped looping and as he watched he could see the back of the train and the front of the train converging upon one another, and it put him in mind of a giant worm, continually devouring itself. He could see the hopping cars with their sacks of substance bouncing on their suspension, and the animal cars where his horse napped standing up, seeming content. Overhead, night had fallen. The snow that fell down now was as fine as ash. The Stranger rose and left the cabin. His feet trod on the soft worn carpet of the hallway. Half of the cabins on this car were empty, as few boarded the train at the Kellysburg end. He made his way to the dining car.

Hot air and the smell of tobacco and gun stew and bread hit him as he entered. Unlike the rest of the train, the car was packed, and the men and women who crammed around the low tables were on the main a rough-and-ready crowd. Bottles of moonshine and some of Sticks sat on the tables and the drinkers were merry but for the Sticks drinkers, who were slumped in their chairs with their eyes glazed open as they visited that other place. The Kid sat near the galley, with his back to the wall, playing cards with three others, two men and a one-eyed woman who winked at the Stranger as he passed. There was a large pile of ducats before the Kid and much smaller ones before the other three. The Kid saw the Stranger and nodded, with only a hint of a grin, and then went back to his cards.

The Stranger squeezed his way among the throng. The only empty seat was across from the card players, near the warmth of the open galley, where a large doughy man and a small, compact woman were working. The man stirred a pot that bubbled over a solid iron cooker, and the woman rolled dough with quick, violent turns. The man, from time to time, reached out and filled a small glass with moonshine from a large bottle, and this he would lift methodically to his lips, wet them, then down the rest in one go. The Stranger slid into the one empty chair. Across the small table from him sat one solitary figure, apart from all the others. It was a short, squat man, in a worn black suit and a rumpled white shirt and a small and rather jaunty trilby on his head. He wore thick-lensed round glasses and a toothbrush moustache. His large eyes were a watery pale blue. The Stranger pressed himself into the seat, hemmed in between the wall and the thick, sweaty back of a woman in a chequered flannel shirt, smudged with pale deposits of substance, who was laughing loudly with her companions. The man in the trilby hat looked at the Stranger's travails with kind amusement in his eyes. The laughter on the other side grew loud in response to a joke the Stranger didn't quite catch.

"Everyone's a comedian," the man in the trilby hat said. He reached across the table to shake the Stranger's hand. His grip was strong. "I'm Mr. Norvell."

The Stranger shook his hand. He said, "If you don't mind me saying, you don't look like a prospector."

The man's eyes twinkled and he said, "That's quite all right, I'm not." He reached under the desk for a black and much battered briefcase and placed it on the table between them, opening it with a click. "I am purveyor of nostrum remedium—that is to say, of patent medicines, elixirs, mugwump, and snake oil. I, sir, am a commercial traveller."

He said that with an air of quiet pride. When he turned his briefcase to face the Stranger, the Stranger saw inside it there many curiously shaped bottles of small sizes, some made of rough glass, and some of clay and some of wood. Some of the glass was an opaque rich blue and some was colourless and grainy. The wood bottles were engraved with sigils and the clay ones with simple marks like crow's feet.

"I have all manners of medicines to cure every manner of ailment," Mr. Norvell said. "And all for a mere handful of ducats. Yes, sir. In my time I have treated with the great and the good of the land. I have been to Xanadu and El Dorado, to Shangri-La and to the Doinklands, yes, sir, I have indeed, and I have healed the deathly wounds of the big boss clown of the Whitefaces. I could have been rich by now, indeed I could have, but it is not the desire for ducats which animates me, indeed it does not, but only the desire to help those less fortunate than I. And you, sir? You have need for succour? Does wart-tongue trouble you, or eagle's claw? A sore tooth? My rates for teeth extraction are most reasonable. Perhaps a love spell?"

"No," the Stranger said, shaking his head. "No, but thank you all the same."

Mr. Norvell folded his hands before him on the table and leaned forward, and pitched his voice low. "You ask me for curses, is that it? I don't . . ." He looked from side to side. "But perhaps . . ."

"No, no, I'm sorry," the Stranger said. "But thank you."

"But what is it you seek?" Mr. Norvell said, frustrated. "You must seek *something!*"

"I am looking," the Stranger said, "for the Ur-shanabi."

Mr. Norvell unfolded his hands and lifted his head and sat back. The motion of the train grew faster then, the cabin rocking from side to side, and looking out of the window the Stranger saw the twin mountain peaks of the Petit Philippe and Grand Philippe approach, as the train headed to the crossing through the saddle.

"The Plant of Heartbeat . . . ," Mr. Norvell said. "No, no, it is I who is sorry, stranger. That flower is beyond even my powers to give." His eyes filled with what looked like genuine sorrow. The glasses magnified them and in their pale blue or-bits one could almost imagine the formation of tears. There was something hypnotic about Mr. Norvell's eyes, as though behind their innocent vista of sky there was a melancholy, chthonic quality. It made the Stranger feel that if only he let himself wander for too long, if only he looked too deeply into those innocent eyes, he would find himself sinking, down into that liquid ocean and farther, into the tubular optic nerve that led not to a brain but to a place of shadow. And he wondered then, again; for the pupae umbrarum had agents among the ordinary and not so ordinary tenants of the Escapement, just as the Colossi did.

◆ ♠ ◆

High overhead, shadowing the train effortlessly, the aerialists leaped and vaulted from branch to branch and hoop to hoop, and Loretta saw the tiny toy train as it puffed its way towards the mountain pass. Loretta had only vague memories of that other place, which she sometimes still visited, on the rare occasions that she used substance. Such visits seemed very real when she was in the grip of them but later, as they faded, seemed cheap and tawdry, for over there she seemed to have been teaching school and returning, each day, to an apartment in the city where she lived alone but for her cat. She did not miss the sound of the television and the ping of the microwave on yet another ready-meal and she wondered often why she kept illicitly taking substance from time to time and visiting that existence, which both repulsed and fascinated her in equal measure. As for the cat, it was often said that felines were neither entirely of this place or another, and could cross the threshold between the real and the not with ease. But for whatever reason that cat in her visions never crossed over, and few cats visited the Escapement. Loretta had been with the aerialists for several years now, ever since meeting Charlie and Simone and Eduardo at Codona. It was a dismal little township and it had been devastated by the Titanomachy in past years, so that its residents were all malleably transformed in unpleasant ways, men with violins for legs, women with aquariums for eyes, the houses all tessellated, and opening in on themselves, endlessly, and linked together by Piranesian drawbridges and the like—it was a marvel the whole place stood up at all. It was a grim grey place and she had danced there alone, for settlers who wouldn't look her in the eye, nor at each other, and even the few ducats they threw her way would often enough change into sickly wasps or wounded birds and try to crawl away.

Then came Charlie with his handsome, laughing face; graceful Simone, who was always so kindly; and the small, intense Eduardo, who almost never spoke and was never still, whose feet never seemed to touch the ground.

They saw something in her. Unlike the others in that town they were whole and wholesome, filled with a controlled energy, and she came with them gladly. They travelled the small towns and outposts, performing, and she learned the adagio and the threefold way of silk, of climbs and wraps and drops, and how to walk a tightrope and how to juggle while standing on her head. Those were heady times but it was only when the four of them returned here, to the mountains, that she met Carl, their leader who awaited them, and then she saw the faces in the stone.

The laughter and the smell of moonshine and the haze of smoke grew in intensity inside the dining car. Mr. Norvell looked at the Stranger with his curious gaze, and he laced his fingers together, and cleared his throat. "That flower I only heard tale of," he said. "It lies beyond the Mountains of Darkness, beyond even the reach of Colossi or pupae. Yes, yes. I have travelled far, stranger, but never there. They lie beyond the Great Salt Lakes, they say. There is a passage underground, where only the dead can walk. Or so it's said." He shrugged. "I could help you forget it," he said. "Your quest. For a handful of ducats, I can give you the gift of forgetting. That much, I can do."

The Stranger nodded. His fingers rested lightly on the butt of his gun, under the table.

"What were you doing in Kellysburg?" the Stranger said. "If you don't mind me asking? It is a little off the . . . beaten path."

Mr. Norvell shrugged. "I go where there's need."

"And was there? Need?"

"Not as much as I'd hoped."

"Have you word of the war?"

"The Titanomachy rages on," Mr. Norvell said, complacently. "What more is there to say?"

"I met a man in Kellysburg," the Stranger said. "I think he was looking for something. A sort of new weapon one side or the other had got hold of."

Mr. Norvell's eyes hardened but he shook his head. "Of that I do not know," he said. Then his look turned shrewd and he said, "Do you, stranger?"

The Stranger drew his gun and cocked it, under the table. Mr. Norvell registered the sound and his lips pursed but he said nothing.

"I don't think I like you," the Stranger said.

Mr. Norvell shrugged.

"Take off your glasses."

Mr. Norvell reached up carefully and removed his glasses. He placed them on the table. The noise of the drinkers was all about them, engulfing them in a bubble of silence. In the galley the two cooks continued to work, oblivious to them. The Stranger did not look directly into Mr. Norvell's eyes. He turned his head, looking at the galley, at the woman rolling dough and the man stirring and stirring the gun stew, and he looked at the snake oil man sideways, from the corners of his eyes, and as he looked the man's eyes seemed to become two black tunnels—

At that moment the lights in the dining car dimmed and went out. The cook swore, softly. The train hit a switch and then the mountains filled the windows of both sides of the train as it entered the mountain pass. The Stranger's free hand shot across the table but all he caught hold of was Mr. Norvell's soft felt hat. The train rocked from side to side and a moment later the lights came back on.

Mr. Norvell's black suit remained in the seat but his hat, which the Stranger had grasped, was nevertheless gone, as was the man himself. Of his briefcase of medicinal samples there was, likewise, no trace. Only the suit remained, as though mocking the Stranger, with its starched white shirt and its black formal jacket, and on the table, he now saw, wedged under a single, stoppered whalebone vial, was a little visiting card. The Stranger slid the card from under the bottle and turned it over. Under a stylised snake curled round a wooden staff, it said, JEFFERSON & NORVELL, MEDICI, and, below that in smaller letters, an address: ASCLEPIUS GARDENS, JERICHO. The Stranger turned it in his fingers thoughtfully, then slipped it into a pocket. He picked up the small bottle and saw that it was marked LETHE. He unstoppered it and sniffed, then made a face. He stoppered the bottle again and put that, too, in his pocket.

The train thundered through the mountain pass. Fat drops of snow fell beyond the windows, and the escaping light from the dining car caught them as they fell. On the other side from the Stranger, a fight broke out between the card players, and they were now short one player.

Temperanza was gone.

And the Stranger had a bad feeling, a feeling that something bad, very bad, was coming.

A large, sweating prospector roared in anger as he tossed

cards in the air, and he pulled out a gun on the Kid, who was sitting with his back to the galley. The Stranger rose with one easy motion and his own revolver pressed against the man's thick neck.

The man froze.

"Is there a problem?" the Stranger said.

The man slowly shook his head. The Kid grinned, swiped the ducats on the table towards him and began to put them away. "No problem," he said, cheerfully. "Me and Chalky here were just having a misunderstanding about the lady's chips, she seems to have vanished and we've just been, err, *debating*, the fairest way to split them, isn't that right, Chalky?"

"S'right, kid," the large man said. There were white traces of substance all over his overalls, and now and then he seemed to go in and out of focus, and the Stranger could see, fleetingly, bits of the room and the furniture through his skin. "S'right."

The Stranger removed the gun from the big man's neck. The Tarocchi cards lay everywhere, on the table and the floor, and the Magician had fallen by the Stranger's feet. He looked at it for a moment before slipping back into his seat and, a moment later, the Kid came over, carelessly pushed off the discarded black suit of clothes, and sat down opposite, still grinning.

"Thanks for that," the Kid said.

"Don't mention it."

"That dame was nice, you know. Too bad she's vanished."

"Too bad," the Stranger said.

The Kid, chatty, said, "He's not a bad guy, is Chalky. No hard feelings. Has three claims down in Kellysburg and environs. When he sells his shipment of substance in Jericho he'll be set for life. Eh, Chalky?"

"S'right, kid," the large prospector said, stopping by their table. He scratched his pale forehead and a thin shower of white substance fell down gently to the floor. "I'm just going to use the jakes."

"You do that, Chalky."

The Stranger watched him walk away. He could see the door through Chalky's back, and the vestibule beyond. The big man went through and shut the door. The train rocked on its bogies. The night and the darkness pressed against the glass. The train's horn sounded, a desperate, forlorn sound. The Stranger said, "Come with me," and rose from his seat.

"What? Why?"

"Because the train's going to be attacked."

The Kid looked at him but said nothing. He got up too, and followed the Stranger out of the dining car and into the vestibule. The door to the jakes hung open, and rattled on its hinges. The Kid drew his gun but the Stranger shook his head, no, and pushed it open the rest of the way. The prospector, Chalky, was sitting slumped over the open hole in the floor. The track rolled below. Chalky's eyes were wide open, his breathing even, but most of him was gone now, had become translucent and ethereal, and through the thick frame of his body the Stranger could see, as through a screen, into that other place. On that screen, images flickered incessantly, showing a lit city, moving cars, garbage bins, people walking, shop windows, a cat that stopped and glared at them through Chalky's skin before slinking away, a boy furtively spraying the walls of an overhang with paint, a drunk in a clown costume urinating at the egress of an alleyway. They could see Chalky, or a version of him, walking down that city street, in a suit and a tie, holding a briefcase. The Kid wrinkled his nose and the Stranger quietly closed the door on the passed-out man.

"Ever since we left Kellybsurg I've had a bad feeling," the Stranger said. "There's something going on, behind the walls of the world. Tiny forms in huge empty spaces. I saw . . . something, out there in the Doinklands, and I think people are searching for it. A sort of weapon. . . ." He shrugged. "This train's carrying too much substance," he said. "I think we're going to get robbed."

"OK," the kid said.

"OK?" the Stranger said. "That's it?"

The Kid grinned and drew his gun. "Sure," he said. "Why not."

"OK, then," the Stranger said. He pushed ahead and the Kid followed, into the next car and past cabins half-empty, and into the next car again. In the last compartment the window was open. He thought he saw a sleeping figure, a pool of darkness deeper than the surrounding gloom; the snow that blew in ringed the figure with a crown of spinose structures, like thorns. But he did not linger, and at the next vestibule they had reached the engine. The door here was polished mahogany. The Stranger pushed against the door but it wouldn't budge. The Kid joined him and together they pressed with their combined force against the door until at last it gave way.

They staggered in.

The first thing the Stranger noticed about the engineer's cab was how very *cold* it was.

It was a clean, surgical sort of cold, and it soaked into the very essence of the room, into its clean white walls and its beige parquet floor. As he became aware of his surroundings he noticed the following in quick succession: the engine room down below and the stoker, working, the large windows in the nose through which he could see the tracks running ahead between the two mountains, and finally the small and irritable man who turned from the board of shining metallic instruments with a frown and said, "What are you doing here? You're not supposed to be here."

The man had tufts of hair sticking out from behind his ears and a bald dome of a head and he wore double-lens glasses, like the apothecary men had worn in Kellysburg. He only looked at them momentarily before returning to his instruments, muttering under his breath figures and measurements of a geometrical nature. But what arrested the Stranger's attention, and made his skin turn cold, was the sight of the firebox and of the stoker beside it, methodically shovelling ghosts.

The car was divided into two levels. They stood in the engineer's upper level, but to their left the floor dropped directly onto a second level, and it was there that, within a small, iron boiler, a cold white fire burned. It was not so much a fire as the antonym of one, an icy vapour that emanated from some mechanical freezer agent deep within the iron firebox. Next to the box stood the stoker, a tall and gangly figure with a skin as white as a Pierrot's. Despite the intense cold the man was nearly naked, and in his hands he held an old and blackened shovel, and beside him there was a large and open drum containing pure crystalline substance. The man methodically reached into the drum with the shovel and hefted up substance and threw it into the firebox. When the material connected with the cold flame it came alive with all the stored and possible permutations of that other place, and the Stranger saw faces and torsos and arms emerge out of the firebox, mouths open in speech or cries, eyes looking—looking at *him*, now, noticing *him*—before they vanished, so quickly he could have almost imagined it. There were so many of them that men merged into women and faces became the fantastical representation of phoenixes and sphinxes and all were consumed in the freezing hungry flames that had to be kept fed, over and over. The stoker never wearied from his task and his skin resembled marble and he kept shovelling ghosts into the furnace of the train.

"Great Harlequin," the Kid said. "Is that. . . ?"

"There's enough raw substance there to blow a hole from here to the underworld," the Stranger said.

The engineer turned on them again. "Get out! Get out!" he said. "What are you doing here? You are not supposed to be here."

"Look!" the Kid said. He pointed, but the Stranger didn't need prompting. The train shot through the dark and suddenly the mountains to either side disappeared as it cleared the saddle, and ahead of them, and lit by the broken moon, was the approach to the Chagrin.

The true and wild Escapement opened up before them then. In a blue-black sky floated the broken moon, wreathed in a milky veil of clouds. The mountains loomed in the distance, fencing in the mighty Nikulin and half-encircling the dark body of water into which it flowed. Straight ahead, the train tracks reached an embankment over the shores of Lake Chagrin, but they did not stop. Rising over the body of the lake was a bridge, mounted on spindly stilts that rose out of the water, and beyond it the Stranger could make out the next pier, where the bridge connected to a small island floating like a dismembered eye in the northeastern part of the lake. There the bridge sloped down before rising again from the pier on the distant bank, linking the island back to the mainland, beyond, at last, the oppressive reach of the mountains.

The train thundered toward the bridge.

The aerialists gathered against the side of the mountain. Carl had pressed his palms to the black rock and communed silently with what he called the esprit de corps. Then he nodded and, seemingly satisfied, returned to their group.

He was not himself, that was all it was, Loretta tried to tell herself. She just had to do what he wanted and then everything would be all right.

Loretta watched the dark island in the lake. The two bridges rose out of it like some sort of malignant growth, not human-made at all but a natural part of the Escapement, over-laid with the train tracks, which seemed puny and fragile in comparison.

Long, taut aerial rope slides ran down from the mountain-side and over the lake, terminating on the black rocks of the island. Loretta held on to the pulley and slid down, following Carl and Simone. Charlie and Eduardo followed her in turn. The small human shapes glided through the air over the dark water as the train emerged from between the Grand and Petite Philippes.

A rush of exhilaration filled Loretta as she rappelled away from the mountain. She filled her lungs and screamed, and in her scream there were all her hopes and fears and dreams, from the moment she was a little girl and first saw a woman do something impossible: leaping gracefully into the air and, for just a brief moment, flying. Her dreams were filled still with that other place and the doppelgänger of hers there, the schoolteacher, whom she barely remembered or knew. But it was her fears she was truly leaving behind her, for her fears had taken on a dark shape and a face, ever since she had followed the others to the mountains. She felt it now, its gaze at her back, the terrible thing that was neither human nor of that other place but truly of the Escapement. And as the distance grew she felt more and more herself again.

They landed softly, like seeds, one after the other on the inhospitable black rocks. There were only a few common loons roosting on the island, and the only habitation, beside the train interchange, was a caretaker's hut, really not much more than a booth. They moved soundlessly, and the unkempt old man who stood holding a lantern and watching the distant lights of the approaching train never even noticed them. Carl, with one graceful motion, drew a knife and threw it at the caretaker, burying it in his neck. Loretta watched the man die, and the blood that was so dark in the moonlight. She didn't want this, she realised, she didn't want to be here, all she had ever wanted was to fly.

They went to retrieve the stilts that had been hidden by the black rocks.

Loretta wanted to flee. Then she looked up, and saw the stern face of the watching mountain, and she did nothing.

Carl motioned for her. He took hold of the caretaker's lantern and gently extinguished it. At Carl's bidding, Loretta went and pushed the switch that would shift the train onto the island's internal loop. Please, she thought. I don't want anyone else to get hurt.

The others returned with the stilts and she donned a pair

too. They began to move with purpose, as graceful as storks, across the shallow water past the island.

"What was that?" the Kid said.

"What?"

"That!"

The Stranger peered ahead. The train rushed toward the lake and then with a *bump* it hit the switch and was onto the bridge. The water fell on either side of them as they rose over the bent stalk structure of the bridge. He caught a glimpse of the mountains on their left, ringing that side of the lake which led on to the wild Doinklands. A dark rock face, for one awful moment, resembled an austere patrician's physiognomy. He turned his gaze from it with an effort. A cold dread clutched at his heart.

"There it is again!"

And now he could see it. The shifting shadows rose over the water, moving with unexpected poise. At first he thought them huge birds of some kind. As they came closer they separated, two to either side of the train, and he saw that they weren't birds at all but stilt walkers.

Then they disappeared, their legs dropping into the black water, and he felt more than heard the dull impact of bodies on the roof. He drew his gun and the Kid did the same. The engineer cursed under his breath and the stoker kept feeding ghosts to the flames.

At that moment a flare burst up into the sky over the island. The engineer cursed again as he adjusted his instruments.

"What is that?" the Kid said.

"An emergency flare," the engineer said. "Why are you two still here?"

"We think the train's about to be robbed," the Stranger said.

The engineer didn't respond, but his shoulders tensed. The Stranger said, "What does the flare mean?"

"The caretaker wants us to go onto the loop," the engineer said. "It's an emergency measure in case the train needs maintenance or there are concerns about the bridge ahead. But I was not aware . . ."

"Kid, cover the entrance," the Stranger said.

The Kid nodded. He moved quietly and stood guard, guns drawn. His cheerful grin was back on his face, the same one he wore when he won at cards.

"Can you take her straight on?" the Stranger said.

"Override the switch? It's too dangerous," the engineer said. He touched the controls and the train began to slow as it rose and then began its descent towards the island. He barked a command in a language the Stranger didn't know. The stoker didn't pause from his job but he began to feed the flames more slowly, and in half measures, and the ghosts seemed to last longer in that fashion, and their faces lingered in the Stranger's mind, and their lips formed silent words he did not wish to interpret.

At that moment the door to the cab exploded inwards.

The Kid was thrown back and the door slammed against the floor with a heavy thump. The Stranger's gun pointed at the invaders but the engineer shouted, "No shooting!" and he withheld his fire.

There were three of them who streamed in, and one standing guard outside. They did not hold guns but rather small and lethal-looking mechanical crossbows, which had been strapped to their backs but now pointed at the Stranger and at the engineer's back. The Kid was on the floor and a small woman stood over him pointing her weapon at his heart. He remained lying.

"Bring her down slow," the woman said. "This is a robbery."

"No shit," the Stranger said, wearily.

The engineer cursed softly, under his breath, but he did as he was told.

"No one has to get hurt," Loretta said, more in hope than in confidence. Simone had her crossbow aimed at the kid on the ground and Eduardo now moved to cover the engineer, making sure there would be no surprises. Charlie stood guard outside, and it left Loretta to cover the tall gangly stranger who wasn't even supposed to be there. No one paid attention to the stoker. "Just don't try to be a hero," she said.

"Trust me," the Stranger said. "No one here's a hero."

"We just want your cargo," Loretta said.

"Shut up, Loretta," Simone said.

"What cargo?" the Stranger said. "Substance?"

"If he talks again, shoot him," Simone said to Loretta. Loretta looked at the Stranger. He had sad eyes, she thought. The train slowed down as it approached the island. Eduardo pressed the arrow's tip into the engineer's back. Everything was going according to plan. At least until the stoker went mad and released the ghosts.

The man had put down the book he had been reading to the boy and now he sat in the kitchen drinking coffee and his head pulsed with pain. The woman moved around with a distracted air as though she simply could not sit still, and the man winced with the bright daylight and with the sound of cars outside, and each time he heard a horn he winced.

I couldn't, he said, I couldn't stay there anymore.

I know.

I had, I had this dream that I could do something, that even now, just sitting here, I should be elsewhere, searching for—

I know, she said. I know. And then she burst out crying. She cried quietly. The tears just ran down her face and she never made a sound or tried to wipe them away. She kept moving, kept pacing the small kitchen from side to side. He rose to her. He put his hand on her cheek, felt her skin wet with tears.

There's nothing, she said, savagely. There's nothing, there's nothing, there's—!

The Stranger came to with a rush of air. Ghosts kept streaming out of the boiler, mouths open in soundless screams. The cab felt freezing. The stoker was on the floor with an arrow through his chest. The drum of substance had rolled and the crystal dust fell everywhere and the cold flames had latched on to it and filled the whole room. The Kid was on the floor, gasping for air. The train's windshield was broken and the engineer was holding in vain to the instrument panel and cursing, over and over, in an unknown tongue. The island rushed towards them. Of the banditti, the man who had watched the engineer had been thrown through the windshield and was somehow holding on to the broken glass with bloodied hands before he finally let go and was sucked away into nothingness. The girl who had kept watch over the kid was dead with a bullet in the heart. The man who'd guarded the door was gone, and the only one remaining was the girl, Loretta. He tended to remember someone's name when they were threatening to kill him.

Loretta looked frightened. She turned, still holding her crossbow, from him to the Kid and back again. "Step back!"

"What are you looking for, on the train?" the Stranger said again.

"I don't know!"

"Is it the substance?"

"I don't *know!*"

The Kid got up. The engineer cursed as the train hit the switch on the island and shifted to the loop, slowing down.

"Don't *brake!*" the Stranger said.

The engineer mumbled something unintelligible.

"What?"

"I can't shift her back!" the engineer said. "There's a—" He subsided again into furious muttering.

The Stranger stared out of the windshield. The dark and desolate landscape of the island gave nothing away. The lake gloamed all around them, trapping them in, looping in on themselves. He pointed his gun at the girl and cocked the hammer.

"Tell me what you are looking for," he said.

An explosion tore through the night. The caretaker's hut was a ball of flame, and the fire snatched at the starlight, casting an eerie glow as the flames danced in a wild tarantella. The Stranger saw a small, lithe figure leap, impossibly, into the air, with unwholesome grace, and then the man was through the broken windshield and inside the cabin with them.

"Carl!" Loretta said. The Kid trained his gun on the man, who was unarmed. Carl smiled faintly at the Stranger.

"The Dumuzi Device," he said.

Loretta stared at them all helplessly. She knew Carl, knew what he was capable of. He'd once tossed her against the wall with a contemptuous casualness when she'd dared ask for a break from the endless practice, and she'd broken her funny bone in two places.

A terrible fear squeezed her insides. The others were talking, they thought they had control of the situation. She wanted off the train. She longed to escape, to go anywhere but there. Even, she thought with a shudder, to that other place.

"What?" the Stranger said. He seemed so slow and dim-witted then. It was happening, she could feel it.

"A chthonic bomb," Carl said, carelessly. It was the way he did all things. It was how the others ended up dead, she realised, Eduardo and Simone. Because he never cared, they were all just tokens to him.

"It's a large piece of materiel. We have reason to believe it is on this train."

"What does it . . . do?" the Kid said.

Carl shrugged. He brought his hands together, then spread them wide, in slow motion.

". . . oh."

The train kept going round and round the island. The care-taker's hut burned bright. It was coming, she could feel it. The Stranger said, "It looks like your plan didn't work."

"How so?" Carl said.

"Your people are dead. You're outnumbered. It's just you, and the girl over there."

"Loretta," she said. "My name is Loretta!"

But they didn't listen to her. They were so arrogant, the men. With their useless guns and the casual way they pointed them about, like it didn't matter! She could hear it, then, that awful laugh from far away, crazed and inhuman and big, so big.

It was too late.

They heard it too, now. That scrawny kid and the man who thought he was in charge of things. He said, "What is that?'"

"But that is it, don't you see?" Carl said. "You had it all wrong, stranger. It isn't just me, and Loretta. It's so much more than us, than any of us. They need it. They need the Dumuzi Device."

"Listen to me," Loretta said. "Listen to me, you have to get out of here, you have to get off the island!"

But they were so slow, so much without grace. They moved so stiffly. Their faces stupid with incomprehension. She looked out of the windshield and then she saw it.

It was coming, at last.

The Colossus.

From high above the lake, from the pitiless gaze of a Colossus, they all seemed so *puny*. The little toy train running round and round on the track, trapped on that little baleful island. The bridges shone wetly to either side. They looked like wings, the island like a beetle. The loons chattered nervously on the black rocks and high above on the Erlandson trees the caiques cowered in the leaves.

No, no, make it stop, make it stop, the Stranger said, but concepts like *sound* no longer existed. On the hopping cars, uselessly guarding the useless substance, armed men went mad and fired gut-shots into the darkness and mostly succeeded in killing each other.

It began to snow then, big fat drops of snow, as the great big mountain shook itself from its bond of rock and roots, triggering landslides, bringing down trees, as the Colossus took one giant step and then another, feet of stones slamming into the lake bed, causing the very earth to shake and triggering a miniature tsunami.

The moonlight caught its face, its terrible and beautiful face with its classical angles of antiquity, and the loons cried on the island and the passengers tried to throw themselves out of the windows of the train, and the Stranger reached desperately into his pocket, for the bottle marked LETHE, to swallow the snake oil inside, to somehow stop this awful, unbearable sensation, to block his ears to the dreadful laughter of the Colossus, to find oblivion.

It was so easy from above for the Colossus to see the humans' fragile, fleeting thoughts as dazzling fireflies flying in confusion, for they were nothing to it, these . . . *people,* mere irritants upon the body of the Escapement, ants that crawled through the cracks in the worlds.

On the train, this limb of the Colossus, this mindless appendage, this *Carl,* as the humans called it, shuddered as it responded to the Colossus's demands. The Colossi had to find it, this thing of the pupae umbrarum, this device. But already they felt they had been misled, that it was not, had never been, on the train, and their rage grew and they took another step, and another, detaching themselves entirely from the mountain range, until the Colossus stood up to its chest in the black water of the Chagrin.

It was Loretta who saved them. She had to. The Kid and the Stranger were shooting at the juddering, inhuman thing that Carl had become. As though its colossal master had reached across the lake and stuck some terrible feast into Carl's insides, stretching and bending the human material of the host like a sock. Now the thing that was previously Carl barely resembled anything human. The creature launched itself at them, knocking a vial from the Stranger's hand onto the floor, before it scuttled away, faster than a bullet could follow, into the train, scenting and hunting for its masters' prey. What made her grab the bottle she didn't know, but its contents seemed to sing to her, a faint white glow emanated from its inside, offering redemption. She leaped out of the broken windshield, landing near the burning caretaker's hut. The snow fell over the flames, sparks shot up, she felt her hair singe and her hands grow cold. It was there, just within reach, the lever, and all she had to do was push it, and she could save them.

Then she turned her head and, under the glow of the moon, she saw it, she saw the face of the Colossus. What sculptor had formed that dark visage? That sneering mouth and that predator's beak, the taloned hands resting in their opal throne? It never *moved*, it never lived or breathed, and yet the mountain was no longer in its place but in the water, and when she looked again it was closer, and then closer again. The snow did not fall on its beautiful and ageless face. It crowded her mind, it drove her out of it. There was only room for the Colossi in the world, there was no room for her in it.

Dark waves raced against the shore. They slammed into the island with the fury of elementals, and perhaps it was that, the spray of Chagrin water and the cold wind blowing in from the peaks that broke the spell, that let her finally, with the last of her power, push the lever.

In the cab, the engineer had never stopped cursing but now he suddenly went quiet, as the track *shifted*, and the little toy train circled one more time round the island, but slow, too slow. The Colossus roared then with a laugh that was pure rage. It was so close, another step, two at the most. The Stranger barked at the Kid, who looked at him in mute horror, but had no choice but to obey. He climbed down to the stoker's cabin and pried the shovel from the dead man's hands. He began to feed the flames.

The Stranger sank to the floor. He could no longer hear and there was blood coming out of his ears and his nose. He trained his guns on the open doorway, and waited. The Colossus took one more step, and then it was by the shore. The train gathered power and the engineer cursed one last time and checked his gauges and manipulated his controls and then the train hit the switch and was rerouted from the loop onto the bridge. The Colossus screamed its laugher again and the very rocks of the islands cracked and sinkholes opened everywhere and the caretaker's burned hut disappeared into the ground. The mad ichorous thing that was Carl burst through the door then and the Stranger shot it, emptying both his revolvers into the creature.

It was not there, the Dumuzi Device. The Colossi had been fed false information, their ancient enemy had played them

once again for fools. In the eternal war that was the Titanomachy, a score for the pupae umbrarum.

The Colossus yanked the now useless lifeline from its ser-
vant-appendage's form. The creature that was Carl dropped
to the floor, black-ink blood staining the walls and the floor
as it died. The ghosts in the boiler screamed, soundlessly, and
then the train was over the stalk of the bridge. Slow it climbed
and then faster as it reached the topmost part and began the
descent towards land. By then the Colossus had boarded the
island and begun to tear it apart. It cared nothing for the fleeing fireflies on their little toy train. It merely wished to express
its displeasure. The train fled— Well, let it flee. The Stranger leaned back against the wall and closed his eyes, for just a
moment. The memory of that terrible face was etched forever
in his mind. Then he forced his eyes open, and his limbs to
move, and he climbed down to the stoker's landing, to help
the Kid with the boiler. The engineer, for the first time, smiled
with grim satisfaction, and his fingers moved dexterously over
the instrument panel. Then the train hit land and raced on,
away from the mountains, and the snowfall, away from the
Chagrin, and into open space again, and the wide expanse of
the Thickening.

On the shore, Loretta was still alive. She felt the destruction all
around her, and the Colossus's anger, and its image was forever
in her mind now, crowding out all others, everything that was
her. There was a thing in her hand, a vial of some sort. But even
the word for vial now escaped her. Without curiosity or thought,
but only instinct, she uncorked it and put it to her mouth.

She drank the waters of Lethe (bottled by Jefferson & Norvell, of Asclepius Gardens, Jericho). The water was colourless and flavourless, but the relief it offered was immediate and lasting. She felt her mind, everything she was, Loretta of the swift dance and the impossible flying, Loretta of the Fabulous Flying Banditti, she felt her go. Her outline grew faint as rocks flew around her, as the Colossus destroyed the island. All that remained for her now was that schoolteacher in her little apartment with her cats, the woman whose name Loretta no longer even recalled. She did then the last and the most terrifying thing an aerialist could ever do.

She let go.

From high above, the little caiques watched the destruction and they were sad, and scared, but they were also creatures of the Escapement, and therefore used to such things. They saw the outline of the woman on the island grow faint and finally fade, and knew that, when she woke up, she would no longer remember them or their song, for she no longer belonged on the Escapement, and the people of that other place had forfeited wonder for the prosaic long ago.

The train raced away from there, and for a time it would be safe, away from the Titanomachy and the machinations of Colossi and pupae. The Kid paused from shovelling ghosts and looked at the Stranger mournfully.

"Well, that's another fine mess you've gotten us into," he said.

FIVE:
THE WAITING PLACE

THE ROOM was very bright and the child frail. He was frail in a sort of doll-like way, like one of those anatomical models where you could see the bones drawn onto the skin surface. The boy's eyes were large and the irises were a guileless blue. It was the blue of waterfalls and deep, clear skies in the late afternoon. How his eyes got their colour the man never knew. His own eyes were green. But he never stopped marvelling at this child, not just from the moment that this tiny bundle first emerged into the world, when the man, for all that he was petrified, was given the scissors to cut the umbilical cord, for all that he tried to protest; but earlier, as the boy grew bone by bone and limb by limb in its mother's belly, when he could feel it moving there, inside. The boy hiccupped a lot in the womb. And the man talked to him, through that thin membrane of skin, and sang to him, too: he did that a lot, back then.

But he never stopped marvelling at this, his boy, and those eyes which he had secretly always thought would fade away to grey once the boy passed his first year; but they never did.

Now the boy lay, patiently, on the sliding table of the machine. He didn't speak and the man held his hand but said nothing, either. He had run out of words long before. The doctors moved about the room like white ghosts. They were brisk and efficient and gave nothing away. The room was kept very cold. A motor hummed and the tray that the boy lay on slowly slid towards the belly of the machine. The machine kicked into life and the boy disappeared inside and the man and the woman waited. They had been waiting a long time and were destined to wait for a long time more.

A cloud of butterflies had engulfed the broken train in the night. The train crawled along the tracks, a wounded, dying beast, and the butterflies hit the broken windows and burst inside and fluttered along the corridors where blood-soaked carpets lay ruined. The Kid and the Stranger were holed up in the engineer's cabin and the engineer kept muttering and twiddling his instrument panel and in the boiler the ghosts kept fluttering half-heartedly. It was possible that the butterflies were drawn to the ghosts, for it was said that butterflies, on the Escapement, were merely the vessels of spirits from that other place, and who was to say whether it was true or not?

The butterflies vanished in the dawn light as silently as they had come. The ghosts in the boiler faded away to nothing and the engineer stopped muttering and his hands were still, and the train came to an ungainly halt at the nearest stop: an outpost of the Thickening in the middle of a great empty plain.

A solitary wooden sign, planted in the hard ground, gave the name of the terminal: LUGAR DE ESPERA.

As soon as the train stopped the engineer collapsed to the floor and remained there. He was fast asleep. The Kid and the Stranger disembarked. The Kid was covered in ghostly substance and the Stranger in black ink and blood. Now they stood there, in the pale light of dawn, and looked on the terminal.

It was not really a town, merely a waiting station on a branch line, and it was miles still from any other human habitation. Nothing around. The sky spread over the grey empty plain like a mirror which only served to enhance the place's isolation. There is nowhere to go, it seemed to suggest. There is nowhere to run. Not from here.

There was a long terminal building built with wooden floors and a sloping tin roof, and a garage, which was shut, and a convenience store, which was also shut. The Stranger looked to the distance and he thought he hadn't looked properly before. Somewhere out there on the plain a group of people, ill-discerned, was digging. But what was there to dig?

There were a few isolated buildings dotted around here and there in what passed for a town, homes or sheds it was impossible to say. The only other large building was made of bricks and looked like a factory though there were no workers he could see nor smoke coming out of the chimneys. Attached to the factory building there was a clock tower and its clock kept beating, and the sound of the seconds reverberated through the town and into the ground and into the Stranger's soul.

He did not like this place. It was hard to look straight at the clock. The hour hand was stuck on twelve and the minute hand on five to twelve and the hand that counted the seconds was the only one moving, but it was trapped against the minute hand and only kept beating out its signal against the same never-ending time, moving in place like a captured moth trying to break free. He looked at the Kid and the Kid shrugged.

"I need breakfast," the Kid said. He stretched and yawned. "Think anyone's serving in this dump?"

"Horses first," the Stranger said. The Kid shrugged again.

They went to fetch their horses, who seemed little affected by the earlier attack. They were creatures of the Escapement, with no ties to that other place and little regard for the affairs of Colossi or pupae. The Stranger's horse nuzzled his face and the Stranger stroked the horse's long neck. They had travelled together for some time and were destined to ride together for a time longer. As they came back towards the front of the train, the Stranger saw a solitary figure approach them.

He was a tall, thin man in the uniform of a conductor, with a head too large for his body, and entirely bald, so that he appeared like a marionette whose head would not quite stay on properly.

"What happened here? Who are you? Where is the engineer?"

"We came under attack over the Chagrin," the Stranger said. "The engineer is in his cabin. He got us this far, but no farther."

"An attack? But this is most irregular!" the conductor said. He looked at a pocket watch and shook his head mournfully. "This is terrible, the timetables will all be out of tune!"

The Stranger noticed that the pocket watch seemed to bear no hours or minutes and that all its hands were missing, but he kept his thoughts private. The conductor muttered to himself, ignoring them.

"You will arrange for the other passengers?" the Stranger said.

"Yes, yes," the conductor said. "It is taken care of."

The Stranger looked back and he saw that the conductor was right. A group of figures in grey, shapeless clothes, perhaps the workers he had seen earlier digging out there on the plain, were now moving lethargically but with purpose across the cars. They helped down the passengers, but what they did with them and where they took them he couldn't tell. He felt disinclined to ask. They were in the Thickening now and this was a job for the railway company. He followed the Kid towards the long cabin and saw that a sign did indeed say WAITING ROOM on the door. They went in.

The floor was clear if unswept. Long benches lined the walls, and he saw with some surprise that there were many people waiting there. They sat with their backs to the walls, the men in worn suits and hats, the women as drab as the men, and all looking down at the ground with dull and listless eyes. They looked as though they had been waiting a long time, and were ready to wait for a long while more. The Stranger himself felt bone-tired and robbed of vitality. He wanted nothing more now than to sit down on those self-same benches and wait. He wondered how long they'd been waiting for. Surely the train came past here often enough?

At the end of the long hall there was a small kiosk. They made towards it. No one looked up at them or observed their passing. He heard no chatting or rustle of pages, nothing but a dull silence. He was somewhat surprised to discover, upon arrival, that the kiosk counter was open for business. A large, pleasant-faced woman stood behind it, though she looked surprised at their arrival.

"Can I help you?"

"What happened to everyone here?" the Kid said. "They look like they've given up the ghost."

The woman looked at him sharply but said nothing. The ticks of the clock reverberated through the building, through the Stranger's bones. He was keenly aware that something was wrong. He just didn't know what. There was no substance here, and the walls between this town and that other place were firm.

"Two coffees, please," the Kid said.

"Coffee?" the woman said. She said it doubtfully, indeed as a woman trying to wake up from a deep and pleasant dream. "There is no coffee."

"Well, what have you got?" the Kid said. "You must serve *something*."

"Porridge," the woman said.

"Porridge?"

The woman looked at him as though trying to place him.

"Porridge," she said at last, with finality.

"But I don't *like* porridge," the Kid said, plaintively. The Stranger turned away from them. He took out a tough piece of jerky and chewed on it as he surveyed the waiting room. None of the waiting people stirred. He tried to concentrate but it was hard.

The woman had her back to them then, and was stirring a massive cast-iron pot in which something pleasant-smelling was bubbling. He stared at her. She had pulled back her long sleeves as she worked, and he saw now what it was that he'd instinctively noticed. Her upper arm, between the elbow and the shoulder, had been hollowed out and the skin had turned to glass. Inside the glass were two further glass chambers, linked to each other by a narrow tube. They were filled with ants. The ants kept moving inside the woman's arm. When she raised her hand, the upper chamber would slowly fill with ants and, when she lowered it, the part nearer the elbow would then fill, as with some forever moving hourglass in which time was suspended in an equilibrium. He said, "You're a veteran?"

The woman turned to him. She dropped her arm and her sleeve came down and covered it. She shrugged.

"Long ago," she said.

"Who did you fight for?" the Stranger asked, curious.

The woman seemed torn in indecision. It was not that her look was unfriendly, or not entirely. It was just that the question seemed to have brought her out of some state in which she wasn't even aware she was dwelling. Some vitality had returned to her face. She said, "We were riding out with General Zavatta to the crystal fountains. It was far from here, at the foot of the Big Rock Candy Mountains. We didn't really know about the war, you understand. Zavatta promised us stew, all that we could eat, and whiskey, and we were hungry, we were young and we were hungry and we were ready for anything. Or so we thought. We rode out that day, leaving behind us tiny homesteads and work on the mines. Our heads were filled with dreams of glory. But instead we rode out for days through the Doinklands. The little food we had was soon gone and the clowns laid traps for anyone intruding on their territory. We lost two riders to a trampoline and Billy Bob got hit in the face by a pie and his face melted clean off. At last we came upon a clown village. It was us or them. It wasn't war, it was a massacre. They tried to run. Some tried to fight back but they were no match for us. We were hungry and ruthless and we wanted blood. That day we slaughtered every one of them and burned down their homes and we rode away from there whooping and hollering and with our bellies filled with food. The smoke stung my eyes, I remember that. We rode that way and Zavatta told us of creeks running with whiskey and trees where cigarettes grew. You have to understand, none of us knew that other place, we were all of the Escapement. In a ravine we came upon a giant stone foot lying severed on the dry riverbed, three of its toes blasted off. We didn't know who we were fighting or why. On the homesteads, some of the old folk spoke of the Titanomachy, but none had been in the war, none but for an old boy, an ex-miner with a parrot for a hand, and he never talked about it at all.

"That night we camped by the giant stone foot and made fires. It was then that I noticed how General Zavatta's shadow, in that light, seemed so much bigger than him, and when they moved, I could not shake off the awful feeling that it was the shadow that moved first, and the man who followed.

"That night two of the boys got into a fight and killed each other under the big toe. It happened so quickly, it was hard to comprehend when it happened, only by that point none of us cared. It was just more spilled blood, for us. It required neither sense nor rhyme. One moment they were friendly, talking about some girl back home that both of them knew. The next there was a knife out, flashing in the firelight, and the shot of a gun. The smell of gunpowder. Blood spilled on the dry riverbed. Two bodies cooling under the big toe of the broken giant. After that Zavatta made us march from that place. We found other pieces of the Colossus on our way: a finger, an ear. It only dawned on me later that the mountain we were traversing resembled a torso.

"The weather grew cold and snow flurries fell as we snaked our way up the mountains. There were clowns there, too, in the ice. Hobos, mostly. We strung them up when we could. More often they would take potshots at us from the high passes, or trigger an avalanche of bright yellow balls. We lost three riders that way, and ate their horses and were grateful for the meat.

"There was no question of deserting. Zavatta led and Zavatta couldn't be questioned. There was nowhere to escape to, only the mountains and the clowns and death on every side. Then we were through the mountains at last and away from the clowns, and we were joined on a great plain by other companies, with other commanders and their shadows. The next night the full broken moon shone down and in its light we saw the line of colossal statues lining up on the horizon, silent figures, huge beyond measure, and behind them the stars in the night.

"We charged. Shadows fled and people died. The Colossi had people, too. I shot and I knifed and I bludgeoned. How many I don't know. My horse was shot from under me. All this time there was awful laughter and it was punctured by pockets of silence that were somehow more terrible in themselves. Back and forth it went, the sound and the lack of sound, and the plain ran red with our blood.

"In the morning the Colossi were gone as though they had never been, and the horizon was empty and clear. There was no sign of Zavatta, and the plain was covered in the dying and the dead. When I came to I was lying under a fallen horse. My shoulder was broken and I had lost two of my toes, and my upper arm was turned into the thing you see now. It itches sometimes, in warm weather. Sometimes I can hear the ants scuttling inside, late at night, but I find their company soothing.

"A few of us, the survivors, banded together. Some had served pupae, some Colossi. It didn't seem to matter, just as the battle we took part in made no sense to us. The plain seemed to me then to have been a sort of checkers board, and we were the pieces being pushed around. For what benefit, I couldn't tell you. I don't think anyone could.

"We wandered the Escapement. Without Zavatta we had no direction. I was affected the least. One man had lost half his body. It did not seem to affect him badly, it's just that the entire left side of his body was missing, as though it had been erased, yet he was able to move normally, as though that missing part was still somehow there, in ghostly form. Another woman had her head turned into a mirrored helmet, and she could speak only with her hands. One person, Rudy, was half-turned into an organ and when he moved he played sad mournful tunes. In this fashion we wandered searching for a home. We could not return to the lonely homesteads and the mines. We were veterans of a war we didn't understand, and just as quickly as we had been used we were discarded.

"I don't know what happened to the others. One day I came here and . . ."

The dull look was back in her eyes and without saying another word she turned and began stirring the porridge again. The Kid and the Stranger exchanged glances.

"I don't think I want any porridge," the Kid said.

"No," the Stranger agreed. The beats of the clock sounded in the still air, *Tick, Tick, Tick, Tick.*

"Let's get out of here," he said.

But there was no respite from the oppressive sense of *waiting* out there either. The sky was grey and the air felt humid and unmoving, and the clock in the clock tower beat louder there, the sound expanding to fill up all that still, unpleasant silence. The Stranger offered the Kid a stick of jerky and the Kid accepted without much grace. They stood there together and chewed.

"There's something not *right* with this place," the Kid said. "Or, for that matter, with that woman."

"I know," the Stranger said. He chewed some more, without enthusiasm. "It's strange," he said. "I heard that name before. Zapata or Zavatta, something like that at any rate. And I heard about that battle she mentions, at the Big Rock Candy Mountains. It was less a battle than a massacre, by all accounts, and the greatest massing of forces in the Titanomachy for centuries. But that's just it. Even with the way time flows differently in different places on the Escapement . . . it must have been more than a century ago."

"But she doesn't look older than thirty," the Kid protested.

"I know."

"I wish that damn clock would stop ticking," the Kid said.

"I do too," the Stranger said.

A man came out of the garage then, wiping his hands on a piece of cloth. He wore long blue overalls and had a shock of unruly black hair and the same pleasant yet somehow vacant smile of the kiosk woman.

"Hello, hello," he said. He looked at them with a polite lack of curiosity.

"Who're you?" the Kid said, a little rudely. The man blinked at him with a friendly lack of concern.

"I'm Lucas," he said. He extended a hand for a shake, which both men ignored. "I'm the mechanic."

"Not much call for a mechanic round here," the Stranger said.

"Tick tock, tick tock," the mechanic said, and giggled. "I used to be a *chasseur de clown*, a bounty hunter," he said. "We rode in the Doinklands, hunting Whitefaces and Augustes for the reward money from the bank. We always avoided the conflicts of Colossi and pupae. What did we need *them* for? Our leader was Zebedee, the greatest of the chasseurs. He could read the strength of the enemy in a dollop of dropped custard, could discern the position of our prey in one careless mark of chalk. For a long time we lived like this, in the wild places beyond the Thickening. We only rode into town with our bounty, and then we'd drink moonshine and Sticks, those of us who still had a hankering for that other place. Not me, Chief. All right, sometimes I would succumb, and I would see hazy visions, a time and a place where it seems to me I was a railway engineer, who drank too much and read dime novels, who lived alone. *He*, that other man in that other place, kept searching for a way out, for a world where he could be something he was not. He was searching for the Escapement, I think. I did not like those visions, which I saw as needless escape into fantasy, and so I eventually stopped drinking Sticks altogether.

"Around that time, Zebedee was caught in a trampoline trap near a Whiteface encampment. Poison custard left half his face mutilated, and he'd broken all the bones in his left leg, but he survived. He changed then, though. And sometimes he carried on conversations with his shadow, and sometimes he would pause at unexpected moments, when peeling an apple for example, and he'd stare at the apple or the knife with a look of complete bewilderment, as though he didn't know what either of them was for.

"Not long after his recovery, Zebedee pushed us farther than ever before into the Doinklands. We were headed beyond any human presence, far away from the small teardrop that was the Thickening. I had never realised before how immense the Escapement was, and how little of it belonged to us. I did then, and it frightened me. We were mere trespassers, new arrivals on this vast and shifting landscape. For a while still we hunted bounty, but where was there to claim it? Soon Zebedee grew bored even with that. All we did was ride, along prairies where the wild Harlequinade ran—a sight I had hoped never to see, which made the blood run cold!—and down valleys where the remains of *las máquinas de sueños* could still be found, and they haunted our sleep.

"Zebedee was searching for something. That became clear eventually, but what it was he never told us. We searched ancient caves dug into the sides of snow-covered mountains. We hunted through brush and forest, in the wild places where the bears still dance. At last we came to a temperate valley below the snow line. Here the air was warm and scented with spring flowers, and there was a brook running through the meadow, where three gnarled and ancient trees cast deep black shadows.

"It was there that we found it, at last. Whatever *it* was. A piece of materiel, left over from some long forgotten battle of the Titanomachy, I thought then. I am not so sure, now. it was a large and curious object. It was a mechanical-seeming large fish, like a carp, with golden scales—"

"The Dumuzi Device . . . ," the Stranger whispered.

"Excuse me?"

The Stranger thought of the fish he had seen, for just a moment, in the tinkerers' cart; and of the aerialists on the train, who were willing to kill to find it. . . .

"What does it *do*?" he said, in frustration.

The mechanic blinked at him with those guileless eyes. "*Do?*" he said. "It did nothing, nothing that I could see, beside being heavy. We had to tie ropes to it and it took four of the horses to drag it along. Zebedee was beside himself. It was then that we truly saw his shadow, and how far it covered the ground, even in the weak sun, and how it moved when the man was still. We were afraid then, I think. But he was our chief, and besides, we were too far out: we didn't know how to get back.

"He led, and we followed. Dragging the thing along behind us. It was not alive but it wasn't *inert*, either. Its mechanical gills moved and its tail thrashed the ground and its mouth opened and closed and it blinked its glass eyes. When the sun caught its scales it shone a golden colour, like summer. . . .

"Through mountain passes that had no name, where not even the clowns went, on and on we went. We lost two men to an avalanche, another we left dying when he fell off his horse in the ice. The horse we kept, the horses to drag the thing were more valuable than our lives at that point. Zebedee's shadow grew and grew until it engulfed the landscape, and it muttered and whispered in tongues we did not understand. We saw Zebedee for what he was, then: nothing but a sock puppet for the shadow to animate. We were afraid of him and did whatever he ordered, but his only command was ever to push ahead.

"Wherever we were going, we never got there," the mechanic said. "We were riding out on the prairies when the first flashes of a storm appeared on the horizon. Crosses, mostly, followed by a shower of asterisms and interrobangs. Zebedee looked concerned at first, then decided to ride on into the storm. The sky looked bruised. There was mud underfoot and the horses struggled onwards, and the fish began to flap excitedly as though the storm had revitalised it in some way. The horses whinnied and tried to run and it was hell to control them. One of the men was hit by a kick to the head and fell instantly dead to the ground.

"At that moment we heard the oncoming battle. The ground shook as though a giant foot stomped on it far away, sending repercussions across the prairies, and the horses broke away and ran into the night. The storm caught us then in its entirety and swallowed us whole. I felt it happen, then, with the Colossi marching in the distance, as Zebedee's body shot up into the air, animated from below by its shadow. . . .

"Flaming hieroglyphs touched my skin, and I felt my abdomen metamorphosing: there were vents in my chest and when I breathed the air came out hot and the vents flapped open and closed. I ran. We all ran, and the fish—the thing—was forgotten in the mud. I saw the shadow race across the prairie holding the thing that had been Zebedee aloft. Then a giant stone foot came down from the sky and crashed it into the ground. It never came back up.

"I ran, through the storm and the flashing symbols, all through the night. I survived. I don't know about the others. At last I tripped over a rock and fell. When I woke it was daytime and there was no sign of the war or of the company and I was alone. After that I wandered the Escapement for a long time. Until, one day, I came here."

He looked up at them then, kindly. "You'll like it here," he said. "You'll see. Just give it time."

"We're not *staying!*" the Kid yelled.

The mechanic looked at him with those same dull, kind eyes.

"Just give it time," he said.

The Kid stormed out. The Stranger shrugged at the mechanic, but Lucas was no longer paying them any attention. He had got up and was happily polishing the pistons of an old broken engine.

The Stranger followed the Kid outside.

"We need to get out of here," the Kid said. "Where are the horses?"

The Stranger looked, but the horses were no longer where they'd been and, somehow, he wasn't surprised. The first stirrings of an answer were coming to him. He thought about the broken maze where the Thurston Brothers had hidden, where he'd first met Temperanza. He looked on the town with new eyes. This was a newly built and ramshackle place, but what did it stand on? He had the feeling of ageless time, suspended. . . . The ticks of the clock were like the desperate knocks of a fly trapped in amber, beating against its prison.

He and the Kid returned to the train. It lay silent on the tracks. When the Stranger looked inside he saw no sign of the passengers, the dead or the wounded. The train rested alone on a single track, and the track terminated at that town. The Stranger said, "Lucas was right, this isn't a main line."

The track extended back the way they'd come. Somewhere there must have been a railroad switch, and they must have hit it on their way, and were side-tracked off the main line to Jericho and onto the spur. Now he looked but all he could see were the grey and featureless plains in all direction.

He said, "We can't leave."

The Kid said, "Sure we can. We'll just follow the track."

The Stranger shook his head. He knew it for what it was then.

"It's a sort of snare," he said.

"A what?"

"It's like a knot, but in the landscape. In the Escapement itself. Like the mazes you come across, sometimes."

"What does that mean?"

"It means the way out isn't out *there*," the Stranger said. "It's in here."

"I prefer just shooting things," the Kid said, morosely.

"Cutting the knot, yes," the Stranger said, and he smiled. But the truth was that he liked mazes, their mystery, the fact that they needed to be *solved*. But he saw the Kid wasn't interested. The Kid was fighting the malaise of the place but he was doing it badly.

The Kid said, stubbornly, "I'm going." Ignoring the Stranger, he began to march back along the tracks, into the featureless plain. His spurs clicked in time with the trapped second hand of the clock, merging with it. He'd never make it, the Stranger knew. But he couldn't stop him. Instead, he headed to the clock tower.

The Kid walked for quite a while and for a time, the going was good. He kept having the sense that there was no *point* in going, that all he had to do was turn back and go into the waiting room and sit down and, well, *wait* and, sooner or later, there would be a train—there had to be one, right? But he didn't listen to the voice in his head and kept ploughing on, stubbornly. He was very stubborn.

The Kid was born in a town called Bozoburg, which sat on the bank of a small river on the Fratellini plains. It was a small, quietly prosperous town on the edge of the Thickening, some three days' ride away from the nearest clown encampment of Whitefaces, and a week by coach to the nearest train terminus. There was a bank and a general store, and a post office that opened once a week whether anyone needed to send a letter or not. The Kid—the kid—had known, in a vague kind of way, that many of the people in the town, all of whom he knew by name, would sometimes use substance, which was a pale sort of powder quarried far away, in places where las máquinas de sueños fell from the skies in ancient times. And that sometimes they drank Sticks in one of the two saloons, and that then they would visit, or go back—the exact distinction was hazy to him—to that other place. What that other place was he wasn't entirely sure.

Once, a travelling entertainer came to the town. He brought with him a machine of sorts, called a praxinoscope, and he'd set it up in the town hall and charged a ducat at a time, and though ducats didn't come easy to the kid nevertheless he had paid admission, to watch *Mercator's Magical Shadow Show!!* as it was billed.

He'd come in, clutching his ducat, and sit down with the rest of the townfolk and the other children—they sat on the floor, while the adults sat in rough-hewn chairs—but in truth, when it came, it was a disappointment.

The adults oohed and ahhed at the shadow play: impossibly tall buildings and vehicles that moved between them at jerky speed as Mercator the Magnificent—a small, whiskered man in a faded, once-dapper sequin jacket—rolled the crank. There were flying machines in the skies and all manners of improbable miracles, and there were no horses to be seen. The kid liked horses.

His mother didn't come with him to see the shadow show. She had a loathing for all and every manner of entertainer. So the kid went alone. Ultimately, he decided, whatever this other place was it was just that: a shadow on a screen. He was bored.

Mercator stayed around for a few days but then he left and took his praxinoscope with him. He had a little wagon and a single, patient horse with eyes kinder than its owner's. The kid ran into him only once after the shadow show. Mercator was drunk and pissing against the side of the town hall when the kid passed by, after dusk. Mercator's shadow, like a grotesque extension of its owner, danced beside the man. For some reason the kid did not wish to step on or near it. He skipped around the dancing shadow and hurried away from there. For a moment the shadow felt almost alive.

The kid read whatever penny books or periodicals came through. His mother was not a voracious reader but she tolerated this habit. He rode horses and he played Hangman's Bluff and Juggler's Ball and Ghost in the Graveyard and, of course, they all played at clowns.

He was quite a happy little kid, for a while.

This all changed after the Rasmussen Gang rode into town.

But the Kid did not want to think about that now. In fact, he realised, he did not want to think about much of anything. A pleasant lassitude of thought prevailed on him. The featureless grey plains seemed never to change and the track just led on and on and on into the distance.

At last he saw something just ahead. He made for it, with that same sort of languor, and soon he saw that it was a small town, really just a collection of several buildings where the track terminated. A train stood at the end of the track with many of its windows broken and heavily sustained damage to its sides, but how it came to that state, or what it was doing there, he had no idea. It was then that a man wearing a conductor's uniform came in his way, and the Kid looked at him with some surprise. The man held an official-looking clipboard in his hands and he looked at the Kid and he looked at the clipboard and he ticked something off on the page.

He said, "You're late."

"I am?" the Kid said.

"Come with me," the conductor said. The Kid followed him meekly. I must be very late, he thought. There was a clock, somewhere nearby, and it kept ticking and ticking.

The conductor led him past the clock tower and into the plain beyond the town. As they walked, the Kid saw a group of passengers standing around in a patch of dug earth. He didn't know why he thought they were passengers. Perhaps it was that they seemed ill-suited for the purpose to which they'd been put. The men wore hats and suits and of the women, some wore dresses and some riding pants, but all of them held spades.

They were digging in the hard ground.

They dug without haste and with seeming indifference to the task they performed. Their spades rose and fell mechanically, dislodging earth, shifting it, then back again, until the spades encountered something in the ground and the diggers would stop, and frown, and lay down the spade, momentarily, in order to clear dirt from the object with their fingers. The Kid watched, and he saw that what they dug out, like turnips or yams, were timepieces.

They were clocks.

The clocks were half-melted, almost malleable, near two-dimensional in form. The diggers handled them with great reverence, brushing dirt from the clock faces before throwing them without ceremony onto a growing pile of similar objects. It was only when they touched the objects that their countenance changed, however briefly, and they seemed more animated.

"Here," the conductor said. He handed the Kid a spade. "Dig."

The Kid took the spade. It seemed natural to hold it. He joined the line and began to dig. It seemed to him he could hear something, on the edge of sound, a soft murmur underground, as though the things buried there were squirming around, shifting, trying to burrow deeper. As though they were, in a sense, alive.

As though, in a way, they were not clocks at all.

The Kid dug. When the spade hit an object he knelt down and with his fingers began to clear the dirt around the clock. When he touched it, excitement quickened in him. The materiel felt soft to the touch, pliable. The clock was like a disc of rubber in his hands. He felt it pulse against his fingertips, tiny ticks, like a baby's heart.

Then he tossed it on the pile and the sensation fled: of being awake, of being alive. He returned to digging, there on the grey and featureless plain, digging in time to the beats of the big clock.

The Stranger meanwhile had the sense that he couldn't shoot his way out of this one. He needed another story and he went to find it. He stood under the clock tower, where time was held captive, the second hand fluttering forever in its place, trapped against the minutes. He saw no one around. At last the doors to the factory opened, as he suspected they would, and a man stepped out. He was tall and wiry and a little stooped, with a thick head of greying hair, a grey-white moustache and twinkling eyes, and he moved like a man used to long days of riding.

He said, "Welcome, stranger."

The Stranger hesitated before replying, and the man did not press him. Indeed, it felt as though the man had time—all the time in the world. An air of amused contentedness emanated from him. An air of cheerful goodwill.

At last, the Stranger said, "May I ask your name?"

"My *name*?" The man's long fingers moved as though playing the piano or itching for a gun. "It has been so long, stranger, since anyone inquired . . . To tell you the truth, I am not sure I would even know it now myself.'

"Was it Zavatta, or Zapata?" the Stranger asked.

"It might have been, it might have been," the man allowed. He frowned. "It seems to me that I had many names, stranger, in my years on the Escapement. But you know as well as most, don't you, that names are not to be taken lightly. Not here."

"That is true," the Stranger allowed, and the man smiled a thin-lipped smile.

"You can call me Zebulon," he said. He offered the name tentatively.

The Stranger said, "I know who you are."

"I . . . see."

"One does not often meet one of the Major Arcana," the Stranger said. "Though I seem to, of late."

The man dipped his head in acknowledgement, but refrained from speaking.

"Tell me," the Stranger said. "What happened in this place?"

The man shrugged. "It was so long ago . . . ," he said.

"But you remember?"

"If I try hard enough. Perhaps. Yes. There was a battle, I think. Yes, that sounds right. A battle of some sort." The man spun in place. He seemed suddenly agitated. "You would not tell so, now. It happened long before the Thickening, long before woman or man set foot upon this place. We were not here, then, or perhaps we were, in a sense, but only in potentia. The land, too, did not look quite as you see it now, for 'land' and 'see' were not fully formed concepts then. There was only the war.

"It is a battle not recorded anywhere but in the grooves it's made in the Escapement. Shadow battles stone; the lizard scuttles from the glare of the sun. There was a battle here, I think, between Colossi and pupae. It created a knot in the land.

"Time passed; elsewhere. The warring factions moved on. Only their discarded materiel remained, burrowed deep underground. People came and they settled and they built railway tracks and they spread out across the Thickening, but they skirted this place. There was nothing here.

"Then, one day, I came.

"I was very tired then, I think. I have been traversing the Escapement for a long time. I have been other people, yes. Those names you mentioned. I was searching for something. Something that seemed important at the time."

"A weapon," the Stranger said.

"Yes. Perhaps," the man said, dubiously. "But then, at last I came here, on my travels. And I *felt* it, then, under the ground. A huge silence, waiting. All that untapped *time*."

Zebulon smiled at the Stranger.

"Um," he said, "would you like to see them?"

Tick, tick, tick, tick, ti . . .
ck.

The wide doors opened wide, on hidden springs, in silence. . . .
Behind them, the dark.

"Come in, come in," the Hierophant said.

The clocks filled every available surface. It was not a factory
at all, the Stranger saw, but a warehouse: the clocks were piled
up from floor to ceiling, while only in the middle was there
a long workbench on which individual pieces resided, where
other residents of Lugar de Espera worked with gloved hands,
cleaning them. There was no sound in that room but for the
distant, trapped ticks of the big clock. But there was a sort of
expectant hush, as of too much time all kept in one too-small
place, the sound of a coiled spring needing desperately to be
sprung. There were hundreds, thousands of the things. They
made the Stranger think of termite eggs.

The Hierophant rubbed his hands together. "So you see," he
said. "There really is no way out, stranger."

The mechanic, Lucas, and the kiosk woman joined him then. They had a vague blank look in their eyes. Lucas held a wrench and the woman a large metal ladle. They hovered on either side of the Hierophant. The Stranger took a step back, and Zebulon and his minions took one step forward.

"What's your rush?" Zebulon said, and he smiled, a little sadly. "We have time, stranger. All the time in the world."

The Stranger backed away from them and they followed. He pushed against the doors and they opened. He noticed the quality of the light outside never changed. It was never night or high noon in that town, but an endless suffusion of grey.

"Ah, I see they're coming," the Hierophant said.

The Stranger turned. And he saw that Zebulon was right. From out beyond the town there came a group of passengers, trudging towards them, and he thought he recognised amidst their number one of the cooks from the train.

And also, quite recognisable among them, was the Kid.

They came slowly and unhurried across the plain and they brought their cargo with them.

"Please," Zebulon said. "Wait."

"Wait," the other two said, in unison. "Wait. Wait. Wait."

The Stranger withdrew his guns. The Hierophant opened and closed his graceful gunman's fingers.

"What are you going to do," he said. It was not exactly a question.

The Stranger turned again as the group of workers came nearer. He tried to cover both sides with his guns, arms spread, but he knew it was futile. The Kid was in amongst the workers. The Kid had the same dull look in his eyes as the others. The look of a person trapped forever in a passenger lounge, waiting for a train that would never come.

The Stranger shouted, "Kid!"

The Kid turned his head and looked at him. He carried a big grey cloth sack like the others. More of the eggs must have been inside.

The Hierophant said, gently, "There is so much coiled time inside of you, stranger. You alone are not yet affected. I can give you what it is you need. I can give you *time*."

He moved his fingers in a complicated gesture. The Stranger felt the tingle of substance in his nostrils. The town faded, and for a moment he was standing in a clinically white room, where a large machine burped and hummed, two tiny legs sticking out from its cylinder. The boy was very brave to endure the procedure. What must he be thinking, trapped inside the scanner, seeing nothing but white walls?

Then it was gone. The Stranger shook his head. "No," he said. "No, it's not enough."

"You seek a cure," the Hierophant said. "But time is running out. I can give you that much. I can offer you the time to wait."

But the Stranger could not abide waiting. He could not abide the smell of hospitals and the shuffle of slow feet, the awful sense of time dripping away. He could not stand being helpless. He turned his gun and he fired, but not at the Hierophant.

He shot the Kid.

The shot merely grazed the Kid's arm. It ripped through the sleeve and left an angry red welt on the skin, drawing blood. The Kid yelled and dropped the sack he carried. Animation returned to his eyes with the pain. At his feet, the sack opened.

The clocks within shuddered and undulated as they tried to crawl away across the ground. The Kid looked wildly this way and that. The other workers turned as one and faced him. They took one step forward, and then another.

"Run, Kid!" the Stranger said. But the Kid didn't need advice.

They chased him. They moved like automatons but they gathered speed. They seemed to the Stranger like a flock of dirty-grey seagulls. The Kid ran and the passengers followed. Bowler hats blew in the wind. The Hierophant, Zebulon, merely watched. The Kid ran until he was at the base of the clock tower, and when he saw they were almost upon him, he began to climb.

The Hierophant looked at the Stranger and made that little gesture with his fingers again. "I built this place," he said. "To find that which was buried. I waited, and they came, those who were lost, those who had nothing left but the waiting. And you would take this from them?"

The Stranger did not reply. The Kid was climbing faster now. The clock tower seemed to elongate into the sky, as though its dimensions were not quite right, and it reached higher and higher into the grey heavens. A wind howled from nowhere, snatching at the Kid, bellowing at his hair and clothes. Down below, the passengers attempted a climb but continued to fall down as others took their place.

The Hierophant advanced on the Stranger.

"I will shoot," the Stranger said. He took a step back.

The Hierophant smiled.

"If you have to shoot, shoot," he said. "Don't talk."

He took another step forward. The Stranger took another step back. Overhead the Kid climbed ever more desperately. When he reached the next level his fingers grasped for purchase and for a moment it seemed he would fall. He flailed helplessly for balance.

The Stranger pulled the trigger of his gun.

The gun clicked with a dry sound like an apologetic cough. No bullet emerged. The Hierophant made that gesture with his fingers. He took another step, and then another.

". . . waiting."

No one was chasing the Kid now. He was almost at the top when he looked down. He must have realised there was no-where to run. His foot slipped and pebbles of broken stone fell down to the ground. He shouted, and just when it seemed he would fall he took one last, desperate jump, and caught hold of the minute hand of the clock.

He hung there, suspended from the big clock above the town.

Tick, tick, tick, tick,
ti—

They were on the Stranger now, the passengers holding him helpless as the Hierophant bore down on him, and the man's fingers pressed against the Stranger's throat as the Stranger's useless gun pressed into the Hierophant's belly. . . .

That useless bullet, trapped inside.

The long, graceful fingers moving on the Stranger's throat, pressing painfully on his windpipe, choking the air out of him.

The Kid, hanging from the minute hand of the clock, the wind lashing savagely at his face.

He cried, "Help me!"

The Hierophant's grimace of savage satisfaction. It would be the last thing the Stranger would ever see, that and the Kid's feet, dangling, high in the air.

A gust of wind blew in from the plains. It snatched a bowler hat off one of the passengers and tossed it skyward. It stirred the grey-brown dust and it tousled Mrs. Lazarus's hair. Overhead, the second hand battled against the stuck minute hand. *Tick, tick, tick, tick, ti—*

ck.

The Stranger was choking. The Escapement came and went around him, fading in waves. He saw that other place and that other man who was there. A machine hummed in a white room. The patient table slid out, slowly, the boy emerging feet first. A doctor said, We'll have to run more tests—

Tick. Tick. Tick. Tick. Ti—

Something had to give. Ancient gears solidified by disuse with rust and dirt, jammed against each other, struggled under this new-found strain, the drop of weight exerting pressure on the mechanism. Something had to give. The clockwork creaked—

Down below, the Hierophant's hands slackened on the Stranger's throat.

The trapped bullet travelled an inch down the barrel of the gun, and stopped.

The Kid's fingers, raw and bloodied, held on but he felt them slipping, slipping . . .

He felt the second hand flutter against the jammed mechanism like a bird trying to escape.

Tick.

Tick.

T . . . i . . . c . . . k—

"No," the Hierophant said. "No, this cannot be allowed—"

Inside the warehouse, the molten clocks whispered and wriggled, shuddering against each other.

And with a hideous screech of gears the big clock broke. The minute hand gave against the Kid's pull and it plunged downwards and up again, and the Kid was tossed and turned in the high wind.

The Hierophant's hands lost their grip on the Stranger's neck.

The bullet, suspended with all that deferred time, was suddenly free. Kinetic motion propelled it onwards. It slid down the tube and emerged directly into the Hierophant's belly. The Hierophant said, "Oof!" and staggered back. His hands held in his belly.

"No," he said. "N—"

Inside the warehouse, the clocks shook and shuddered, their time finally come.

Tock.

He pushed the Hierophant off of him. The shell of the man was dying, and the grey clouds parted and sunlight burst through. The body—of the man who had called himself Zapata, or Za-vatta, those and all the other names—fell to the ground. The

Stranger pushed himself upright. Overhead the hands of the clock spun and spun, free from the rule of their escapement. The Kid dropped through the air. The passengers stood there, blinking stupidly, as though they had just woken up from a long and pleasant dream.

"Oof!" the Stranger said, in unconscious imitation of the Hierophant, as he caught the Kid in his descent and broke his fall. They ended up in an undignified pile on the ground, and it was from that position, lying on his back, staring upwards, that the Stranger saw the clocks at last take flight.

The clocks broke out of the roof of the old warehouse, flapping against the currents of the wind, and their dials moved and were transformed into talons, their escapements opened and became dark wings. Their mainsprings turned to beaks. In silence they streamed into the sky, a dark cloud of clocks turned into birds—ravens, or crows, or perhaps they were storm petrels. The Stranger didn't know. They rose into the sky in a swarm, forming a shape that could have been an hourglass before it broke, re-formed and changed.

The birds, newly hatched, flew against the sky and fled away from the waiting place.

"That *hurt*," the Kid complained.

"You're telling me," the Stranger said, rubbing his side. "You're heavier than you look, kid."

They left the townsfolk where they were. Some, the Stranger

saw, had simply gone back inside the waiting room. Others stood, uncertain, under the open skies. They might be there still tomorrow, or the next day, or the next day after that. The Stranger didn't know.

They found their horses ambling near the broken-down train. The horses whinnied greeting. They seemed unconcerned with all that had transpired.

"I hate waiting," the Kid said.

The Stranger nodded. He climbed on his horse and the Kid followed suit on his.

"I think we'll just avoid the railways for a while," the Stranger said.

"Seems sensible to me," the Kid said.

They rode out of town, following the setting sun. And if he listened very hard, the Stranger thought he could just hear something, faint, on the edge of sound . . .

The things still buried deep underground, burrowing, murmuring . . .

Tick. Tick. Tick. Tick—

Tock.

SIX:
BIG TOP

THE TOWN of Big Top lies some one hundred miles from the main estuary of the Grimaldi River, and over seven hundred, as the jackdaw flies, from the city of Jericho in the heart of the Thickening. It was to Big Top that the Kid headed after he'd left Bozoburg, and it was there that he first tried to kill the Conjurer.

The Kid really *was* just a kid back then. The guns hung heavy on his waist. He was a skinny thing, a backwater country boy fashioned into a weapon by circumstances, and with only one thought on his mind, which was to kill the Conjurer. The circumstances surrounding this instinct lay back both miles and years, in Bozoburg. Around his neck, the Kid wore the old silver thumb tip that bore the legend VERNACULUS. He had rescued it from the burning homestead, on the night the Rasmussen Gang hit the bank.

Big Top, burning. They mined substance nearby and as it burned it cast shadows into that other place and back again. Bright coloured flames . . . the smoke rose up, a permanent fog over the town. It was a liminal sort of place, a lonely, lawless outpost beyond the Thickening, half-way into the Doinklands themselves. There were clowns in the streets, and things that only looked like clowns. There was no law but there was a sort of . . . *decorum*. There were things much older than people on the streets of Big Top. Shadows that talked. It was said that if you took the wrong turning you might run into Harlequin, pissing in the street, and if it turned and looked at you with its grin it would be the last thing you ever saw. They said members of the Major Arcana could still be found in human form, passing through the dusty streets of the town.

Open fires burning in drums . . .

Figures dancing, drinking, swearing, fighting, sweating, hugging, the shadows of cars passing through the streets of that other place, ghostly illusions imposed upon this world. The fading siren call of an ambulance in the distance. The Kid cared for none of that. He stepped into the town with his spurs jangling and his guns hanging low and his hat over his eyes. His mother was dead. The town bank was in ruins, the safe blasted open, ducats falling down like silver rain . . .

Out there without a friend or money, he searched for the Conjurer in a city full of conmen and magicians.

He saw a one-armed bandit performing the three-card monte, and a bearded lady pouring water out of a giant ear held high in the air. He saw giraffes walk high on wires strung between the rooftops. He saw clouds coalesce at head height and rain down pennies. He trudged on. This meant nothing to him. He was a child of the Escapement, he had an instinctive mistrust of the land and its illusions.

Now, this is the thing about conjurers: they're inherently honest about their intent to deceive you.

The Conjurer must have known the Kid was coming, even

if he didn't exactly know *why*. People sometimes tried to kill him. He was not the world's nicest guy. The Kid hunted him through streets covered in muddy straw, dodging between burly prospectors, bounty hunters, clown posses, snake charmers, street vendors, vagabonds, and clochards. He traced him methodically, without passion.

It was the doves that gave the Conjurer's location away.

He had always had a flair for theatrics. His doves were almost a part of him, hidden as so much of him was hidden, nesting warm and comfortable in his clothes. He would raise his arms dramatically and release them, a flock of white doves bursting out of him and into the air.

He performed in a town square with the broken toe of a Colossus towering at its centre . . .

His audience were drunk on Sticks or moonshine. But he was used to that . . .

He was tall and thin and wore black evening clothes, white gloves, a tall black hat, and pistols black and worn with silver handles. He smiled, and his teeth were white and even . . .

The Kid came strutting into the square with his guns on his hips and a dove flew overhead and shat on his shoulder. He barely noticed.

"Listen," he said. He felt there was a need to fill the air with voice. "I've come to kill you—"

With that same smile on his face the Conjurer shot him. It wasn't a killing shot, exactly. It hit the Kid in the shoulder and spun him round and tossed him like garbage on the ground, where his blood dirtied the straw. The Conjurer came and stood over him for a moment and just looked at him and then after a moment he shook his head, as though he were disappointed. "Words are slower than a bullet," he said. Then he was gone, in a puff of smoke, from a canister that was hidden in his sleeve: he always did have a flair for the dramatic.

The Kid survived. Someone relieved him of his possessions. Someone else cleaned and bound his wound. His pride took a knock and he had a neat little scar after that, but he survived and he learned his lesson.

By the time he'd recovered, the Conjurer was long gone.

"What happened in Bozoburg?" the Stranger asked. They rode slowly through the Thickening, to Jericho. Geographical positions were more fixed, in the Thickening. Directions often stayed the same. Elsewhere on the Escapement compasses were generally useless, and the sun did not always set where it should. This area of human settlement was the first to be mined for substance, and old mineshafts and broken country stood side by side with fields and orchards. More than once they came across train tracks, which crisscrossed this part of the Escapement, and more and more often now they came upon small, prosperous towns, with rose gardens in the front of houses and white picket fences all neat and orderly, orderly and neat. The Stranger had been travelling for a long while, and he was destined to travel for a long while more, and the flower he sought remained forever out of his grasp.

"The Rasmussen Gang came riding into town," the Kid said, "and there was no one to stop them. They were mean and hungry, more wolves then men, with faces painted white and noses painted red as though they had tried to go native out there in the Doinklands. They shot whoever got in their way and set fire to the town . . ." His voice faded away and he looked elsewhere, into a place that was no longer there. "They blew up the bank and, well, I was only a kid."

"You tried to fight them?"

"I knew how to shoot, stranger." For a moment, a rueful smile illuminated his face. "I nicked one of the brothers' arms with a lucky bullet. That was as far as I got before they caught me. I don't think they liked me much. Maybe it was being just a kid, maybe it was telling them that I would kill them if it was the last thing I ever did. They put the money into saddlebags, and then they threw a rope over the beam of the old courthouse, and then they strung me up. I was choking when I saw the fire on the edge of town as they rode away. I thought I was dead . . . then the beam broke. It was an old building."

He still looked elsewhere. The sun was setting, and the blue sky deepened into purple, the flames of the setting sun streaking it in vivid red bursts. The air felt fresh and clear. In the distance they saw a farmhouse, but as they rode closer they saw that it was abandoned, the roof caved in. Beside the main building was a smaller one, the roof intact but the windows broken, and the Stranger saw that it must have once been a balloonery.

They dismounted. The sun set, and the Stranger built a small fire by the side of the balloonery building. The Stranger watched the Kid's hands. They moved in a practiced, absent-minded pattern: the old disappearing handkerchief routine. As much as he looked he couldn't see the silver thumb-tip as it was being used in service of the act.

"When I recovered I ran to the fire. The house burned. I ran inside . . ." The flames illuminated the Kid's face.

His eyes were open and he stared into the flames. "My mother was inside. I was too late to save her."

"I'm sorry," the Stranger said.

"Yes." The thumb-tip was back around his neck. "There was nothing left for me in Bozoburg. There was hardly much left of the town. I picked up a pair of guns, and followed the Rasmussens into the Doinklands."

"Did you ever catch them?" the Stranger asked.

"No." A bitter smile twisted the Kid's face. "I did find them, though, eventually. By then they were incarcerated in the local jail of a town called Soo's Creek. I was just in time to see them hang. . . ."

The silence settled around them. Insects buzzed around the fire. The horses neighed softly. And the Stranger thought of the Escapement.

It was a land where people lived and laughed and loved and died, a land like any other land. It did not require people for it to be there, but nevertheless people came, and changed it by their being. He thought of the farmhouse, and who might have lived there once, and had they been happy, and whether they had children. It felt like a place that once echoed with the laughter of children. And he thought about his quest.

He did not know if the Escapement were real, for what was real? The world was filled with impossible things, like the joyful laugh of a child. He closed his eyes. Behind them were only white walls, an antiseptic smell, the hum of machines. A doctor whispered something, there was a hand on his shoulder, shaking him awake. Sir? Sir? Visiting times are over.

He shook them away. When he opened his eyes the Kid was there, still, staring into the flames. His hands moved through the old routine, making a handkerchief appear and disappear.

"And the Conjurer?" the Stranger asked. "Did you ever find him again?"

"No," the Kid said. His hands moved, the thumb-tip hidden. The handkerchief disappeared and reappeared.

"No," the Kid said. "But I will."

SEVEN:
CLOCHARDS

WHEN HE CAME OUT of the hospital gates he just stood there for a good long while and breathed. Cars went past and their smoke filled the air. An ambulance drove by with red lights flashing. A taxi dawdled at the curb, letting out two elderly visitors who paid and disappeared into the gates and the taxi took off. He remembered other, better, days, a walk in the park with the boy when the sun was shining. The sun always seemed to shine, in those days. The boy had held his hand and he said, Daddy, Daddy, a butterfly! and the man nodded, not really paying attention, and he wished now that he'd paid so much more attention, that he'd been fully present for every single, fleeting, precious moment.

We're going to need to run more tests. The grey light pressing against the smoked glass windows. The whisper of nurses' shoes on the linoleum floor. Elevators pinging softly. He took a gulp of air and crossed the road to the shop on the corner and bought another fifth. The liquid burned his lips. A fire down his throat. Fog rising in his mind, he needed it like a blanket. He staggered home through dark deserted streets. Traffic lights winked green and red, green and red.

The city like a checkers board with squares of light and dark, the shadows whispering. Near his apartment he saw a group of homeless folk standing in a huddle looking at something on the ground. They seemed transfixed. He pushed near to see what it was. Some were holding bottles in brown paper bags just as he did. He pushed between two figures, a slight man with long curly sidelocks and a girl with wide shoulders and short cropped hair dyed with purple stripes. They made way for him. Their attention was focused downwards. He followed their gaze to the open drain.

A giant carp was lying in the gutter.

How the fish got there was a question none of the observers felt inclined to ask. It just was. It was huge, and the man vaguely remembered reading once how carp were near immortal, that they could die of violence or disease but not of old age.

The fish was still alive. Its glassy eyes stared up at the onlookers and its tail beat against the shallow running water and its gills opened and closed. It was just stranded there. The man felt somehow bad for the fish and yet the creature was too alien to inspire real sympathy. It was just *there*.

Hey, man, the guy next to him with the long sidelocks said, can you spare some change.

He reached in his pocket, brought out a handful of coins. He handed them over.

Thanks, man.

The fish flopped in the open drain.

Hey, I know you, the guy with the sidelocks said. I've seen you, man, here and in that other place.

I don't know what you mean.

Is it real or is it a shared reflexive manifestation of the sub-conscious, an endless battleground of Eros and Thanatos, do you think?

Excuse me.

The man left them there. An old word came to him. Clochards. It meant, vagrants. He walked away from them, under awnings, stepping in puddles, and soon he was lost from sight.

The clochard, whose name was Mathieu, looked after him and shook his head. He took out a can of paint and pointed the nozzle carefully and sprayed the wall with a message that was replicated elsewhere, on other walls, in other parts of the city. Then he put the can away and took a swig from his bottle and smiled, and he and the others left there and went through the shadows and into the cracks between the stones of the world, and then they were gone from there and to that other place.

They sat on top of a cliff that, from a distance, looked like an exclamation mark. Mathieu drank from the bottle and passed it to Esther and she in turn passed it to Mikhel, and so on. Their numbers never stayed exactly the same. The clochards never worked, only travelled, and they begged when there was begging to be had and they stole, if there was anything worth stealing. As they moved across the Escapement their numbers sometimes swelled and sometimes dwindled. They were driven only by the desire to keep on moving, and by their need for substance or Sticks.

They were currently out there in the Doinklands. A ghost road glowed white and pale in the distance, snaking across the plains. Mathieu took another glug from the bottle, passed it round again. They'd scored substance a few days' hike away in Kellysburg. They'd made their way from there across the plains and to the low mountains, though it seemed to Mathieu that they'd spent a part of the way traversing a city in that other place, dodging cars and taking shelter in abandoned buildings or under bridges.

The two places got mixed up in his mind more often than not. It was hard to keep track of what was where, and when. Clocks exploded into birds, shadow battled stone, lizards shed their skin and scuttled on the sands with rattling bones. Now the clochards sat on the big rocks and drank just enough so that the world thinned around them and from time to time, beyond the dark, he could see the glaring lights of shops from that other place. They were sitting like that, quite comfortably, when they saw the approaching storm.

It was not a rare occurrence out there and they were not unduly worried. The clochards continued to drink and watched as the first golden symbols began to dance like fae lightning on the horizon. Tildes and pilcrows and polygons burst and popped as the storm moved across the plains, and in its wake they began to hear the sound of swords clashing and enormous feet slamming against the ground. Esther slumped and curled down on the ground with the bottle of Sticks held in her hand, and it was empty. Mathieu could see her, walking away, crossing the street at a green traffic light as cars waited like beasts of the plains, puffing steam.

Some of the others were slipping away, too. It was only he perhaps who remained mostly there. He thought he saw a small wagon traverse the ghost road, following its crazy curlicues, pulled by donkeys. The donkeys strained to run, and behind them he thought he saw giant stone feet rise and fall, rise and fall, until at last the wagon was forced to abandon the ghost road and travel in a straight line, and then it was engulfed by the storm and he did not see it again.

In the night he heard inhuman laughter fill the air, and awful silence, and the baying of animals. At last he drank enough of the Sticks that he, too, went to that other place, and there he huddled with the others under the awnings of a shut store, until morning rose about them and a policeman shooed them away.

Then they hopscotched and jump-roped through the cracks of the world and woke up a second time, blinking sleepy eyes at the plains. A snake slithered under a stone and was gone. They drank their breakfast and chewed on dried beef and old bread and then by unspoken agreement they left the high places and went back down to the plains. They were natural scavengers and it was well known one could pick up materiel in the passing of a storm, the incomprehensible leftovers of the battles of the Titanomachy.

But it had not been a battle, Mathieu thought uneasily as they descended. And indeed, when they began to search the ground, they found no transmutations or metamorphosis, not even a cockroach turned on its back. It was only later, when Bill spotted the crater, that Mathieu realised that what he had witnessed in the night wasn't, indeed, a battle at all. It had been a hunt.

From a distance the crater almost resembled a giant foot. Coming closer, the details faded into nothing and it was just a large hole. Inside the hole, turned on its side, was a wagon that had been crushed by some immeasurable force. Its wood had snapped. Its wheels lay buried in the ground. Of the two don-keys, one was dead, flung against the side of the crater, while the other was still alive. It raised its head and looked at the clochards with large innocent eyes as they approached, and whimpered softly when Esther stroked its neck.

The sun was by then at an angle over the horizon, and the shadows cast by the clochards lengthened into blades. The wagon's shadow was like a squashed maggot.

Beside the wagon, lying as peacefully as two rag dolls, were the corpses. They were small and rotund, their bodies wrapped in long coats. They could have been brother and sister, but really it was impossible to tell. Whatever force had come down from the heavens and pressed down on them had neatly severed their heads from their necks, and their long scarves had unravelled and fluttered on the ground in some invisible breeze.

There was no sign of the heads.

The sun was low and the shadows long and Mathieu shiv-ered as the temperature dropped, and he took a swig from the bottle for comfort. This was the problem with scavenging, he thought. Sometimes you found things you weren't exactly looking for.

"Search the wagon," Davide said. He was a recent arrival to the travelling troupe. A short, compact man who seldom joined them when they went beyond the shadow-play screen to that other place.

"Search it yourself."

The clochards sniggered. Davide shrugged, and then he went and began removing broken wood and tattered cloth, looking for what lay beneath. After a moment, Esther joined him.

They dug and dug, and Davide cursed, but soon the broken pieces of the wagon were cast in one pile, and out of the rubble they began to pull out dented old pots and pans and other useless junk, and more of the clochards drifted away, from the Escapement into rain-soaked roads and streetlights shining wetly in the night. On the Escapement, the sun dipped farther to the west.

"Hold on," Davide said. "What's that?"

Esther tilted her head, birdlike; listening to the hidden sounds of the dusk. Then her fingers moved, gently brushing dirt and wood chips out of the way, and a glint of gold shone through out of the dark ground. Mathieu caught his breath as a metal fin was exposed, burning gold in the dying rays of the sun.

He went to join them, skirting round their shadows. The other clochards awoke to this new discovery. With sounds like chirping birds they all joined in, digging and clearing out the rubbish, until scales were exposed, a long, heavy tail, a body, glass eyes.

It moved.

The tail beat against the ground. The eyes moved, blindly. The thing was immense, a carp or, more specifically, a koi, some sort of mechanical contraption resembling such. Yet it seemed alive.

"What *is* it?" Mikhel said.

"Materiel," Mathieu said, quietly.

They dug. It seemed to Mathieu that it was Davide and Esther who dug the hardest, who were most insistent on bringing this monstrosity out into the open, but they were all caught up in it by then. It was the biggest find they'd ever had, if only they knew what it was or what price they could get for it.

The sun had set. The fish was still only half out of the ground and they set fire to the heap of broken wood, and the scales of the fish glinted in the firelight. A wild mood took them. They drank moonshine and danced as the stars came out and the smoke of the bonfire curled upwards, and Davide and Esther tied ropes to the body of the fish and then they all joined forces in hauling it out, until it *popped* out of the hole with a sudden wet sound and flopped on the ground, moving in some mechanical way like a clockwork automaton, its mouth opening and closing and its artificial eyes reflecting the fire back at them.

They proceeded to get very drunk.

In that other place and a long time before, Mathieu imagined that he was a scholar, and he studied holy texts. He had a wife he imagined he must have loved, and two children that he knew he had. He and his wife had married young, by arrangement of their families. The children he had loved wholeheartedly, but something happened, he no longer knew what, and after that event he was no longer married nor had he any children. It was in that period immediately after the tragedy that he took up drinking. He took to drinking the way he took to books, earnestly and wholeheartedly.

It was at approximately that time that he began to experience delirium tremens, and then merely delirium. After that Mathieu kept to himself and little by little departed wholly from his old life.

In his delirium he was no longer in that other place but in a land called the Escapement. He lived, not sure if he were a scholar dreaming he was a clochard, or a clochard dreaming that he was a scholar.

In that time he had seen all kinds of things he had once thought impossible. He saw the living statue of a woman, turned to granite, the eyes still clear and tracking, trapped within. Flesh-clad skeletons stretched into accordions. A rain of bowler hats.

But after a time the sight of every battleground fatigued him. He withdrew by degrees. Nights in that other place he read cheap books pilfered from drugstores and late-night gas stations. He read by candlelight in the abandoned buildings where clochards sought shelter. Days on the Escapement he spent walking, or riding the hopping cars on the rails, or hitching rides on slow-moving wagons. All he knew was that he had to keep moving.

Gradually, by degrees, he got to know the others. Esther, Bill, others who belonged in neither place. Liminal, they moved like ghosts, unseen by passers-by. They banded together for comfort. They drank by open fires and slept under the clear and distant stars. They had no purpose, no ambition but to simply be.

"Bring it up, bring it up." The ropes tied round the fish made it easier to drag it along, but it took their combined force to pull it out of the footprint-like crater and back onto the horizontal plains. Finally they brought up the surviving donkey and it was the donkey who was tasked with pulling the fish, and the rest of them took turns helping.

Mathieu didn't mind the labour. He welcomed the exertion,

the fact that with the weight of the fish each step became a world, and there was no room left for anything but the act of pulling. It made him uneasy, the thing, and when he wasn't pulling alongside the donkey he was troubled by the way Davide and Esther walked close together, and how their shadows trailed behind them, and how the shadows seemed larger than their source. And he was troubled by the fish itself, and how it seemed alive, this elaborate, mechanical contraption, inimical, a mimic, a simulacrum of life.

They walked days across the plains and saw not another storm. On the seventh day they saw an edifice rising far in the distance, a giant structure that jutted out of the ground as though, long ago, it had crashed into it. Currents of lightning flashed in complicated shapes all across the dark body of the edifice, which cast a long shadow over the plain. It took a two-day hike to reach it, and they were glad, for it was known that substance could often be found near such an edifice.

This close, it almost resembled a passenger ship, buried nose-first in the ground. The metal looked strangely organic, and it occurred to Mathieu, unpleasantly, that it could have been something else entirely, something alive: like an egg. They camped under the edifice that night, and the fish, agitated, kept flopping on the ground where it lay, its mouth opening and closing as though it were trying to bite prey or bait that wasn't there. All through the night the blue electric lights flashed as they snaked over the body of the edifice like living tattoos. They trudged on across the plains.

The land rose by degrees but the forces of vastation and revel acted upon the Escapement and on the eighth or ninth day after they left the edifice they woke up in the morning with the sun rising from the north and it set that night beyond the mountains. The air was colder and the fish as heavy as before and there were no towns or any sign of human habitation, and Mathieu thought that they must have shifted farther into the Thinning. It was then also that he began to discern the hidden marks of the denizens of this wild land. A squiggle of chalk on the bark of a tree; boot marks in the ground, of long, flat feet; a dollop of rancid custard.

They were deep into the cedar forests at the foothills of the mountain range when the clowns attacked.

They came like pale ghosts out of the trees. Hobos, Augustes. They carried baleros and diabolos and cream custard pies. Long red boots and pale wide faces and red round noses and eyes that reflected your own inhumanity straight back at you.

Leading them all was a boss clown. It was a giant Hobo clown, with hobnailed boots that thudded into the ground with each step it took. The clowns surrounded the clochards, though they avoided the shadows that congealed around Davide and Esther. The clochards were not armed, and it was Mathieu who faced up to the clowns. The giant gestured. Davide replied with gestures of his own.

"You must not trespass," he translated. "This is no place for that which was lost."

"What does *that* mean?" Bill complained. Davide and Esther communicated silently, or so it seemed to Mathieu.

"It's the fish," he said. "I think."

"All we want is to find our way back to the Thickening and sell the damn thing," someone else said. But the clowns would not move, the road ahead blocked to the trespassers, and the clochards turned and left the forest the way they'd come, and the clowns shadowed them silently until they were far away from that place.

They came upon a river that snaked between the mountains and followed it instead. There were no maps and they were running low on substance and Sticks, and that other place was no longer there for them to imagine. There was only the Escapement, and the snow-capped mountains which resembled stone giants, and the loons that cried by the riverbanks in low lingering moans, and the flurries of snow and the harsh shadows shed by the sun. Rise and fall, rise and fall, and they carried their burden onwards until they came at last upon an old bridge that spun the river, the first sign that they had seen of human intervention in the landscape.

Onwards they went with a giddy sense now that their sojourn in the Thinning was over. Stones flaked from the bridge like scales and fell down to the river far below, and the fish's belly made a screeching sound as it was dragged along the rails, but they persevered. On the other side of the bridge they came upon an old rail terminal, and Mathieu thought that it had been long abandoned. It must have once been a part of the Thickening, some inlet of human habitation deep into the Escapement, but for whatever reason that excursion by humans had failed.

There was a small ghost town on the other side of the bridge. The loose assortment of buildings was assembled with sheets of metal hammered together, wooden poles that were stuck into the ground. Tears of rust ran down the walls, and the paths that wound between them were as black and barren as the exposed roots of burnt trees. Who had lived there, Mathieu could not tell. He pushed open the door of one such dwelling. A rough-hewn table sat in the middle of the house. The table was set with a meal for four. Food that had long ago rotted into gunk smeared black spots on the plates. Colonies of mould prospered in the enclosed space and the air smelled fetid and worn out. The chairs had been pushed back, as though whoever had sat here, long ago, had merely got up at an interruption, and never returned. On the otherwise bare wall hung the ikon of a Harlequin. Its eyes mocked Mathieu.

A giant banyan tree grew in the centre of that town, and it was under its canopy that they put the fish. That night they built a bonfire out of rotted old wood and fence posts and they danced in its light and their shadows danced beside them, all but the shadows of Davide and Esther. Those crept over the town and over the old homes and they nestled in the cracks. There was familiarity there.

By the side of the tracks was an old engineer's shop and it was there that they found the kalamazoos. There were five of them, and still in good working order, large flat handcars with manual pumps, and these they set back on the tracks. They placed the fish in the middle cart and Mathieu and Bill took the front kalamazoo and Davide and Esther took the rear. Their shadows flowed after them like wide-winged birds of prey. They went slowly, operating the arm, seesaw, seesaw, up and down and up and down. It was back-breaking labour.

In this way they departed that nameless town by the bridge and followed the tracks. They looped and curved through the mountain pass. It was hard going and with no Sticks, and what little food they had was all but gone. Overhead the sky became a blank window. Far ahead Mathieu thought he could hear gulls. They drove the handcars over a last bridge spanning the river between two mountains. The distant smell of salt and tar, and he felt a longing awake in him, a desire to one last time see the sea. The handcars creaked across the chasm, see-saw, eew-aww, the gears creaking, the wheels sliding, a shower of sparks.

Thunder overhead, and Mathieu looked up to see a moun-tain wake, an icy rock face like a torso, a snow-capped head, shaking.

"Hurry! Hurry!"

And faster and faster they went, the avalanche overhead gathering, a rain of stones beginning to fall, slowly, so slowly, an inexorable decline.

"Quick! Quick!" Bent double like the old and the infirm they went, clochards, with their golden treasure. A falling rock caught Mikhel, tossed him off the trolley like a rag doll. Down, down into the depths, a splash of foam like a white question mark his only tombstone.

"Hurry, damn it, *hurry!*"

He risked a glance back. Behind him, the shadows of Davide and Esther spread giant wings of ink. Shadow battles stone. He heard inhuman laughter. Falling rocks. The opening of a tun-nel in the mountain straight ahead. He looked only forward.

They'd made it. Somehow they were through, into the safe-ty of the tunnel. Dark, dark. They worked the trollies till their hands bled and their breath dribbled out of their bodies. On-wards. Until they were through, and on the other side, and into sunlight, and for just one moment, he saw the sea.

It was easier after that. A gentle slope down into farmland, and the smoke rising from chimneys, and neat roads, and the railway tracks were new and gleamed in the sunlight. In the first town they came to they found a bar and proceeded to get so drunk that the Escapement disappeared entire, and for one long glorious day he explored the streets of his old neighbourhood, with posters on the walls warning residents to keep decent, and once he went past the cemetery with the pointed stars on the tombstones but he did not go in.

After that they hopped a junk car, going deep.

Clown's Gulch, Stark's Holborn, Grieblingsburg, Skelton's Landing, Blackstone, Geller's Bend, Balducci's Levitation, Downtown Wagon, Freak Alley, Mud Show, Pitchman's Stand . . . the small hamlets and towns fled by as the slow cargo train went past them, past checkerboard fields and tidy orchards, bubbling streams and sleeping beehives. The sights evoked in Mathieu a nameless longing, for all that could have been and wasn't, for a homestead, for a home. For children playing in the yard, their laughter. There was nothing more pure and more holy in all the worlds, he thought, than the sound of children laughing.

Bells pealed as they went past chantries and chancels and clown missions. Whitewashed walls and good black earth and flowers growing in profusion. The smoke of foundries and trains, and herds of cows in the distance. The fish like an intimation of things to come. Something external, something that had a purpose all its own.

In this manner they traversed the Thickening, until at last they saw the famed walls of Jericho rise ahead of them in the distance. He felt like a sailor in a crow's nest, sighting land.

The city came upon them and they passed through, and it swallowed them, it swallowed them whole, and they passed from sight of the world.

EIGHT:
THE FALL OF JERICHO

"The peace has held for a thousand thousand years," the petit Pierrot said. He—if it was a he—tugged nervously at his bells. They made no sound, or rather, they made an absence of sound, a peal of silence that spread outwards from the diminutive Pierrot. "No, not *years*. Time didn't mean the same then as it does now. And no, not *peace*. What is the word I am searching for? Ah, yes. *Stalemate*. The stalemate held for a long period of untime. Until people came to the Escapement."

The Conjurer hid a yawn. He sat at the table of the dimly lit Bull Tub, drinking moonshine. He was a great believer in moonshine, and hogswallop, and bunkum. If you could drink it, the Conjurer believed in it. He was most devout, in that regard.

He wore his beautiful white gloves, and his beautiful black top hat. He was very tall and very thin. The top button was open on his pristine white shirt. There were thumb-tips and Svengali and Bicycle cards in his jacket; invisible thread and elastic eggs and cut-and-restore ropes and linking rings; silk handkerchiefs and cups-and-balls and all manner of cut and restored papers which, frankly, he'd forgotten about and could no longer remember what they had been for. On his hips he bore twin six-shooter handguns with silver-plated handles.

The Conjurer liked conjuring. He always said you had to be good at at least three things in this world to have a happy life, and he was good at exactly three: conjuring, drinking, and killing people. Now he pulled out a small brown cheroot, struck a match on the sole of his boot, and lit it. He drew in breath, and blew out three perfect smoke rings in succession. He stared at the pitiful little Pierrot.

"Well?" he said.

"There'd been . . . *consciousnesses* here before," the Pierrot said.

"Ah, yes," the Conjurer said. "Whoever left those fucking dream machines scattered about."

"Yes, perhaps," the Pierrot said, though he didn't seem sure. "But anyway, sooner or later, they all went away."

"So?"

"The p . . . the *stalemate* held, for a thousand thousand—"

"Yes, yes, you already did that part. You need to work on your patter, friend."

"May I?"

The little Pierrot gestured beseechingly at the bottle of moonshine. The Conjurer sighed, conjured a tumbler, and poured one exact measure for the little creature. Jericho, he thought. It used to be the flotsam and jetsam of the Escapement kept well away or, anyway, hid themselves thoroughly in the nooks and crannies of that weird old city. Now they seemed much more . . . *visible*. As though they knew something the Conjurer, as yet, did not.

The Conjurer did not like that particular feeling. Knowing things other people didn't was his business.

The Pierrot drank. His little white hands held the tumbler like an offering.

"*Well?*" the Conjurer demanded.

"A thousand th—ah, yes. Sorry." He coughed. "But when the people came, the balance shifted. It seemed the stalemate could be broken, with the right tools."

"The right tools being . . . ?"

"People," the Pierrot said, surprised at the question.

"Forgive me. Of course."

"Shadow battles stone; the lizard scuttles from the glare of the sun."

"Indeed."

"And so the . . . *opponents*, they began to, err . . ."

"Recruit?"

"That's right. That was the word."

The Conjurer wondered how *old* the little Pierrot was. Those creatures weren't like *people*, not exactly. He wondered how far back the creature's memory went. He wondered if he remembered the Battle of the Big Rock Candy Mountains. The Conjurer *was* old, and he remembered that one, though he'd elected, then, not to take part. He had merely been a . . . a *witness*. That, if he recalled, was the last time that the pupae umbrarum and the Colossi had attempted to redress the balance.

The result had been a massacre.

"So what's changed?" he said.

"Eh?"

"What's changed? Now?"

"Ah," the little Pierrot said, and he tapped his nose, and winked, or tried to, his features didn't quite work right. Then the Conjurer's gun was in his hand and the muzzle was pressed to the small creature's deathly pale face.

"Yes?"

"That which was lost is believed to be found!" the Pierrot said.

"What?"

"That which was l—"

"I heard you the first time," the Conjurer said. The Pierrot made another beseeching motion at the bottle. He seemed unfazed by the gun to his face.

"Tell me first."

"Doom! Doom! Doom cometh to Jericho, and Jericho must—"

"Fall?"

"Fall!"

"Piss off, you little twerp," the Conjurer said. He kicked the stool from under the Pierrot and the little creature fell, but nimbly enough.

"No drink?"

"No drink."

The Pierrot shrugged. He wended his way to the next table, where a couple of grizzled ex-miners sat half-slumped over Sticks.

"The peace has held for a thousand thousand y—" he began.

The Conjurer sighed.

He sat there for a long time, sipping his drink. It had been years since he'd last visited Jericho, that oldest and grandest of all human settlements on the Escapement. It was a strange old stone town, filled with narrow cobblestoned alleyways that took twisting turns, and tall, narrow houses that obscured sunlight, and it was surrounded by sturdy stone walls, which had withstood numerous attacks over the centuries. It was a solid place. One very seldom caught even a glimpse of that other place, and even drinking Sticks, one found it hard to penetrate the veil of shadows and into that other, more mundane existence. Though the Conjurer had no use for that other place. He was firm in who and what he was.

He was, first and foremost, a conjurer.

The Conjurer had been born into the great Boreal Circus on the outskirts of the Désert de Soleil, a thousand years before. He could have been as young as twenty or as old as a hundred, and he distinctly remembered at certain times being much older, and at others very young. He had grown up by the great salt marshes that lie on the very outskirts of the inhabited world, and beyond which lie the Pillars of Nisir, which are inhabited by fearful serpents, and are, or so it is said, the gateway to the Mountains of Darkness.

The Boreal travelled slowly along the Thinning and the Thickening of the Escapement, performing less for an audience than for the sake of performing, and it laid down train tracks ahead of itself and removed them again after the great lumbering cars passed, and in this fashion it traversed the edges of the desert.

The sun shone very brightly there. He remembered it, still, a huge ball of fire in a cloudless sky, and the heat, and the haze over the Great Salt Lakes, and that smell of bromine. And the tracks being laid and pulled out again, and the Big Top erected over inhospitable land, and the elephants shitting in great steaming piles, and the hunters coming back cursing and grumbling, for there was no meat to be had.

Still there were others living in that distant and inhospitable land. As a child, the boy who would become the Conjurer was fascinated by the ancient ruins that could be found in the lonely places of the Escapement. He had made a friend in Professor Federico, the Magnificent, whose dazzling displays of alchemical marvels were in truth nothing much more than fizzy potions made with water, vinegar and baking soda.

The Professor was a short, stocky man with thinning black hair and a thick moustache, and when he spoke he spoke with an accent that came from that other place. He let the boy accompany him on his excursions, and it was thus that the boy first saw the great broken pillars of the dead Colossi.

The first dead Colossus he saw lay in a valley crusted with salt seams in the walls. The Colossus had fallen on its side, and its body broke into many parts, and trees and desert shrubs grew on its scalp and in its ears and sprouted out of its nose. Its pelvis was shattered, and its fingers had broken into many smaller pieces, and the Professor said, "A great violence had been perpetrated here."

The boy stood on the heights and looked down on the Colossus. From above, one could see its overall shape, and there was something sad, even noble, about the stone. When they descended, it was impossible to discern that image: the Colossus broke into fragments of vision, so all that one saw were curiously-shaped rocks.

"Who did this?" he had asked. The Professor puffed on a pipe which merely produced soap bubbles, and the boy watched the bubbles rise high into the sky. They broke the sunlight into rainbows.

"Us, I think," he said.

"Us?"

"People. We carry our violence within ourselves."

The boy did not understand the answer; not then. The Professor showed him how history was often erased and rewritten in the flesh of the Escapement. How where once the maps said was a river was now a part of the plains, or how hills became mountains, how paths disappeared. He showed him the old ghost roads, which came and went on the Escapement, but it was when one appeared, more often than not, that an old place would be revealed nearby, and it was in this way, too, that the boy saw the first of las máquinas. You saw it long before you reached it, if you ever did. It rose out of the hard, dry ground and seemed to travel up for miles, an ovoid shape of metal and glass that reflected the sun out of cubic mirrors that could have been windows and could have been eyes.

It could have been a luxury liner, or the egg of some giant, flaming bird.

"Now these," the Professor said. "These truly are intriguing. *Las máquinas*. Organic or machine? Are they even real? Are they natural structures of the Escapement, or are they of an alien origin to it? Some say, you know, that the Escapement had been colonised at different times by a different peoples—a different *species*, perhaps? That each successive immigration reawakens the dormancy of the Escapement, and in the interaction changes it, shapes it to that race's *perception*. What do you think, boy?"

"Me?" the boy said, surprised. "I don't know, Professor. I was born here, to me this is as real as . . ." Words failed him.

"As that other place is to some of us, you mean?" Professor Federico, the Magnificent, said.

"I suppose . . ." the boy said, mumbling a little, for he did not understand what that other place was, and why some people went there.

"Which begs the question," the Professor said. "Are *you* real, boy?"

"Am *I?*" the boy said. It was then, perhaps, that he first began to consider the nature of reality itself, and how our perceptions, and that which is perceived, may not match. Which is to say, it was when he first got on the long road to becoming a conjurer. A conjurer fools perception, after all. That is his job, and his joy. And in such a manner, perhaps, he therefore acts as a minor agent of the Escapement, in which all manner of Fools, and of fooling, proliferate.

Life at the circus was hard and work-heavy but the boy never complained. He was happy as a boy can be happy, out there on the edge of the world, far from the battles of the Titanomachy and the machinations of pupae and Colossi. In such a manner, and with the gandy dancers leading ahead, pounding the spikes for the rail tracks into the ground, over and over, the great circus traversed the shorelines of the great salt lakes that lay there, and skirted the edges of the desert, there where even the clowns hesitate to go, for the Mountains of Darkness lie beyond.

Yet this part of the Escapement was not without denizens; nor without danger. And it was on one day, all but identical to all the other days, with the sun a fiery ball of fire in the sky, and bromide in the air, and the elephants calling and the pots filled with stew slow-cooking on open fires, and the Big Top erected, that the wild strongmen attacked.

The boy saw the dust they raised before he actually saw the attackers. There were tribes of strongmen and their bearded ladies who roamed the Escapement in those days, though most went extinct in the great inter-circus war between the House of Boreal and the House of Mercator a couple of centuries later.

The battle that day was long, and bloody, and several times in the melee the boy heard, or imagined he had, high-pitched, inhuman laughter, and this was punctuated by terrible silences, as though the battle was merely the microcosm of another, bigger battle which took place on a different plane of perception entirely. When it was over, all he remembered from that time was the taste of dirty cloth in his mouth as he bit on a sleeve, someone's sleeve, an arm flopping from above him in the pile of corpses. He lay there like a mouse in a cave, biting on cloth to stop himself from screaming. He could hear the strongmen moving through the rubble of the camp, and the laughter of their bearded ladies as they looted the circus's belongings. All through that day and into the night the boy lay, delirious, under the pile of dead. It was before dawn, when the night is darkest, that he crawled out, as quiet as a mouse, and made his getaway. The strongmen and their bearded ladies lolled here and there, drunk on moonshine and innocents' blood. The boy who would become the Conjurer made his way to his parents' wagon, but it lay on its side, its roof burned to cinders, and lying in the dust he saw his mother's corpse.

One more thing must be mentioned, though the Conjurer never liked to do so himself. On his way out of the encampment he came to what is called the Backyard, the space behind the Big Top where the performers prepared. There he came across a strongman slumped before a cage in which two of the big cats still prowled. How he did what he did, the Conjurer never explained, though the story went ahead of him and grew in the telling. The first hint of the boy's presence and subsequent escape from the camp came to the strongmen at dawn, when they found the mutilated body of their companion lying inside the big cats' cage, with the cats nowhere in sight, and with the door locked from the inside.

It was the Conjurer's first act of conjuring, and its bloody spectacle would come to define his work in the years to come, as he traversed the Escapement, performing sleight-of-hand and making coins and handkerchiefs appear and disappear for delighted children in one-clown-towns; all while earning his living, more quietly yet lucratively, by shuffling off the mortal coil of various targets for various clients: it was said that he always carried a job through to the end.

That night, or predawn day, he had slit the strongman's throat as the man lay snoring, then had pushed him into the cage and watched the cats feed. Only when they were sated had he gone inside, and petted them, and taken substance. It was easy to come by, in the circus, for many of the performers were addicts and bought it at every stop where prospectors and miners could be found, and sometimes they discovered veins of the stuff in the desert, and worked it for a while by hand. So the kid who was soon to become the Conjurer had taken a pinch of the dry white powder, and then another, and even though he was not *of* that other place—he did not have an *equivalent*, or a him-shaped *absence* of one, or however that worked—even though he could sense it at first and then glimpse it, and he'd seen that where he stood was not really a desert at all but a sort of highway, an eight-lane vast road that rose over a second, intersecting road down below, and that lights moved all along those highways in every direction, and he'd known then that there was no cage, and there were no bars. And so he had locked the cage from the inside and pocketed the key, and he had walked through the walls and away from the encampment and the wild strongmen and their bearded ladies, and into the dawn.

It was miles from there, in a ravine where he'd thought he could hear it calling, all through that journey in a twilight between the one place and the other, that he had found the machine. A sound like the peal of crystal bells . . .

And there, sitting around a small fire, he'd found Professor Federico, the Magnificent.

But all this had been a long time ago, and far from Jericho. The Professor was long gone, dead or vanished into that other place. He had often told the Conjurer that he believed in his own existence on the Escapement less and less. With the passing miles and years and doses of substance, he felt he was fading ever more. Until one day, when the boy who had become the Conjurer went to gather wood for their fire. When he came back, the Professor was gone. For the Professor, that other place had become the only real one, and he'd escaped back into it with a sense of quiet relief. To him, the Escapement would become nothing more than a pleasant daydream, a fantasy of escape.

Or so, at least, the Conjurer imagined. When he thought about it at all.

Right now, sitting in the Bull Tub in Jericho, what the Conjurer thought about was that little speech the petit Pierrot had given him.

"Doom," the Conjurer said softly, trying out the sound on his lips. "Doom cometh to Jericho."

He discovered he quite liked the sound of that. The truth of the Conjurer was not that he was *entirely* an amoral character, but rather that he had his own, somewhat idiosyncratic notion of morality, and one that did not perhaps chime exactly with the ideas other—or even most—people had. The wild strong-men and their bearded ladies had robbed him of something— something precious, something ill-defined—and though you cannot miss what you do not have, nevertheless, from time to time he'd feel a pang in the place where his heart should have been, an itch of the sort that you get from a ghost organ. And it was not *compassion* that made him get up, and make his way, stealthily, out of the bar and into the dark streets, but *curiosity*, a curiosity as dark as the streets of Jericho and as empty as the salt plains beyond which lie, or so it was said, the Mountains of Darkness.

The Conjurer was what one may term a purist. He killed cleanly and efficiently and only for money, and he applied the same methodology to his magic routine. Underlying both occupations was the most important thing one could do to achieve first proficiency and then excellence, and which is, of course, *practice*. There was no one whose patter was better perfected, no other whose linking rings routine seemed so flawless and natural, and no one better to dispose of a corpse than the Conjurer. He was not prideful. He always sought to become better than he was.

But this purity—of practice, of purpose—was the same aspect of him which made him loathe the city of Jericho as much as he did. For he was born on the edges of the world, and for all that he now dwelt in the Thickening, it felt to him an unnatural intrusion upon the body of the Escapement, like a malignant tumour that needs must be removed. Worst of all was its very heart, this fortified town, with its great train terminus and its garlanded avenues, its towers of solid stone and its cheery and practical and hardworking façade, which hid the truth of itself behind walls and deep in the ground. The Conjurer was an expert in misdirection, but even he was fooled, at first, by this city, which had been built, he had come to realise, as an exact and rather sinister act of manipulation of interest, so that one's eyes were always drawn elsewhere, and it was only with effort that one could tear away from the illusion to see the ancient truth.

But he knew it now—some of it, at least. Enough to steal out of the Bull Tub that night, just behind the petit Pierrot; and he watched how the little creature straightened himself and stepped with quiet purpose much at odds with the persona he had put on in the bar; how he faded into the brickwork and the shadows, so that he all but vanished. But this was child's play for the Conjurer, who turned his gloves inside out so that the bright white was replaced with pure black velvet, and he utilised what magicians call the "black art," the act of vanishing when a black object is placed against a black background, which conjurers use in their stagecraft; and he moved softly, like a big cat.

He followed the petit Pierrot down the alleyway.

The city of Jericho stood at the heart of the Thickening, that tear-shaped stain of human settlement on the Escapement, and it had grown, as they say, in the telling. It was a rough prospectors' town in the old days, and sat on the confluence of substance mines that even when the first people came had already been extensively mined by other, vanished peoples. Whoever *they* had been, they had left some of their curious remnants behind them, these machines which trouble the dreams of those who pass too close, and as the city grew and prospered it worked hard at the subterfuge of hiding its foundations. Vast ship-like structures jutting out of the ground had been built over with wood and stone, in graceful spirals of stairs and homes that floated in the sky, bridges that linked rooftop to rooftop and on which the denizens of the pleasure quarter gaily strolled at nightfall among hanging gardens. Down below, the wide avenues that intersected each other in a series of bright circuses nevertheless gave birth to a host of narrow, twisting alleyways that had come into being through the unregulated construction of dwellings of all sorts, many of the buildings rising several stories high, many leaning alarmingly and some even merging into each other as individuals found themselves sharing homes that had, through the actions of gravity and time, slowly fallen into each other. Those alleyways, in contrast to the main thoroughfares, were dark and narrow and hid many things that respectable citizens of the Thickening would not openly tolerate, and indeed would shake their head in amazement to find dwelling, still, in their midst.

Beyond the avenues and the towers lay the enormous train terminus of Jericho, into which all tracks led. It was a place of wrought iron and paved platforms and high windows of coloured glass which broke the clear pure light into rainbows, and it was filled with bustle and steam and the sharp whistles of trains, the hurly-burly of passengers and conductors, the transport of people and goods.

The city was gaily decorated with many balloons.

Unbeknown to the Conjurer, he was being followed.

The Kid and the Stranger had split up upon arrival, each intent on his own private goal. The Stranger went one way and the Kid another. The Kid could sense that his quarry was there. He fidgeted with the silver thumb-tip that hung round his neck. He had not seen a town as large as Jericho before, and for a time he was seduced by the bright shopfronts, where they sold every manner of fabulous things, from bales of multicoloured twine and miniature train sets remarkable in their detail and vivid in colour, and pedal-operated machines for the washing of clothes, and in the streets the horse-drawn carts intermingled with penny-farthings swishing to and fro, and pedestrians in clothes smarter and brighter than he had ever seen doffed their hats at each other as they passed. The Kid strutted down the street confidently enough. He fancied himself a sort of alley cat, ready for anything and everything, and he grinned cockily at the young ladies who passed him, who could not resist but glance back at this dashing young man, with his spurs that jangled on the cobblestones, and the guns on his hips jutting from their holsters.

But the Kid had other things besides women on his mind, and underneath the cheery and untroubled façade there coiled the same dark, jagged anger, like a hanging rope coated in broken glass. Which was what he kind of had in mind to use when he finally found the Conjurer.

The Kid diverted from Bim Bom Boulevard down a narrow road that ran perpendicular to a long, old wall. Something about this wall, the way it seemed to swallow the light, so that the road seemed gloomier than perhaps it should, disturbed him. He paused and ran the tips of his fingers lightly across the brickwork, and was surprised to see dust smudge along the path, exposing underneath not brick but a faded metal, warm to the touch. He cleared more dirt from the spot and saw that it was the kind of metal one found in the giant edifices that littered the Escapement like downed ships. It could be a fin, he thought. Which would mean the rest of the edifice was buried deep down below. . . .

He tried the bars and hostelries of the city in his search, and each became shabbier and more decrepit as he wended his way deeper into the clown quarter. In each bar he asked for the Conjurer, and in each bar he was met with dark looks and muttered excuses and shakes of the head, but still he persisted. The daylight grew dim and then disappeared entirely, and a thin, wan moon rose like a broken sickle blade over the towering minarets.

Street lamps came into life then, burning a yellow flame that cast the alleyways in shivering chiaroscuro. The Kid felt suddenly how very *alien* the place became at night; how none of the shadows quite corresponded to the objects casting them; how in the passageway between two decrepit buildings he could swear he saw a tiny figure, not quite human, in a three-point jester hat with bells on, whose wide yellow eyes stared at the Kid with malevolence. He saw the night riders come out then, scruffy, scrawny youths who skulked into the alleyway and hastily pasted posters on the mock-brick wall. The austere face of a patrician man stared at him from the poster, but the eyes had been daubed with black paint, with the corneas, irises and pupils erased, and the scrawled letters below said, MAYOR WILDER IS LYING TO YOU and DOOM COMES TO JERICHO.

As he watched them, from the shadows, one hand on the butt of his gun ready to draw, he saw the ushers stream into the alley, official men in uniform, carrying billy clubs, their clogs rat-tat-tatting on the cobblestones. The fight that ensued was swift and brutal and at the end of it the night riders ran off but for one unlucky soul who was captured by the ushers and kicked on the ground, viciously and without sound, all this while without a sound from anyone at all.

The Kid holstered the gun he had almost unconsciously drawn, and then he faded into the space between buildings where the Pierrot had been. This city's problems were not his own. He followed the narrow gap over to the next alley and then the next, getting lost in a maze of impossibly twisting streets. He passed a wide gate, to what might have been a garden or a pavilion, on which was etched the symbol of a serpent entwined around a staff, but he paid no attention, and he passed it by, and did not notice the Stranger as he entered that strange place, for which the legend above the gate read, simply, ASCLEPIUS GARDENS.

Everything will be all right, the man said. He stroked the boy's hair. The boy lay in the bed under the clean white hospital sheets. His hair stuck to his forehead yet his skin felt cold. He breathed evenly but his eyes were closed. The machine by the bedside beeped. There were always machines these days and they always beeped. Do you remember this book, the man said, taking a worn copy out of his bag, we used to read it all the time when you were smaller.

The boy didn't answer. By his head, the man had placed the boy's favourite stuffed toys, an elephant, a cowboy and a clown. Outside the window the lights of cars passed endlessly, like a river. The man opened the book and he tried to focus on the first page but he couldn't see the letters clearly. The book had black-and-white ink illustrations. He leafed through the pages wordlessly.

Tiny forms in huge empty spaces.

A man disappearing through an arch into a shadow of ink.

The Stranger *did* notice the Kid's passing, but he had other things on his mind just then. He'd noticed many things since their arrival, for like the Conjurer he, too, was uneasily attuned to the changing vagaries of the Escapement, if only as a mechanism of survival.

He'd noticed, for instance, that the pitchmen were out in force that night across Jericho. A cross between show criers and vagabond preachers, they stood on street corners and ranted at the world, warning of the coming doom. A sense of anticipatory celebration was building up in the city. On the sky-bridges overhead and in the floating gardens people were drinking and dancing, their voices loud and gay, if a little edged, and little caiques caged in hanging baskets screeched and barked and mimicked the shrill whistle of the trains.

The Stranger passed into the night. On Moe Lane he found a shop selling materiel. For a moment he stood and watched the objects behind the glass, avidly, almost with hunger. Behind a window he saw the mummified corpse of a bee eater, its beak transformed into a set of golden scissors; a clock with seven hands, each human; a pair of dice formed of the skulls of rodents; a plant with human hair; a coal iron filled with blinking human eyes—the usual assortment of materiel discarded in the wake of battle. No use. No use to the Stranger, no use to the man behind the Stranger—

A nurse said, Could I get you a coffee?—kindly, startling him awake. He shook his head. No, no, he said. But thank you. In his hands, the book he used to read the boy. The one about the flower. But when he'd asked in shops about it no seller ever recognised the name or the description, he'd never seen another copy but his own. No, thank you. He was so tired. He had such important things to do. He let the book slip from his fingers to the floor, and settled in the chair. The beep, beep, beep of the machines. The boy unmoving. He had to find the flower—

The Stranger shook his head, warding off bad dreams, and set off again, into the night. It did not take him much longer. The twisting alleyways led him unerringly to his destination. Cats fled in his passing and watched him from a safe distance, a juggler juggled fire under ancient ivy. The Stranger looked at the card the man on the train had given him. He found the gate and entered.

A garden thick with vegetation welcomed him inside. A sort of hothouse. He saw orchids and cacti and Joshua trees. Skunk cabbages and giant hogweed. Corpse flowers and Venus flytraps. Strangler figs and witches' butter. The air stank with a hundred odours. Behind foliage he could see the signs of alcove stores, all dark yet he could sense them open. DREAM REPAIRERS, said one. THE EMPORIUM OF PERPETUUM MOBILE, said another.

MUMMY DUST AT ATTRACTIVE PRICES, said a third. LIGHTNING BOTTLED HERE, said a fourth. HERR HAHNEMANN'S ELECTROHOMOE-OPATHY CLINIC was yet another.

But these did not interest the Stranger. He searched, going deeper and deeper into the gardens, which seemed to go on forever, as though they somehow existed in a space in which the city itself did not; or perhaps it was that, by some curious property of alchemy or the Escapement, they bent the dimensions around them so that they seemed bigger on the inside. The Stranger stepped softly, his fingers resting lightly on the butt of his gun, for all that he sensed that it would not serve him here. He was aware of other lives all around him. Not merely the rustle underfoot of tiny beetles, or the hum of bees, but other people, or things like people. But though he several times thought he saw a silhouette, he never came into full view of those traversing the gardens as he was. And it seemed to him that perhaps each came alone into the gardens, and alone they travelled it, each to their own and isolated destination.

He checked the card again and it was then, at last, that he saw it, the sign peeking out from behind an unruly growth of nightshade and hemlock: JEFFERSON & NORVELL, MEDICI.

The Stranger skirted the poisonous shrubs and made his way to the door. He hesitated on the threshold; as well he should. It was only for a moment, and then he shrugged and pushed the door open and went inside.

The shop was dimly lit with only a few burning candles. With their folds of wax and their halos of flame the candles looked like fat, balding monks. The air smelled cloyingly of candyfloss and sweet cherry tobacco, and the walls were dirty with years of nicotine stains. Only a handful of potted plants decorated the room, but they were all wilted, and nothing hung on the walls but for a faded, cheap-looking print of Baphomet from a pack of Tarocchi cards.

A short counter separated this antechamber from the gloomy depths of the workshop beyond, and on the counter there was an old steel summoning bell. The Stranger, seeing no one, pressed the bell several times. The sound it emitted was not at all a ring, but rather the sort of gasping, eventually despairing sound of a person drowning.

"What? What! What do you want! Is this a delivery? Deliveries go through the back. What is this? Has it started yet? We're closed. Oh." He peered at the Stranger. "It's you."

The man had a long, thin face and mischievous eyes and spikey black hair and he wore a tweed jacket and a bowtie. He was not the man the Stranger had met on the train.

"Do I know you?" the Stranger said.

"I don't see why you would."

"Do you know me?"

"You? You're a stranger."

He said that dismissively.

"Is Mr. Norvell here?"

"Norvell? No. He's not here. Busy. Long time. Gone on a journey. Commercial traveller. What do you need, stranger? Pectoral drops? Anderson's pills? Sagwa? Catarrh snuff? Radium water? Stanley's snake oil? I'm Stanley, by the way. But you can call me Mr. Jefferson."

The Stranger said, "I am looking for the Ur-shanabi."

Jefferson stared at him. "Ah, it's *you*," he said again. "Yes, yes. By which I mean, no. Sorry. Don't have it. Never have. Beyond even my powers, etcetera, etcetera. Bugger off."

"I need," the Stranger said, and his gun leaped into his hand

and the muzzle was pointing very directly at Mr. Jefferson, "to find it."

"Then find a fucking cartographer!" Mr. Jefferson snapped, not at all concerned with the appearance of the gun. "There's one next door."

The Stranger still did not lower his gun. "You," he said. "You're a mask, aren't you. Not a . . . person."

"Great Harlequin," Mr. Jefferson said in exasperation. "Does it *matter*?"

The Stranger holstered his gun.

"No," he conceded. "I suppose not."

"Only we're very busy back here, on account of the . . ." He stopped talking and waved his hand airily. "Things, you know? Everyone's a little tense right now."

"The doom and—?"

"And so on. So you understand . . ."

"Next door?"

"Mercator's Conventional Signs. Can't miss it. Now piss off? Please? We're closed."

"All right," the Stranger said. He touched his trigger finger to the rim of his hat. "*Adios*."

"Just go."

The Stranger smiled, though there was nothing warm in it. Then he stepped outside, where tendrils of mist curled lazily around the planted cacti.

He did find the cartographer. And he did obtain a map. But what price he paid for it, no one could tell you, though it was a steep one, it was bound to be. For one does not make bargains easily with one of the Major Arcana, for all that they knew the Stranger and the Stranger knew them.

On the bed the child shivered, and the machine ping-ping-pinged wildly, and the man, distressed, cried, Nurse! and he held the child in his arms, and put his coat around him as though he could in this way keep him safe and warm. Then came running feet, and hands pushed him aside, and the boy's bed was wheeled outside. The man stared at the clock on the wall, and at the second hand crawling on its face.

Then it was done. And with that the Stranger left the cartographer's shop, but he did not go back the way he came. For there were grooves in the world and in such grooves a man must follow. And so he snuck round the back of the witchy shops, heedless of the poison ivy and stinging nettles, and a long way it seemed to him until he reached the back. He forced open a side door, kicking it with his boot, the wood splintering, and then he slid inside with his gun in his hand until he made it to the back room of Jefferson and Norvell's, and there he stopped, at the sight of something familiar.

The Kid was just headed to a bar called the Bull Tub when he spotted the Conjurer as though the man had stepped out of nowhere. He stopped in his tracks but the Conjurer hadn't seen him, and even if he had, he would have had no reason to suspect the young man was any kind of threat to him. The Conjurer merged into the shadows, but the Kid had taught himself the black art which magicians use, and he could follow.

And so he did.

Far beyond the city, trains thundered along old and newly-laid tracks, coming and going across the Thickening. On the Chagrin, the wrecked remnants of what had once been an island shuddered and for a moment the broken rocks in the water seemed to resemble a face. Beyond, still, in the Doinklands, silent clowns streamed across the land on top of painted ponies, their white expressionless faces staring up in wonder at the sky. Over the town of Kellysburg a symbol storm was brewing, ankhs flashing and octagons and dittos, and the town's residents locked up their doors and closed the blinds, and a bad wind blew in from the Doldrums.

The same storm that those prospectors in Kellysburg could sense was building over the Big Rock Candy Mountains. In the Désert de Soleil, dry wind picked up sand and tossed it this way and that until it built into a full simoom, and the ancient máquinas de sueños, disturbed from slumber, rang uneasily with the sound of wind chimes.

Beyond Jericho, forces were awakening that had been dormant for centuries, and they assembled now with something like anticipation, and something like glee. They came from the east, the north, the south and west, for all that directions meant nothing to them. And a child peering out of a moving train saw something impossible, a Colossus rising in the dark,

and behind it another, and another, faces in the stone unmoving, austere, cruel. But when she looked again, the figures
were no longer there.

The Conjurer saw the little Pierrot slip into a deliveries yard for
what must have been a row of shops, and he followed him in,
and threw open a door that had been left just so slightly ajar.

Behind him, softly, came the Kid, and he snuck behind the
Conjurer and lifted up his gun, but he never took the shot.

"Kid?" the Stranger said, on the other side of the room.

"What are *you* doing here?" the Kid said.

The Conjurer looked at them both, first at one, and then at
the other, but he made no comment. Then he looked back at
the centre of the room, and at the thing that lay there.

He stared.

"A fucking *fish*?" the Conjurer said.

The three men stood in the room facing each other with guns
drawn over the giant flopping mechanical fish. The Stranger
had not seen the fish since that single glimpse within the tinkerers' cart. The thing seemed more alive, somehow. Its glassy
eyes stared up and seemed to glow from within, with some yellow, inner light. Its powerful tail thrust against the floor, over
and over, and its scales shone wetly, as though it had just risen
from a swim.

"What *is* that thing?" the Conjurer said. "And who the fuck are *you?*"

The Stranger shrugged. "I'm a stranger here myself," he said. "And you, kid?"

The Kid stared at the Conjurer with something like loathing, and something else, ill-defined, something like desperation, or longing.

"Hello, Dad," he said.

It was quiet in the room. In the silence the only sounds were the men's breathing and a sound that materialised slowly, on the edge of hearing, but became more and more pronounced as one tuned in to it, until it seemed to dominate the world: the slow, relentless ticking of a mechanical clock. It seemed to come from within the body of the fish.

The two men stared at each other across the room. The Conjurer, for once, looked taken unawares. He stared aghast at the Kid.

". . . What?" he said.

The kid removed his necklace and showed the silver thumb-tip to the Conjurer.

"Do you recognise this?" he said.

"*Vernaculus* . . . ," the Conjurer said.

"Do you remember a town called Bozoburg?" the Kid said. "A small town on the Fratellini plains. I doubt you even re-member. There was girl who worked there once, in a bar. Her name was Ethel." His right hand was very still on the butt of his pistol. "She was my mother."

The Conjurer stared at the Kid, but for a long moment he didn't say anything. He remembered a one-clown town and dun-coloured plains that stretched in all directions, some-where on the edge of the Doinklands. He remembered a young woman who laughed at all his jokes, who had eyes that shone with the light of the sun, he remembered long after-noons stolen out of time, and a sense of *completeness*. A rare time of peace, and all the more valued for that . . .

"You're Ethel's *son?*"

"Yes. Dad."

"But I didn't . . . I can't . . . How is she?"

"She's dead, Dad."

"Stop calling me *Dad!*" The Conjurer stared at the Kid, and he seemed oblivious to the gun pointed at him. "Wait, dead? How did she die?"

"How do you think she died? She was murdered."

The Kid remembered again when the Rasmussen Gang, mean and hungry, more wolves then men, with faces painted white and noses painted red, had come riding into town.

We're looking for the Conjurer, they kept saying. We're looking for that bastard, he owes us a life, we know he's been through here, there was a woman, they said.

Then one of the townsfolk, he must have said something to them, and the biggest of the brothers smiled. A terrible dread filled the kid's heart then, worse than the fear of dying.

They'd strung him up and he swore he'd get them and they laughed. Then they left him to die, but the rotten old beam collapsed under the kid's weight and he lived, still. But when he ran after them it was too late.

He reached his home only to see it on fire.

He ran inside. . . .

"It was you," he said now. "They were looking for *you.*"

"The Rasmussens . . . ," the Conjurer said. "Ethel's *dead?* I never meant . . . When we parted . . . it was only meant to be for a few months, but time flows differently in the Thinning, and when I returned she wasn't there, the whole town was gone. But that was years ago, and as for a kid, I never . . . she never said . . ."

"I've been looking for you for a long time," the Kid said. He aimed the gun very steadily. "I've waited for this moment."

"I didn't kill your mother!" He stared at the Kid. "And I don't want to have to kill you. Put down your gun."

"You think you can take me?" the Kid said, and the Conjurer laughed.

"I know I fucking can," he said.

The Stranger backed away from them both. His ears were filled with the even ticking sound of a clock. It felt to him that the seconds were speeding up, and that time was running out. A sense of giddy exhalation . . .

"I hate to break this touching family reunion," he said. "But I think we have bigger—"

Two shots were fired at once. The Stranger stared at the others. He could *see* the bullets. See them emerge from the barrels of the guns. See them cut through the air like slow-moving larvae. See them *shed* the casing, like pupae emerging, like popping corn. The bullets spread wings. Two butterflies rose into the air. They circled each other, then fled out of the open door into the city beyond.

"—problems," the Stranger said.

The Conjurer stared down at the giant mechanical fish. It whirred now, from some internal mechanism, and it glowed, light escaping through narrow slits under its scales. The ticking sound grew louder.

"*What* did you say again this was?" he said.

"I didn't," the Stranger said. "But I've seen it, once before."

"The Dumuzi Device . . . ," the Kid whispered. "Right?" He

turned to the Stranger. "Those aerialists on the train, *this* is what they were looking for?"

"I think so, yes," the Stranger said.

"Well, what *is* it?" the Conjurer said.

"I think," the Stranger said. "I think it's a chthonic bomb."

They stared at the fish. Its movements became more rapid, and clinking and hissing sounds began to emerge from it over the ticking of the hidden clock.

"I *think*," the Stranger said, meditatively. "I think it might go *off*."

"A chthonic bomb?" the Conjurer said. "Great Harlequin, not *again*!"

"You've seen one before?"

"Long ago, and far away, and only the aftermath," the Conjurer said, grimly. "And that was enough, once was enough. We have to get out of here."

"Can't it be disabled?" the Kid said.

"*Disabled?* It's a *fish*."

"We could, I don't know, shoot it."

"You couldn't even shoot *me*, kid. And it's not like you weren't trying."

The Kid kicked the fish.

"Ouch!"

A tongue of light had darted out of the fish's body and wrapped itself around the Kid's ankle.

"Hey, let go!"

The Stranger looked at the fish, which seemed to grow *larger*, or to twist the dimensions around itself so that the walls and ceiling of the room seemed to bend down and around it, and he saw that a miniature symbol storm had begun to form in the air overhead, and obelisks and pilcrows and crucifixes burst in tiny flashes of light.

"Step away from the fish, kid," he said.

"I'm *trying* to!"

"Oh, for crying out loud," the Conjurer said. He grabbed the Kid in one arm and the Stranger grabbed the other and they pulled. The Kid howled in pain and protested with some profanity, and the tentacle of light tightened around his ankle but then, at last, released him abruptly, and the three men staggered and fell through the open door, and outside.

Inside the room, the ticking of the mechanical clock grew faster and louder in intensity and then, just as abruptly, stopped.

The three men stared at each other in the silence.

"It's *definitely* about to go off, isn't it," the Conjurer said.

"What do we do?"

"Run?"

"Run where?"

"I know a way," the Conjurer said. "Come on." He hesitated, glanced at the Kid. "Son?"

"Don't call me *son*!" the Kid said.

But he followed all the same.

The three men moved fast and with deadly purpose, guns drawn, and the burghers and good citizens of Jericho moved swiftly out of their way. The streets were thronged with revellers drunk on moonshine; a fat man on a piano struck "Entrance of the Gladiators," and a mime troupe locked in an invisible glass cage writhed and floundered as though they were choking on invisible gas. A cat chased a mouse down the street. The Stranger wasn't sure, but for a moment it seemed to him the mouse wore a bow tie.

The Conjurer led the other two men over a low stone wall

and into an unlit courtyard and from there to a twisting stone staircase that rose high up into the upper echelons of the city.

"Hurry, fools!"

They huffed their way up the stairs, going round and round, and the Stranger was absurdly glad they weren't carrying anything heavy with them, like a piano. They found themselves at last on the roof of the building, and the Conjurer led them in a leap across it, and in this way they traversed the rooftops over Jericho, which were themselves filled with revellers. The Stranger felt the city shifting then. A rumbling just beyond the edge of hearing, a subtle rearrangement of the elements all about him. He stumbled, but the Kid caught and steadied him. Wordlessly, they ran on.

There was a high tower ahead. Below, the Stranger could see wide palatial gardens, a water fountain, mimes . . .

More mimes.

The mimes crawled along the walls like spiders. They climbed up, holding knives between their teeth. Their hands were like geckos' adhesive toes. Their eyes were black and empty holes. They weren't human, the Stranger realised.

He said, "Pupae umbrarum."

"Those *fuckers*!" the Conjurer said. "Shit!"

"Friends of yours?"

"Just . . . shoot them, will you?"

"Gladly," the Kid said, and he took off his rifle and began to fire, picking out the white-skinned creatures one by one. They fell from the walls without sound.

"I fucking hate mimes," the Kid said.

The Conjurer grinned in savage appreciation, but more and more mimes were converging on their trail.

"We have to go higher!"

"Where!'"

"That tower, it's Mooky's Spire! If we get to the top we can get away!"

"How!"

"Magic," the Conjurer said, and grinned again.

The Stranger fired methodically, running, stopping, firing, resuming. So this is what it came to, he thought, chilled. The pupae at last had the device, and it was their agents who'd brought it into the city.

If so, their opponents would not be far away.

They reached the tower and he and the Kid leaped after the Conjurer, onto a sturdy metal ladder that rose up to the top. They began to climb and it was then, from high above, that he at last saw the Colossi.

They were ranged beyond the city, illuminated by the moon. Vast figures carved of stone, with sneering visages of cold command. Behind them came the storm. He heard inhuman laughter, punctuated with awful bursts of opposing silence.

"Colossi . . . ," he said.

"Climb, you idiot! Climb!"

A hand grasped the Stranger's boot. He kicked, then fired down, and a mime fell soundlessly through the air. There was no way out, he thought. No way out but death.

Still, he climbed. They reached the top and fell inwards through a window. Winds howled against the tower walls.

"Ain't she a beaut?" the Conjurer said, fondly.

Standing in the middle of that turret was the deflated enve-lope, gondola and burner of a hot-air balloon.

The Stranger took one window and the Kid another. They fired methodically at the mimes climbing the walls. The mimes mimed getting hurt. The mimes fell, hitting invisible obstacles. The Conjurer attended to the *Fat Lady*. Her envelope inflated slowly. Gas jets hissed from the burner. The roof had fallen down years in the past, and been covered over with a tarp to keep out the elements. Now the Conjurer tore it off (with a flourish that went unnoticed by his audience, who were otherwise engaged) and the envelope expanded outwards towards the dark skies.

"Come on!" the Conjurer said. He hopped inside the gondola. The other two kept firing. One of the mimes had almost reached the turret. The Kid was out of bullets and with a shout of disgust he pulled out a knife and stabbed the creature in the neck. The mime gave him the finger, then clutched his neck, which was bleeding an unhealthy green.

"Got something to *say?*" the Kid screamed. He plunged the knife down again and the mime let go of the wall and fell, hitting two others on his way down. The Kid abandoned the window and climbed into the gondola. The *Fat Lady* was rising fast.

The Stranger sighted down the barrel of his gun. He hesitated, his finger on the trigger. Caught in his crosshairs was a human figure rising into the air towards him at some speed. It was the man he had last seen playing "March of the Gladiators" on a piano. The man rose into the air, his mouth open impossibly wide, and his shadow fell down below him like massive entrails spilling from an animated corpse. The shadow congealed and shuddered as it held up the man like a hand puppet, pushing him higher and higher into the sky.

The Stranger took the shot.

The bullet caught the man clear between the eyes and went clean through the back of the skull. The corpse shuddered, hanging in the air like the condemned at the end of a rope. But it didn't stop, and the shadow below opened the corpse's mouth and a scream of rage, or perhaps it was triumph, burst forth as the shadow operated the dead man's lungs to produce it. The Stranger took out a stick of dynamite, bit the fuse to shorten it, lit the fuse, and dropped the stick of dynamite without even looking. He ran for the gondola.

There was a small explosion. Hands reached out for him as he stumbled. The gondola hovered overhead, but the Kid and the Conjurer, working in tandem, got hold of the Stranger and lifted him up. He flopped down to the floor as the *Fat Lady* rose, higher and higher into the air.

When he rose to his feet again and looked down, all he could see was a fine red mist falling down. It fell on the mimes and painted their faces crimson. A pool of shadow lay far down below, and as he watched it flowed, like water, down the street. The mimes looked up, wordlessly.

The hot air balloon rose up into the sky, far above the city.

They felt rather than heard the second explosion. Somewhere to the east of them, in what had until very recently been the back room of Jefferson & Norvell, Medici, of Asclepius Gardens, the fish had finally detonated.

It manifested first as the taste of purple. They felt it on their tongues, against their inner cheeks. It set their teeth on edge. The rooftops wobbled like cloth. In the avenues down below, the revellers stopped and stared. A man pushing a food cart looked briefly puzzled and then turned into a pink flamingo. He spread his wings experimentally and took to the air.

The towers of the city began to melt. A horse-drawn cart swerved sharply to avoid a swirl of tomatoes which had drawn together into a humanoid shape and ran down the street, leaving juicy footprints in its wake. The horse reared back and its legs turned to glass in the air and it remained there, suspended, only the eyes still alive and blinking.

Mimes spread through the city then, cradling weapons only they could see. Beyond the walls, there arose a terrible laughter, and the sound of giant stone feet treading. They came down on the walls and tore them to the ground. From high above the city, the Stranger could see it all. The rows of Colossi ranged against it, and the awful shadows that fled into the city from the north and west, a sea of dark. Each opponent reached within and animated people like puppets in its war. A water fountain burst and shot up multicoloured streamers. A man's nose melted down his face and he wiped it clear off with a hand that was turning by degrees into a trumpet. The cats, who knew when things were going bad, slunk into the holes between the city and that other place and vanished. A woman's head turned into a flower. The flower grew, extending roots deep inside her. It bloomed beautifully, rising as tall as a building. Men turned to ants and lay helplessly on their backs.

Civilian resistance was bloodied and ineffective.

Veterans, of which the city hosted many, already transformed by previous skirmishes in the war between pupae and Colossi, took up assorted arms, pistols, rifles, hoes and hammers. They smashed and stabbed and shot the invading materiel. Walls disappeared, opening onto sudden chasms. Ivy with tiny snakes' heads choked homes and palaces. The

Fat Lady rose above them, rose above it all, drifting on the strong cold winds. The Stranger watched the city transform, eldritch lights bursting forth, shadow battling stone. The Colossi moved across the city methodically, treading on people, buildings, carts and horses, flattening trees and anything that stood in their way. The shadows of the pupae umbrarum grew over their own side of the city, snuffing out lives and lights like useless candlewicks. The Stranger watched the city's destruction. For too long it had stood there, an open sore, an irritant on the flesh of the Escapement: fat, arrogant, elegant, doomed. Now the war had come at last to Jericho, and those who had thought themselves secure, impregnable, discovered too late the awful truth. All human life is solitary, brutish, nasty and short.

Another pink flamingo rose awkwardly into the sky, and then another.

"I guess the doom really *had* come to Jericho," the Conjurer said. "Well, I'll be damned." He spat over the side of the gondola, meditatively.

The hot air balloon drifted away from the city.

The last the Stranger saw of it, the city resembled the crushed skull of a lizard, crudely drawn in shadow and stone. Then it was gone from sight.

NINE:
THE PREACHER

AT NIGHT, hospitals feel like shadowy, deserted wastelands inhabited mostly by machines. The man stood alone in the elevator and he pressed the button to go down, over and over, until the machine announced Doors *closing!* with a sort of unwarranted cheer, and the doors slid shut and the elevator began its descent, like a mine cage going down a shaft. When the doors opened again they did so onto a wide corridor where, in the daytime, numerous visitors, doctors, nurses and patients came and went, not to mention deliverymen and postmen and administrators and attendants and cleaners and cooks, the lifeblood of a hospital, its people. Now there was no one in sight and the lights were dimmed to conserve power, and in this twilight empty world the man walked, his feet treading the parquet floor. They made a little squeaking sound with each step he took, like a clown's.

Another corridor connected to this one and it was along it that the various shops and amenities for visitors ran, though most closed down at night and would not be opened again until morning. A janitor mopped the floor by the men's public bathrooms. The only place open was the café, which like the hospital never closed, and so it was there that the man headed. There was something almost comforting about hospitals at night, he'd discovered. In his long sojourn he had grown to loathe the daytime hospital with its ceaseless movement of people and eternal busyness, the constant babble of voices. People died in the night much as they did in the day but nights were quieter: one could hear oneself think. He ordered a coffee and paid and sat by the window. A wan moon shone behind clouds. It had rained earlier. A dark figure stood and watched him from outside, by the public benches. He could not make out its face. It raised a hand in greeting. Just a random passer-by, a teenager returning from the clubs late, or a homeless person. The hospital offered them a kind of comfort. He tore a sachet of sugar and then another and another. The sugar spilled over the counter. He drew a shape: walls, windows, a roof. A house. He took out his hip flask and poured into the coffee surreptitiously. A word came and went in his mind, something to do with the end of a railway line.

Terminal.

He told it to go away.

Terminal.

No, he said. There's a flower and it lies beyond the Mountains of Darkness and—

Shut up.

He wondered if he was talking to himself. It didn't matter. It wasn't long now. He had the map now.

A doctor and three nurses came and sat at a table. They spoke in low voices, occasionally glancing at him. He thought they were glancing at him. The doctor laughed. The sound was jarring in the room. It was probably nothing, they had probably just come off a shift, or were taking a break. It didn't matter. The figure outside whose face he couldn't see was gone. The Stranger looked over the railing of the hot air balloon.

They had been sailing over land for days, ever since the deliquescence of Jericho. In that time they had seen the Colossi range across the land, the railway lines broken, towns and hamlets abandoned or grotesquely transformed, and vast shadows congealing like pools of dark ink across the Thickening. They pissed and shat from on high, never touching ground, drinking when it rained and subsisting on a tin of dry old biscuits that the Conjurer uncovered in the *Fat Lady*'s basket. One night a symbol storm burst overhead and as they passed it St. Elmo's Fire ranged the gondola, pale luminous plasma taking form as grotesque animated puppets dancing on the railing, blinking at them with huge round eyes. They'd felt the directions change then, and in the morning when the sun rose the landscape was new and the compass needle swayed like a drunk. There were fewer and fewer signs of habitation then, and at last they passed over ground entirely uninhabited and the view changed to low-lying hills, with a smattering of viridescent shrubs and trees, into which no train tracks ran. And they knew then that they were come to the edge of the Thickening.

They'd passed that invisible boundary in the night and in the morning they were truly into the Thinning. There, where the true Escapement began, the Conjurer's device for the measurement of time was still and lifeless.

"It isn't permanent," he said, looking sheepish. "It's just a slipstream."

He meant the way time was not neatly homogenous on the Escapement but could flow, like hot and cold currents which sometimes overlaid each other. They'd hit a patch of slow time, that was all. Or perhaps it was that the Conjurer's clock was merely broken.

The next day and the next took them into what should have been clown country, but they saw none. Only, here and there, the hidden dwelling places of the clowns would come into sudden and unwelcome sight: funhouses burned, ballooneries trashed, trampolines lying torn and half-buried in the ground. This trail of devastation continued for miles and the three men, uneasy, kept scanning the horizon and held their guns, but there was nothing to shoot at.

Another day, another night. A storm rose from the east then, a regular yet violent storm. A column of air twisting and turning like a majestic predator, crossing the land. The tornado threatened to swoop them up and carry them elsewhere. The Conjurer cursed and fired short bursts of flame from the burner. The hot air balloon dropped but the edges of the storm had them then and they were helpless in its grasp. It twisted them round and round, high and then low. Below, the Stranger saw a curious procession. A small white chapel stood on the hard ground beside a wide cemetery in which were laid rows and rows of headstones. Beside the chapel stood several figures, and it occurred to him that one man was about to be hanged from a tree, and that another man, astride a horse, was directing this execution. He saw all this in but a moment as the storm brought them up again and then, by what forces of nature he could not tell, decided abruptly to change direction again and violently released them. The *Fat Lady* hurled downward at speed. The three men were tossed and turned within the *Fat Lady*'s belly. The Stranger held on to the sides of the basket, which badly shook. The air rushed all about them, and they hit the ground with a terrible cracking sound and a terrified whinny, and the deflated envelope came down on them, burying them in a dank darkness.

"Screw this lot!" the Conjurer said. He must have reached for a knife, for next thing they knew the envelope had been sliced open and sunlight poured down along with fresh air. The three men emerged through this breach, guns at the ready, but they were not prepared for the scene that greeted their hatching.

A man's legs stuck out from under the hot air balloon's gondola. Over by the dilapidated chapel, several men and women stood like mourners at a funeral, dressed in sombre black clothes and wearing whiteface makeup. They stood peering at them stoically with hands crossed. Standing facing the hot air balloon in an uncertain semicircle were four rough-looking men holding guns. From a thick branch of the solitary tree there hung a thick rope. It, in turn, was looped around the neck of a man.

The man was desperately pedalling a unicycle to try and stay upright.

The four armed-men drew their guns, but the Conjurer, the Kid and the Stranger were faster. Three shots rang out, and then three more, and then a final seventh shot, which severed the hanging rope. The man on the unicycle shot forward, hit a trampoline, bounced up into a full aerial cartwheel, and landed improbably on his face in a custard pie that had been lying there.

The mourners clapped, politely. A murmur of appreciation rose and fell among them like the chatter of crickets. The Stranger stared at the scene: four men lay dead on the ground, and a fifth must have died under the *Fat Lady* when she'd landed.

The Stranger climbed down. "Get their weapons," he told the Kid.

A woman ran up to him then, sobbing. He saw she wore an eyepatch. She threw her arms around the Stranger's neck. "We thank you very sweetly for doing it so neatly," she murmured into the Stranger's ear. Her breath was hot on his skin. She lingered there a moment longer, as though unsure of protocol. Then she released him abruptly and retreated to be with the rest of her congregation—for that was what they must be, the Stranger saw. He had seen such chapels before.

The Kid and the Conjurer moved among the corpses, collecting the dead men's guns. The Stranger went to the fallen man on the unicycle and helped him up to his feet. He was a large, imposing man, the Stranger saw, with broad shoulders threaded with muscle. His grey hair was cropped short, in almost a military fashion, and his deep unsettling eyes were the colour of Tyrian purple.

"Thank you, stranger," he said. His voice had the gritty coarseness of broken coral. "I am Jedediah Baily, preacher to this poor congregation."

The Stranger looked up at the small chapel. It was a clown ministry, of the sort that dotted the Escapement on the edges of the Thickening and into the Doinklands.

A stylised Harlequin, garrotted with a diabolo, hung over the steeple. The Harlequin's eyes, disconcertingly alive, bulged comically out of their sockets as the wire cut into its throat, and a single drop of blood was visible. Gravel neatly covered the ground before the door. The whole place had a neat and well-kept, if worn, appearance.

"You seem to have incurred someone's displeasure, Preacher," the Stranger said.

"That would be the General's man, down under your gondola, General Barnum's man that is," the preacher said. "And

I thank you kindly, you and providence, for despatching him when you did. I could not have pedalled that wheel for much longer."

"But why is it that you were about to be executed?" the Stranger said.

"Yeah," the Kid said, swaggering over to join them. "And where's your congregation, Preacher? I don't see any clowns."

"Yet plenty of tombstones," the Conjurer observed, more quietly, coming to join them. "Your ministry appears to be nothing more than a graveyard, Preacher."

"My story is a long and sad one," the preacher said. "But come inside, strangers. We have little enough, yet what we have we'll share gladly."

"I'd like a drink," the Kid said.

"A big fucking drink," the Conjurer agreed.

"We may have some moonshine . . . ," the preacher said. "I could do with a drop myself, now that you come to mention it. Coming this close to death makes a man thirsty."

The Stranger said nothing. He watched the barren landscape, and the rows and rows of tombstones. He listened to the silence of the wind. Now that the storm had vanished, the air was still, and it had a stuffy, oppressive quality to it, and on his tongue the Stranger thought he could taste the vestiges of substance. He glanced again at the hot air balloon, and at the legs of the dead man that protruded from underneath it. He checked his gun. The preacher's congregation had vanished inside the mission house, and for a moment the Stranger remained alone under the big and empty sky. Jericho had fallen, but this was the nature of the cities of men. Sooner or later, they fell. Out on the Escapement, stone and shadow endured. He tasted again the substance on his tongue. It was in the air, he decided. An open mine, perhaps. But this was redfeet country now.

Wasn't it?

He followed the others into the chapel. They walked down the pews and past the altar, and through a wooden door into the sacristy, where the preacher kept the tools of his service, the big red nose and face paint and wigs, and from there through a second door to the secular part of the mission house. A small but pleasant kitchen with a long oak table in the middle, and already on the table was a pot of coffee, and eggs were cooking on the stove, and the smell of it, homely and familiar, awakened in the Stranger some terrible longing, and for a moment he looked away so that the others could not see his face.

The preacher sat at the head of the table and the three men sat down as well. A quiet worn-down man in a worn-out suit brought them plates of eggs and flatbread and beans. The men ate enthusiastically, for this was the first meal they'd had in days.

Sitting side by side, the Kid and the Conjurer did resemble each other. Throughout the long ride in the hot air balloon they had spoken little, and only of practical matters, such as there were. Most of the time on board the *Fat Lady* they simply played cards. Since both of them constantly cheated, the Stranger had mostly refrained from participating. The two men had bet fortunes neither had, but that did not seem to dissuade them. As far as the Stranger could make out, at the time of their crash-landing the Kid owed the Conjurer two million ducats and the shoulder bone of a fallen Colossus. Or perhaps it was the other way around.

The Stranger ate, too. But he kept a careful eye on the door all the same.

"My name, as I told you earlier, is Jedediah Bailey," the preacher said, when they had done eating and were drinking their coffee. The coffee was bitter and strong. "I was a wild youth, given to sudden rage and acts of violence which I now regret. When drunk one night I killed a man. It was a fair fight, and he'd swung for me first, but I killed him all the same and he was a judge's son. The ushers were after me then, and the old man had hired the Pilkingtons to do for me, but I ran, and I ran far and I ran deep into the Doinklands, where even the Pilkingtons wouldn't go. I wandered, alone. One day I came, starved, half-mad, upon a party of Auguste clowns. Perhaps I was the first man they had ever seen. I tried to speak to them—I begged for food—for help! They looked at me with incomprehension. Finally the boss clown, whether out of pique or pity, I never knew, struck me over the head with a juggler's club, and I lost consciousness.

"When I awoke, they had gone. Only the marks of their giant feet were left in the ground. But I *saw*, then. I had been *reborn*. It was as though a tiny window had opened, and the light poured through into the cell that had been my life up to that point. After days of walking, I reached a monastery on the Maskelyne range. They are snow-peaked mountains above the Copper Fields, far to the east. There I became a novice."

The Stranger listened for other sounds, but there were none. He heard no birds outside, nothing living. The man finished his coffee but was reluctant to get up from the stool. He stared out of the window into the night. He could see the city skyline beyond the river. The radio was on somewhere in the background. He felt both tired and alert. He couldn't face going back up to the room, he could not face to see the boy just lying there. He got up, walked past the water fountain where the same lethargic janitor was moving the mop back and forth, back and forth, with a listless determination. Through the revolving doors, and into the night and a blast of cold air. It didn't revive him. Traffic on the road, the lights moving slowly, like so many eyes of so many buffalos in migration. The man lit a cigarette, drew bitter smoke into his lungs, exhaled. He coughed. You can't keep going on like this, she'd said the night before. The drinking and . . . this throwing yourself into oblivion. You have to be strong. For him, if not for me.

What is being *strong*, he said, or wanted to and didn't. What did it matter. Being weak or strong in yourself made no difference at all. He could not manipulate the clouds to rain nor the traffic to halt nor the boy to heal. But things were different now. He'd not told her that. He had the map now, he'd never had the map before. It could lead him where he needed to go, to cross to cross the great salt lakes marked there and though the tunnel and beyond the Mountains of Darkness to the place where the Ur-shanabi grew. If only he could stop being assailed by distractions and side-quests, and other people telling stories. Stories, always stories! But they were all he had. He tossed the cigarette on the ground and crushed it with his foot. Over the river the city lights shone.

"When I was ordained, I was sent back out into the world to spread the good word as written in the Funny Pages," the preacher said. His fingers, thick and tan, rested on the surface of the table. "I walked from town to town, visiting the lonely homesteads of the Escapement on the way, preaching the word. Mostly I was mocked and jeered at. More than once I had to make a hasty retreat, or use my pistols to defend myself. Once, I arrived at a place called Benders' End, named for the family who lived there. A place never touched by a clown's smile, as they say. Dark and dismal homesteading land, nothing but a flat plain in all directions, as far as the eye could see. What anyone thought they could grow there is anyone's guess. Fool's parsley and devil's snare and thistles. Those bloody Benders had a sort of encampment out there, an inn they called it, and at first they welcomed me pleasantly enough. Their matriarch, Ma Bender, claimed sympathy to Harlequin, and I dare say she may have meant it, for there is a dark side to every clown, and there was none darker than the Bender family. I stayed for dinner, at their urging. The daughter, too, attempted to distract me. It was then that I noticed the scuff marks on the floor, the outline of what I thought a trapdoor directly underneath my chair. As I was looking, Pa Bender swiped at me with a hammer. I was lucky, having swooped down, and he missed. Then the womenfolk came at me with knives. No doubt they planned to cut my throat, rob me, then dump my body in their cellar.

"Strangers . . . I killed again that day. I killed every last one of them and when I was done I opened that trapdoor. How many unwary travellers had wound up down there I could not in truth tell you. The stench made me retch. That night I dumped the Benders' bodies into that same communal grave and when I was finished I set fire to the place and watched it burn.

"I felt cleansed by the fire. In the outline of flames I thought I saw the Harlequin, looking back at me, telling me I'd done the right thing. There is so much wretchedness, on the Escapement as much as in that other place. The innocents die while the wicked celebrate. You have to laugh or you'll cry. Or so I believe. I have to believe."

The preacher excused himself abruptly. He rose from the

table and for a moment the three men were left alone in the room.

"Barmy as a barn owl," the Conjurer said.

"I say we rob him and get out of this place," the Kid said.

"Rob him? Of what?"

"Fair point, Dad."

"I told you not to call me that!"

The Stranger listened to them bickering. The map was in his pocket. He knew his way now. He was getting closer. The Stranger had been travelling for a long time, but perhaps he was no longer destined to travel for such a long time more. Only a little farther, he thought. Though he had begun to feel that he was running out of time.

"I walked the Escapement for a long while," the Preacher said. When had he come back to the table? The air felt too still, the familiar cooking smells felt cloying. "Spreading the word of the Funny Pages, eliminating evil with extreme unction. In that time I saw Colossi move across the sands, I heard the awful silence of the pupae umbrarum as their shadows pooled in haunted valleys. I gathered true believers unto me. Some, veterans of the Titanomachy. Others were former bounty hunters and outlaws, clown killers who had found redemption. Together we ventured beyond the Thickening and into a remote and unexplored part of the Doinklands, and it was here that I at last set up my mission. With my own two hands I built this house of faith, my people and I, and it is here that we dwelt, among the clowns, for all that they treated us much as a circus-goer might treat an ostrich. I had hoped for a long and tranquil life here, to end my days here, under the infinite sky, far from the world of men. But that was not to be."

It really was so very hot in the room. The smell of grease made the Stranger nauseous. He said, "Excuse me," and stepped outside. He could not hear a living thing, no birds, no crickets. All he could taste was substance on his tongue. The man paced outside the hospital. He thought he saw the same shadowy figure as before and went towards it, out by the shrubberies. The Stranger walked amidst the tombstones in the graveyard, looking at the names. HERE LIES MASTER JESSUP, ESQ., LATELY OF THIS PARISH, WHO WAS KIND TO CLOWNS. The same one-eyed woman from earlier approached him.

"You must help us," she whispered. "The General has enslaved all the clowns, he's taken them for slave labour."

"Lady," the Stranger said, "my path lies away from here and to the Mountains of Darkness, wherever they may be. I have no time for the affairs of men and clowns."

"You have kind eyes," she said. "And I seem to recall a stranger, much like yourself, distracted from the purpose of his quest once to exact justice for a troupe of massacred clowns. . . ."

She raised her face to him then, and winked.

"*Temperanza?*" He'd not seen her since she vanished on the train. "What are *you* doing here?"

"There has been *unrest*," she said. "The Colossi and pupae are renegotiating the balance, and the Major Arcana are once more loose upon the world. Justice and the Devil are up to their old tricks once again. I'm after the Devil's fortune, myself. General Barnum's." She winked again. Her eye was very blue. "Don't get in my way. It's taken me forever to infiltrate the preacher's congregation, and I had hoped today to make the switch and go with the General's men to Hole. But you ruined *that* plan . . . so I'll have to do it the hard way."

"Do *what?*"

"Kill the General and steal his fortune. Were you not *listening?* Oh, and you might want to go back inside. The preacher's just about to murder your friends."

She punched him in the shoulder and disappeared down the row of tombstones. He stared after her, then rushed back into the kitchen.

The Kid and the Conjurer were half-asleep in their chairs. The preacher held a hammer and two of his congregation women were creeping up on the men with razor blades in their hands. He could see now the outlines of a trapdoor underneath the chairs. He drew his gun and fired.

The women died first, and they died quietly and without a fuss. The preacher was hit in the shoulder and he fell back but he was like a mountain. The Stranger shot him again, and then again.

"*You* were the Benders?" he said.

The preacher, on the floor, smiled through the pain. "A preacher like that did once come through our home," he said. "His story was as fatuous as his mission so we killed him and ate his flesh, though it was gamey. Listen, stranger. There's a seam of substance that reaches all the way under this house. My brother, damn his soul, controls the mine. Go to Hole. Kill him, for me, for he stole my clowns for his own and robbed me of my share and tried to have me hanged. . . . I can give you money."

"I don't need money."

"Then fetch me my medicine." He coughed, and blood frothed out of his mouth. "There is a . . . leather satchel in the sacristy, hidden in the book. Bring it to me. It has the last vestige of dried petals from the Plant of Heartbeat. Not enough to revive me, but to offer comfort. . . . Yet I do not need it. I welcome pain. Take it, instead, for your payment. You have the look of a man who . . . needs it more." He tried to laugh, puked out more blood and then, with a final heave of his chest, expelled the last of his breath and died.

The Stranger went to the sacristy. He opened the book and saw that the Funny Pages had been cut through and a small hiding place had been made and inside it was the satchel. He opened it, carefully. There was only a smidge in there. The man rode the elevator back up to the floor and went into the boy's room. Was it his imagination, or did the boy's breathing ease, just now, did some colour return to his face? He sat in the chair, resuming his vigil. It was only a smidge, dry leaves, close to dust. The Stranger closed the satchel carefully and went back into the kitchen, where the preacher's body had disappeared. He dragged first the Kid and then the Conjurer outside, where the air was cleaner, and watched them recover.

"That son of a . . . !" the Conjurer said. He massaged his throat.

"He wanted to hire me," the Stranger said. "Hire us, I suppose. To kill his brother."

"Why would we want to do that?"

"He has a fortune."

"Oh. Well, did you accept the job?"

"Yes," the Stranger said. "I suppose I did."

"All right," the Conjurer said. He rubbed his head and blinked. "All right, then, good."

♦ ♠ ♦

The three men rode out of the mission later that day, on three docile horses that didn't have names. Before they left, they set the church on fire. It wasn't much, but it was something.

The Kid and the Conjurer still looked a little woozy. They swayed in the saddles, this way and that. But it would pass, the Stranger thought. Most things did, sooner or later.

Low-lying hills, far in the distance. The shrubbery was sparse. The more they rode the stronger did the smell of substance linger. Ghostly cars swept past the lonely prairies, ghost men walked past ghostly shops, ghost traffic lights, ghost city streets. Far, far in the distance, the Stranger imagined he could smell salt. Imagined he could see dark rising mountains.

Onwards they rode, until they came to Hole.

TEN:
HOLE

THEY HEARD and they saw it for miles before they reached the place. The fires burned endlessly, bright white flames hungrily devouring the horizon. They looked like albino lizards crawling on a vast black screen. There were no stars above Hole. The sky was written and erased endlessly. Only occasionally they would see a ghost plane from that other place fly through and disappear. The Stranger wondered if the passengers inside could see the Escapement. Perhaps, cruising at high altitude, someone would look out of their window, expecting clouds and stars, only to be granted a glimpse of this other place, an image to carry with them through all the years ahead, a moment of wonder at something inexplicable.

The burning fires were fuelled by substance. More substance than the Stranger had ever imagined could be found in one place. The fires were like the thieves' lights one found in prospector towns, but on an unprecedented, industrial scale. It made the Stranger uneasy. There were many blights and snares and traps on the Escapement, buried debris from bygone ages, and the unfathomable machinations of pupae and Colossi in their endless war. Yet they were all *of* the Escapement, and woven into its fabric. This was something else, a hole in the matter of the world. He had never before seen a region where the walls between this and that other place were so thin. Even in prospector towns where they mined the seams of substance, such as could be found, the concentration was only relatively small. Mining towns were like half-open windows . . . but this place, the Stranger thought, was more like a door.

Then there was the noise. The *thump . . . thump . . . thump . . .* like the beating of a giant, living heart buried underground. It sent tremors through the earth. It vibrated in the Stranger's bones. After a time, he almost began to think it was his own heart that was beating, out of body.

They rode in uneasy silence. The Kid chewed on a stick of jerky. The Conjurer kept rolling ducats between his fingers. The Stranger just watched, and thought. The man sat in the room all alone but for his thoughts and he looked at the boy, who was not sleeping and not awake. He thought that the dry leaves of the Ur-shanabi might have given him comfort. It was hard to know, in truth. The Stranger blinked and the world swam back into focus. They rode until the sound swallowed them and they became as one with it. Until the white fires erased every trace of shadow, and within it could be seen the streets and houses of that other place, and the people who dwelt there, for all that they moved the way ghosts do, and did not make a sound, and seemed unaware that they were being passed through.

When they came at last near to the place—to Hole—they began to see tracks in the ground, looping and twisting on each other. The tracks led to giant warehouses built of stout wood—all the wood that had been chopped off for miles in every direction. As they came near they saw a mining cart emerge just ahead. It was being pulled by four Whitefaces, whose legs were shackled by chains. The cart was laden with bags and bags all filled with substance, the white crystals spilling out as the cart shuddered and was jogged forward, one step at a time. The clowns never made a sound and their faces were impassive. Only their eyes showed the strain.

"What is this?" the Stranger said, aghast.

"Hold on, wait," the Conjurer said, as the Stranger reached for his rifle. "Don't be hasty—hello, what do we have here?"

The Stranger let go of the rifle. The clowns, he saw, were not alone, for ambling behind them came a ferret-faced individual, and he held a long and nasty-looking whip which he let whistle through the air idly as he walked. He saw them, and winked. It was then that the Stranger realised they had not been alone for some time. Out of the haze of substance the men came sliding like tightrope walkers, from all directions, and they surrounded the three travellers.

They wore oversized striped blazers with too many pockets and too many buttons sewn on them. They wore straw hats that looked like plum cakes, and large bow ties, and bright yellow fake gerberas in their lapels. They carried knives up their sleeves and guns on their belts, under the blazers, and they wore sharpened spurs on their boots. Their faces were uniformly gaunt. In their eyes, the pupils were mere pinpricks of black swallowed within a dirty-pink iris. They looked like they always spoiled for a fight.

The Conjurer groaned. "Oh, no . . . ," he said. "Not fucking *carnies.*"

"Friends of yours?" the Kid said.

"No one's friends with a carnie, Kid," the Conjurer said.

"They ain't got no friends and they ain't got no *moral compass* and they'd knife you as soon as look at you. I don't know *what* they're doing this far into the Doinklands. They live on the edges of the Désert de Soleil and war with the strongmen tribes and their bearded ladies. Shit, Kid. Nobody likes a carnie."

"Keep your hands nice and loose where I can see them."

The man who stepped forward was taller and lankier than the others and his hair was long and dirty, and a scar ran down the left side of his face. The four clowns went past with their cargo of substance. Behind them the Stranger could see the next cart, and the one behind it, already emerging out of the mist.

"And who might you three gentlemen be?"

"Just travellers, passing through," the Stranger said, pleasantly enough.

"Armed like this?"

The Conjurer barked a laugh. "Wouldn't you be?" he said.

The carnie inched his head, acceding the point.

"Jericho is fallen," the Stranger said. "Colossi and pupae are battling once more in the Thickening. We had no desire to become embroiled in the war, so we headed as far away as possible. . . . We're looking for work."

"Work? What sort of work?"

"The sort a man can do with a gun in his hand," the Conjurer said, and laughed.

"Or a pack of cards," the Kid said.

"There ain't no work here," the carnie said, and spat. "Not unless you're a carnie . . . or a clown." He laughed. His teeth were white and even.

"Just what *is* this place?" the Kid said. "It's not on any maps."

"Hole," the carnie said.

"Hole?"

"Hole," the carnie said, with finality.

The carnies edged them along. The three travellers had no choice but to be led. They moved deeper into the territory. More and more carts arrived and more and more clowns. Some pulled the loaded carts and others ferried rocks and others carried large planks of wood, and all this while the air was thick and hazy with fine powdery substance, and it was not long before the men came to the ledge and then they finally saw it.

The hole gaped out of the broken land like a giant wound in the Escapement. Even the Colossi would have been dwarfed inside it. The walls on the far side were visible only as a hazy, unreal cliff-face. It looked as though a giant's fist had come out of the sky and punched clear through the abdomen of the Escapement, tearing it open and bleeding.

The hole was filled with clowns.

There were more clowns down there in that crater than the Stranger had ever seen. Whitefaces, Augustes and tramps, Grotesques and Pierrots, Bozos and Dinks and jesters and Fools.

Boss clowns, shackled like the rest, moved among them, shoulders slumped in mute defeat. The clowns trod the white earth with their long red feet. It was hard to tell them apart. Fine substance clung to their clothes, their arms, their faces. They held drills and spades and shovels. Tracks led down the slope into the hole and came back with cargo, and every few seconds, in the distance, the Stranger could hear a carnie shout, "Fire in the hole!" and this was followed by an explosion, and then another. Drifting through the floor of the mine he could see ghostly cars, ghost men walking, and cats that slunk between the mine and the streets of that other place. Planted in the ground down below he could see a traffic light.

It was not ghostly but solid, firm. He realised with horror that it must have somehow slipped from that other place to the Escapement and there it remained, an impossible relic. Somehow, the sight of that traffic light, in all its ordinariness, was worst. It did not belong here, its presence was a wrong, it was like a splinter in a pussing wound. The sight of the enslaved clowns filled the Stranger with rage, but he controlled it with an effort, and the face he turned on his captors was bland and pleasant, as though he had not a care in the world.

"A mine, eh?" the Conjurer said. He rubbed his white-gloved hands together, as though to keep them warm.

"Not just any mine," the carnie said. "This is the mother lode."

It had to be. The Stranger had been traversing the Escapement for a long time, and was destined to travel for a little while more, but in all this time he had never seen a mine such as Hole. It should not have existed, it was more than a hole in the ground, it was a breach between the Escapement and . . . other places. The man woke with a shudder in the hospital room and looked about him helplessly, spooked by some nameless night terror, and when he looked out of the window he saw not the city streets but the white dusty plains of a crater like something on the moon, and it was full of clowns.

The Stranger looked around the rim of the crater, and he saw the carnies positioned in their little booths, with rifles pointed down at the slaving clowns like shooters at a duck gallery. He said, "You seem to have everything very much under control round here."

"Pride ourselves on it," the head carnie said, and spat again. A cat materialised a few feet away, slunk to the carnie and purred against his leg, then vanished. "Now get a move on."

The Stranger was keenly aware of how close they were to the edge. How easy it would be to topple down there. One push . . .

"Where are you taking us?" he said.

"Up to the mansion," the carnie said. "Let the General decide what to do with you."

"Can't we just shoot them, Charlie?" a younger carnie, face scarred with acne, said.

The head carnie shot him an angry look. "We don't shoot shit without the General's say-so," he said. "You *know* what he's like. And you lot, move it. Ain't got all day."

The Stranger and the Conjurer exchanged a glance, and the Conjurer gave him a wary grin. The Conjurer didn't have an ace up his sleeve . . . but he did have the dynamite. The Stranger gave him a tiny shake of the head. Not yet. Instead, they let the carnies lead them on.

They walked, through the haze of substance. It burned in furnaces scattered all about the place, ghost faces forming out of the smokeless emanations of the cold fires, mouths open in silent screams. They walked, past shackled clowns on the chain gang, past carnies holding rifles and a boss clown being whipped against a spinning wheel of death, but never uttering a sound. They walked, along white-smudged dusty trails that resembled the paths slugs make as they pass. They walked, past cranes that dipped and rose, dipped and rose, lifting up rocks and chunks of crystal substance from the mine. They walked past tents where the carnies lived, past older, abandoned excavations, past the severed giant foot of a Colossus, past a broken dream machine half-buried in the ground. And the Stranger began to realise just how *old* this place was, how long this part of the Escapement had been worked. The flesh of the Escapement was at its most tender here, it had been prodded and poked and dug out since long before humanity's arrival. A Cadillac drove towards them, its lights burning. It passed harmlessly through the carnies' bodies and disappeared into thin air. Something else, at the edge of vision, was less easy to quantify. For a moment he had a dizzying sense of wrongness, as though he were beyond the atmosphere, in outer space, and something vast and balloon-like and semi-dead floated like a mote of dust in a giant eye. . . .

They walked, and they walked some more, until they reached at last a hill that must have formed in millennia past from the debris of earlier, more primitive digs, and on top of that hill there stood Hole Manor, and it was to its doors that they wended their way.

The men were very tired and very thirsty by the time they reached Hole Manor, and their clothes were dusty white from the substance, and though they kept their weapons about them they could not use them for the carnies always had them under watch. The carnies were well organised and moved with easy purpose, and there was a practical viciousness in their eyes and in their casual contempt for the three travellers. This was *their* claim, they seemed to say, and they ran it as they saw fit. It could not have been easy enslaving the clowns, for clowns are not naturally given to obedience or order.

There is nothing funny about a clown, but there is perhaps something funny about seeing a clown fall, or so some say. Be that as it may, the men came to the doors of the mansion and there they paused, as the head carnie disappeared nervously inside. On his return he was accompanied by three young girls, in summer dresses, and these apparitions descended on the travellers with cries of delight.

"Look, Constance, he has a top hat! Oh, mister, mister, can you do magic? Show us a trick, make a ducat disappear!"

"With pleasure," the Conjurer said, for he was a man not so much given to vanity as with rightful pride in his skills, and he charmed the girls with all manner of card flourishes and coin vanishes until they clapped in delight.

"Oh, look, Florence, look how *handsome* he is!" and the Kid blushed as the girls pulled at his shirt and admired his necklace with the silver thumb-tip, which they pronounced "Divine!"— and took out his pistols with not a care in the world and spun their chambers round and ooohed and aahhed, "But where did you *find* them, Charlie?"—with delighted amazement.

"On the perimeter, miss. Intruders, miss."

"Oh,bish*bosh*, Charlie! Look at them, Boo, real men. I bet they've been to the city, and know all the latest songs!"

The Stranger watched them warily.

"Oh, stranger, what a frown!" said Florence. Boo and Constance held his arms and pushed their trigger fingers at his cheeks, lifting the corners of his lips—"Turn that frown up-side *down!*"cried Constance in delight, and Boo squealed as the Stranger smiled, for all that he itched to lift up his pistol and shoot them. The carnies watched but kept their distance, and seemed relieved to be dismissed, though the head carnie, Charlie, did put up token resistance—"But the General . . ."— to which Constance said "But of *course* Daddy must see them at *once!*" and that was that.

They were led or dragged inside. It was a very stately home, Hole Manor. The three girls led them down corridors where the carpets were as thick and black as layers of ancient mould. The wainscoting was mottled with spider-web cracks so fine they looked like artisan etchings. The corner posts were crusted with crystals of substance. The ghosts of men in suits and ties walked the corridors holding briefcases. They vanished into closed doors and in the midst of conversation, as though, in that other place, this grand mansion held a bank or some other large seat of commerce. The corridors were lined with doors of different makes and colours, but all were closed. On and on they went, deeper into Hole Manor, until the Stranger began to despair of ever reaching a destination. The mansion was just another snare in the Escapement, he realised. Like the maze where he had first met Temperanza.

Which made him wonder where Temperanza herself was. She'd be somewhere out of sight, yet close. The three men had discussed their strategy before reaching Hole, and they had chosen to ride in openly. "You can catch more flies with honey than you can by skulking like a clown in a mine, as the saying goes," the Conjurer had argued, and when they'd looked at him, confused, he'd said, "Whatever it is we're facing, we won't be able to take all of them by force."

So here they were. Another corridor and another turn and another, and just when the Stranger thought they would never escape, that they were doomed to wander endlessly down the maze of corridors, they reached the reception hall.

Glittering chandeliers hung from the high ceiling. A warm, cloying breeze blew through the hall. Wan sunlight pierced the haze on the far side, and bookshelves lined one long wall, reaching from floor to ceiling, though all the spines had warped and the letters ran down the leather like smudged tears. The marble floor was dusty with substance and marked with count-less footprints. A long table sat in the northwest corner, laid with plates and cutlery for twenty-odd. It was unoccupied but for a solitary figure at the head of the table, and it was to this man that the three girls led the travellers.

"Papa, we have guests," announced Boo.

"Guests? I've invited no guests, not in centuries," the man said. He took out his left eye and polished it on a napkin before popping it back in its socket. He was short and thick-armed and with a neat, trimmed black beard. He stood at their arrival.

"What new playthings have you found, daughters?"

"A stranger and a conjurer, and one is all but a kid!" Florence said.

"Aren't they fetching?" said Constance.

"Sir, we are but poor travellers passing through—" the Conjurer began, but the old man waved away his explanation.

"Save it," he said. "It matters not whether you're saps or schemers. You're here. The girls do like new toys to play with. Be welcome, for a time. Will you be joining us for dinner?"

"Sir?" The Stranger did not like the implications in the old man's speech.

"Dinner," the old man said. "You do eat, don't you?"

"Yes, sir."

"My name is General Barnum. You may address me as General."

"Yes, General."

"In your journey, have you encountered a preacher, some days' ride from here?"

"We did. There was a battle. He is dead, but so are his killers."

"Ah. I wondered why my men did not return. Very well." He waved his hand. "It does not matter, for all that he was my brother. No doubt he'll pop up again, sooner or later. He always does."

"But sir—I mean, General—the man is dead."

The General smiled. His teeth were white and even. "Yes, yes," he said. "But this is Hole."

In the white corridors with the parquet floors the man walked, to and fro, to and fro. The early morning shift had come and dawn broke outside the windows. The hospital felt livelier, awake. The kitchen workers were preparing meals and the shops on the ground floor had all opened, and visitors began to crowd to the elevators, some to see the new babies born throughout the night, others to visit those relatives who had only just departed. In all this world only the boy was still and unchanged. The machines monitored his heart rate and his blood pressure, fed him liquids, evacuated waste. The nurses came and went with brisk if compassionate efficiency. Nothing had changed throughout the night. The man paced, his old routine dictating the same unchanging movements as the mechanism of a clock. Which stall to use in the public bathroom, which sink to wash his hands in, which nurse was at the duty station, which elevator rose and which went down. He counted windows, people, plastic plants. He counted airplanes passing in the sky. He counted shoes, how many black, how many brown, how many sneakers, what colour socks. He counted two pairs of flip-flops. He counted seven hats.

The clock on the wall was a cheap plastic clock and the hands moved so slowly but they moved all the same. Then it was noon and the ward was busy, and he retreated to the café and had a sandwich. He went down and up the elevators. He paced the corridor. He sat by the boy's bed and tried to read to him, but the words soon stopped making any kind of sense and he ceased in his futility. Time! He was running out of time. He had to find the Ur-shanabi or the boy will—

"More candyfloss?" Florence said. Overhead the chandeliers shone, bathing the dining room in soft yellow light. A ghostly truck passed through the wall and disappeared down the other end. "Is the food to your liking, stranger?"

"It is very nice," the Stranger said. "And thank you." He stared at his plate of bone-white china, and the soft pink cloud of candyfloss that sat on it. He turned the stick forlornly between his fingers. Across from him, the Kid was very close with Constance, sharing strands of spun sugar between them. The Conjurer entertained Boo with card tricks.

"More popcorn?"

"If you don't mind."

"Of course not."

Florence hefted a heaped spoon from the bowl and ladled the popcorn onto his plate. The Stranger chewed without enthusiasm. The Kid laughed childishly as Constance fed him a gummy worm.

The Stranger could smell nothing but substance. It was everywhere, in the air, in the clothes, in the furniture. Outside, the din of the mine never ceased, the machines humming and burping and digging, always digging, and the sounds of distant, underground explosions at regular intervals, and the rustling of the chains.

"Bring me a damn steak," the General said. The Stranger sighed with relief when a servant materialised (though it was just another carnie, in an ill-fitting suit), pushing a service cart. He plonked down several steaming plates on the table and decamped. The General helped himself (with a long three-tined fork), and the Stranger, too, took a steak and began to eat.

"Do you like it?" Florence said, eagerly. "It's rump."

"It's tasty but . . . I've seen no cows?"

The girls giggled. There was something very old and very false about the sound, at odds with their youthful looks. Their dresses, too, were very old, like brides' gowns that had gone mouldy in an attic.

"Did I say something funny?"

The General put down his knife and fork and glared at the girls, and they subsided into a frightened silence.

"Not cows," he said. "Zebras."

"*Zebras?*"

"And sometimes bear. This is clown country, kid. If you can ride it or you can make it dance or you can stick your head in its mouth, then you can eat it."

"Clown country," the Stranger said.

"Was," the General said. A cat came and sat under the Stranger's chair and rubbed its head against the Stranger's leg, then padded softly away and vanished through the wall. "Mine, now."

"The Hole," the Stranger said. "It's very large."

"Biggest substance mine ever discovered," the General said. "A star that fell down from the sky. Made this hole. This Hole. Sacred to the clowns." He snorted. "Clowns," he said. "Makes you laugh, doesn't it."

But no one laughed around the table. The Stranger had lost his appetite. There was punch, served in giant jugs, and he drank from it though it never sated his thirst. It was red and smelled of mouthwash and gin and shatkora. It had large crystal chunks of substance floating in it but that seemed to make no difference. Everything in that place was covered in substance. The Stranger drank. A band, still made of carnies, struck up a dance. They played fiddle and harmonica and the washtub bass, stovepipe and kazoo. First Boo drew the Conjurer to his feet, and then the Kid was doing a wild ragtime with Constance, and then the Stranger too was on his feet, dancing with Florence, and the beat grew faster and their steps more frenzied, and the chandeliers twinkled in the candlelight and the punch flew freely and the ghosts, too, were dancing now, in that other place, like mimes in a mirror. The Stranger had a vague sense of unease, but there was nothing to pin it down to, there was nothing but the music and the candlelight and the girls in white moving like cloth in the wind, like white dresses on a clothesline, like scraps, faster and faster and fa—

The flash of a nervous grin as the last of the carnies scuttled out warned him. The Stranger sidestepped the dance and for just a moment he looked upon the scene not as he thought it was but as it was. He saw the Kid and the Stranger shambling, and the three creatures—things—these women in white, how crude their features were. Crystal substance grew upon their skin and colonised their eyes. They were like pillars of salt, like rotted driftwood crusted with sodium chloride. And yet, in a fashion, they lived. And yet, in a fashion—they hungered.

He shrank back from Florence with a muted cry of horror— of revulsion!—but she laughed, and drew him to her, and he was powerless to resist. Her lips touched his. He tasted emptiness—an awful coldness—a bright explosion—

Then nothing. The Stranger was falling, in a black emptiness where giant forms of light glared. Space, he thought.

Perhaps it was outer space. The Escapement was a fleck of dust in the distance, yet so lovely: he could see all its features so clearly, the flowing Nikulin and the wide Chagrin and the Désert de Soleil and the Great Salt Lakes and beyond them the Pillars of Nisir.

Beyond the Pillars there was no light, and he knew then that he was staring at the Mountains of Darkness. He focused, and the Ur-shanabi came into view, the Plant of Heartbeat, growing all on its own at the highest peak. How lovely it was! he marvelled. He could see each of its petals, its quivering leaves. The Stranger had travelled the Escapement for a long time, and he was destined now, he saw, to travel just a little bit farther. With a sign he returned to his body, held still in the dance by lovely Constance, and he smiled at her, tenderly. How happy they could all have been, in Hole!

"No," the Kid said, "no, no, Boo, I don't want to, I don't *wanna*—"

The Conjurer was making those strange little noises small boys make when in the grip of a bad dream.

"Wake up, you fools," he said. "Wake up!"

The Conjurer stumbled. The Kid, with a frightened cry, said, "Daddy!"

It gnawed at the Stranger's soul, that cry. The man left his bedside vigil by the boy and went into the bathroom and he stared at himself in the mirror and his vision blurred. In the reflection he could see a grand ballroom, a table strewn with dirty plates and gnawed-at gummy worms, the stained tablecloth splotched with red ichor. In the reflection three men shied away from three deathly white creatures dressed in ruined wedding gowns. The man reached and rubbed the mirror but the image didn't grow any clearer and it was only when he wiped his eyes that the image sharpened. He stepped back across the divide. The Stranger drew his gun. Florence and Constance and Boo advanced on the men. The Stranger shoved the Kid in the back and yelled, "Run!"

They ran. They were good at running, these men. There are men who stand their ground and fight to the last, and there are those who run and live to tell the tale.

The three girls followed. They moved fast, jerkily, with a certain joie de vivre, hopping after the men, hopping onto the walls, and Boo hung from the ceiling, and stuck out her tongue after the running men, like a frog catching flies. Her tongue was very long and very pink. The Stranger and the Conjurer and the Kid ran down the corridor and turned and ran and turned and ran. But the girls cheated and passed through the walls and appeared ahead of them, laughing and calling out, "Alakazam!" and "Aunt Sally!" and "Ballyhoo!"

The Kid took potshots. They missed, or if they hit they made no damage. The Stranger and the Conjurer saved their ammo. They ran with frenzied determination, not speaking, breathing heavily. But the maze of corridors seemed endless, and they could find no way out.

All mazes, it has been pointed out previously, are ultimately solvable. There is the random mouse approach, and there is wall following, there are the Pledge and the Trémaux. But mazes on the Escapement were not always *static*, and the unwary traveller using one such method might find that the maze could shift unexpectedly around them. The three men kept trying doors on their way, and on one such corridor the third door on the left opened and they disappeared briefly into a large wardrobe filled with heavy fur coats, much eaten by moths. The Stranger felt a cold draught, and made his way deeper into the wardrobe, to seek an exit, and for a moment he smelled fresh pines, and distant snow; but he found nothing but the back of the wardrobe and he retreated back with a vague sense of loss.

"We need to find a way out of here," he said.

"What *are* those things?" the Kid said. "My head hurts."

"You hit the punch?"

"Well, it was *free*."

"Only yourself to blame, then."

"When are we going to rob the mine and get the treasure?" the Kid said.

The Conjurer and the Stranger exchanged amused glances.

"How do you propose carrying it all away, kid?" the Conjurer said.

"I don't know, *Dad*. In a cart or something."

"I don't think you've quite grasped the *scale* of the problem, kid," the Conjurer said. "What happens when a place is too big to be robbed?"

"I don't know, what?"

"If you can't rob it, you have to *own* it," the Conjurer said.

"Own it? What are you going to do with a *mine*?"

They pondered the question. Beyond the door, they could hear the three girls call out, sometimes distant, sometimes near. Their voices echoed down the corridors, multiplying and trailing off on their own.

"There's a way out," the Conjurer said. "Come on."

They listened at the door until the girls' voices, more frustrated now, faded into the distance. The Conjurer opened the door cautiously. "Clear."

They stepped out into the corridor.

"Look for chalk marks," the Conjurer said.

"You marked the way?"

"This ain't my first time at the rodeo."

No maze is unsolvable. But it is a forward-thinking person who makes sure to mark their passage as they go into one. And a conjurer is never short of chalk.

They ran. But this time, they ran with purpose along the endless corridors, searching for a mark. Soon they found one, and then all that remained was to follow the trail. On and on they went, while the wails and cries and laughter of the General's three daughters gradually receded behind. Until at last they burst out of the front doors of Hole Manor, and into silver moonlight.

They stopped, and stared. For this was Hole, but this was not the place that they had left when they first entered the mansion. This was not . . . Hole.

The Stranger looked down at his arms and they were transparent, but when he looked at the other two men they were solid, and he realised that they had no parallels.

They stood on the side of the road of a busy intersection. The moon hung in the sky, but it was the only thing visible above, and unlike on the Escapement it was not broken. There were no stars, and the streetlights shone in a soft eternal yellow. Cars and trucks crawled along the four-lane roads, their lamps shining. A cat emerged beside the three men, purred, rubbed itself against the Stranger's leg and wandered away along a pavement strewn with cigarette butts and broken bottles. The traffic lights flashed red and green and yellow. The cars crawled and crawled and music blared out of the speakers of a white Buick. The Kid looked at the scene with awe on his face and said, "What is this place?" and then he looked at the Stranger and said, "Hey, you're a ghost!"

"I am not a *ghost*," the Stranger said, but the Kid wasn't paying attention. "This must be what the circus is like," he said. "I've always wanted to visit the circus."

"The circus isn't what it's cracked up to be," the Conjurer said. He looked very out of place in his black suit and top hat and his very white gloves, and his silver-handled pistols. The Stranger worried a police car would go past and see them with their weapons. But there was no one around, they were on some no-man's-land, a traffic island, and an overhang for foot traffic made of rusted steel was the only way out. He began for the stairs.

"When did he turn into a ghost, Dad?"

"I told you not to call me that."

"Where are we?"

The Conjurer sighed. "We're at that other place, Kid," he said.

"I never thought it was real," the Kid said.

"No," the Conjurer said. "It does seem far-fetched."

They followed the Stranger up the stairs and along the bridge. Overhead on a low hill there stood a grand old bank building with stone columns, and on the other side, one block away, the Stranger could see—

The hospital, he thought, with a sudden chill. This had never happened before. Should not have happened. It was Hole, it had drilled a hole so far down the substrata of the Escapement that it came clean through the other side, into that other place. He could go there right now. He could see the boy, he could tell him everything, about the Titanomachy, and las máquinas de sueños, and what happened in Jericho, and, and . . .

But he saw that his form was fading even further as he

walked. He was becoming translucent, and when his hand accidentally brushed the railings it passed clean through them. He was not meant to be there, he was a reflection of the man in the hospital or the man in the hospital was a reflection of him. He did not know if he dreamed that man or if that man dreamed him. He hastened his steps and almost tripped coming down the stairs on the other side of the footbridge. The other two chased after him but he paid them no mind. He reached a road lined with shops. All the buildings were very tall and rose overhead, blocking the sky. A newspaper blew past in the wind and a homeless man went clear through him and grinned with a toothless mouth. He could hear the Kid's delighted sounds behind him and the Conjurer saying, "Leave him, we'll have to make our own way back—"

He paid them no attention. I'm not even really here, he realised in horror. A couple walked towards him, the man pulling up an umbrella and the woman laughing at something he must have said, and they too walked through him as though he was not really there. His feet sank into the ground. He had to get out of that place. He saw a plain wood door leading to one of the above-shop apartments and tried it, but his hand kept slipping through the handle. When he at last gained purchase it was locked. He ran with increased desperation, tried door after door. But the buildings themselves began to lose definition and he could see the naked skeleton of pylons and beams, wires running everywhere. Why were there so many *wires*?

He reached the front of a convenience store. He could see the counter inside, a turbaned man behind it, a row of cigarette packets, gum, condoms. The shop was awash in light. He stepped in through the open door. The door pinged, once. The Stranger stepped into the light.

◆ ♠ ◆

He emerged into a long dark tunnel. He could not see the other two. The tunnel was hewn deep into the rock. The walls shone with wet substance. He could see the crystals embedded in the rock. He ran his finger over a seam, lightly, and tasted it. Hole. He was back in the mine. Lights were erected along the tunnel and he made for the nearest one, not knowing whether he was going deeper into the mine. He heard a deep humming sound. At first it meant nothing to him. He reached the light and plunged back into the darkness. On his way he saw the first clown.

The clown was a Hobo and he was alone. His feet were chained and he dug into the rockface with a pickaxe. And as he dug, he hummed.

The Stranger passed the clown and as he reached the next light fixture he saw a group of shackled clowns digging into a rich seam of crystal, and they all hummed in unison, a deep and thrumming sound that ran through the rock and was magnified in the crystal substance until it seemed it could alter the very shape of the world. And he realised then that, in their own, curious fashion, the clowns were singing.

It was this eldritch subterranean song that carried him, deeper and deeper into the mine, along that dark tunnel, traversing the twilit world from one lamp post to another. Into the song he went, into a sort of wakeful dreaming, and his shadow travelled by his side. He began to see the crystals blossom along the walls as new seams were found and not yet exploited. He saw there traces of the ancient Escapement, its hidden layers. The silver fin of a struck ship, the earlobe of a Colossus, a broken wind chime still making eerie noise and shifting the air and light around it in disturbing ways, the skeleton of a giant, ossified boss clown with seven elongated toe bones. The darkness sang to him ahead. He walked between the lights along the darkness, until there were no more lights, and no more relics, and the clowns' song vanished behind him, and he was all alone in the total, all-consuming dark.

There was no more ground, there was no more floor. The Stranger fell, into Hole.

What he saw there, in that null-space, he couldn't, later, recall. Only vague and fleeting sensations, somewhere far older than humanity's newborn existence, out there between the stars, where huge, black machines floated, dead and unresponsive, in the vastness of space. The Stranger floated there, in that ancient graveyard. He could make no coherent shape out of the vast objects he passed. They were larger than worlds, and dormant, all—all but one. For one of these ancients opened an eye as large as a moon, and *saw*—saw *him*! And it spoke to him, in some alien fashion, and whispered tales of a younger age, and of machine minds which fell from the sky one day onto the Escapement, through some hole torn out of space and time and dream, and for an era made it in their shape. They had wakened the Colossi and the pupae umbrarum, who took on their shapes as they took the shapes of whichever generation of species came upon the Escapement, as all living, dreaming beings do.

But nothing lives forever . . . , the ancient thing whispered, there in the null-space. *What is it you seek, stranger?*

215

The Ur-shanabi, the Stranger said, *The Plant of Heartbeat,* which can cure even time.

The healing plant, yes, yes, the ancient machine said. *We had a different name for it, and in our minds it took a different shape. I had smelled of the flower, stranger. In my youth I had undertaken the long and perilous journey to the Mountains of Darkness, to seek that rarest of blooms. And I alone remain, here, in this desolation, with my people all about me as still and cold and lifeless as the ice-moon of Amarok. Is this what you wish for?*

Tears strangled the Stranger's throat. *No,* he whispered, in that place of null-sound. *Only a moment, a single breath, for the boy, for the boy to live.*

The old machine was silent then, for a long while. Then it sighed, a single, drawn-out exhalation, of cosmic ice, and dust, and X-rays. Then it closed its eyes, and it was still. The current caught the Stranger and lifted him up and tossed him away. He fled towards a small red sun. It opened and he plunged towards it, and once again he fell into the hole.

He emerged out of a tunnel mouth. He was inside the giant crater. He heard a shout overhead and saw one of the carnie guards take aim at him from the rim. The Stranger drew his pistol and fired, and the carnie's head exploded and he toppled over the rim and rolled down into the crater.

A hail of bullets rained down on the Stranger from on high and he ran, found shelter behind a storage shed. Shackled clowns ambled around him, oblivious. He held his fire. There had to be a way out of this hole. He risked a look out.

For just a moment, he thought he saw the flash of white

gloves, a silent gesture. A carnie fired and hit a clown. The clown fell and lay on the ground, close by the Stranger's hideout. He stared at the clown and the clown stared back, and the Stranger felt a terrible, burning anger as the clown died. This could not go on, he thought. He rose from his hideout then, oblivious of the danger. His guns were in his hands and he ran, and as he ran he fired back at his attackers, sending carnies toppling down.

They fired on him. They tried to take him out, but something else moved up there, something silent and unseen, and it killed the carnies like a vengeful Harlequin. A mining cart descended down on him at speed, loaded with carnies, all firing, their faces twisted in jubilant hate. He pulled out a stick of dynamite and lit it and tossed it into their cart and threw himself away, rolling. The cart exploded, throwing shards of wood and pieces of metal and chunks of flesh in all directions. Dust stung his eyes. When he could see again he found himself at the feet of a giant clown boss. The clown looked down on him with an inscrutable expression. His feet were shackled. The Stranger lit a second fuse and stuck the dynamite between two links of the chain and ran from there. The explosion tore the metal with a horrible wet sound. When the Stranger looked again the boss clown was free.

Something flitted across the face of the boss clown. He bent down and picked up a giant axe. He held it in his hands as if uncertain. Then he set to work.

The Stranger made it to the slopes. The shooting was more sporadic now, the carnies firing in disorder while return fire threatened them. He began to climb. Down below, the clowns had unshackled one by one. They held the tools of their forced trade as though unsure of what to do with them: axes and lanterns and spades. Some held the metal chains that had bound them. The Stranger scrambled up the slope and though bullets pinged near him, the shooters were soon silenced. He reached the rim and hands pulled him up, and he found himself staring at Temperanza's grinning face.

"You're the nicest goddamn dame that ever lived," the Stranger said.

"The more I see of men, the more I like dogs," Temperanza said. "Come on. You lot really messed this up again, didn't you."

"I thought everything was going brilliantly," the Stranger said. He pulled out his gun and fired at Temperanza. She didn't move. The bullet hit the carnie behind her, who fell to the dirt with a little surprised sigh.

"Did you take care of the General?" the Stranger said.

"You were supposed to do that," Temperanza said.

"We got . . . distracted," the Stranger said.

"Of course you did," Temperanza said. She sighed. "Never send a man to do a woman's job," she said.

She walked and the Stranger followed. They traced the rim of the crater, searching for carnies, but many of the carnival men had abandoned their posts by then. On the other side of the rim, the Stranger thought he could see two tiny figures moving with a similar purpose, and he felt a sense of relief that his two comrades had come back from that other place. It was not meant for them.

The clowns were humming again. They had gathered down in the crater, a mass of Hobos and Augustes and Whiteface clowns, led by the boss clowns, armed with chains and axes and spades. The Stranger had never seen so many clowns all gathered in one spot. It was a full circus. And as they gathered they hummed, but it was a different sound now, a new, strong, joyous vibration that shook the rocks and burst the substance crystals, and then the clowns began to climb their way out of the hole. The remaining carnies saw what was happening, and the fight left them, and they ran. The Stranger and Temperanza met with the Kid and the Conjurer and the four of them made for the mansion. The clowns emerged from the hole and flooded across the desolate landscape of the mine, parting around the four travellers. They moved silently but with grim determination. The mansion towered above them on its hill. And as they marched across the plains to reach it, the great doors of Hole Manor opened, and the old general stepped out, and his three daughters were beside him.

As they stepped down to the plains, a hush fell over the circus of clowns. The General looked at them with his single good eye and sneered.

"You're nothing but a bunch of clowns!" he screamed. "Nothing but a bunch of . . . a bunch of . . . !" Words deserted him. The Stranger watched him, and saw him then for what he truly was. Not a man at all, but an embodiment of an idea, just another denizen of the Escapement, re-enacting a role. The Stranger had travelled the Escapement for a long time, and he was destined to travel on it for a little while longer, and he had met those of the Major Arcana before.

"Nobody likes a clown!" the General screamed. "Freaky, creepy, twisted, maddened, evil, strange, *other*! You awful white-faced, red-nosed monstrosities! You, you . . . !" Words abandoned him again. The General pulled out his guns. His daughters laughed, a maddened shriek of sound that filled the air.

Then the clowns were upon them.

◆ ♠ ◆

The Stranger watched Hole Manor burn. It burned in white cold flames, and the faces of ghosts from that other place kept emerging out of the billowing fire, mouths open in silent shrieks, but other than that it was strangely peaceful.

The Conjurer had disappeared in the melee. The Kid had gone looking for him but returned empty-handed. When he looked in his pocket, however, he found a short note, scribbled on an ace of spades, the contents of which he kept to himself. And a present: a miniature set of gold linking rings.

"I guess that's that, then," the Kid said. He tried to pull the rings apart but they just clanged against each other. He stared at them for a moment longer, then shrugged and put them back in his pocket.

"Did he say where he went?" the Stranger asked.

"Somewhere where there's an audience," the Kid said. "Somewhere where they still like magic."

"I never liked magic," Temperanza said. "All that pulling coins out of ears and breaking clocks and, you know . . ." She shuddered. "Spoon-bending."

The Kid shrugged again. "I'm not much of a fan either," he said.

The clowns had gone. Hole was left abandoned, its treasure piling uselessly where it fell. All that mined substance. It would be best, the Stranger thought, to disperse it widely. So much of it in one place distorted things.

"What will you do now?" he said.

The Kid looked at Temperanza and she smiled. "We thought we might ride together a while."

"Oh," the Stranger said, and he smiled too. They looked good together, the bounty hunter and the Kid, he thought. He hoped they wouldn't get into too much trouble together—though he rather expected they will.

The Stranger bid them farewell as the sun set low over the horizon. He gave the Kid an awkward hug. "I'll see you, Kid," he said.

He tipped his hat to Temperanza, who nodded back. "Stranger."

He left them then.

The Stranger rode out of Hole on a horse that bore no name, traversing the silent, now abandoned, ghostly landscape. The map was in his pocket. It felt good to ride alone again. He knew where he was going, and he knew who he was. The Plant of Heartbeat was within his grasp, he knew that now. It was close.

There was yet time.

The Stranger rode out of Hole and into the west, towards the setting sun.

ELEVEN:
THE HERMIT

THE STRANGER rode for many days and many nights in the wilderness. The land was red rocks and dry creeks, which the Stranger crossed, and dead and blackened trees.

The sun rose each morning and set each night, and the Stranger's shadow followed him from dawn until dusk by his side. He began to scent salt in the air and he thought he must be coming close to the Great Salt Lakes beyond which lie the Mountains of Darkness.

One night the Stranger saw the flashes of asterisks and curlicues and ankhs on the horizon that meant a storm was coming. He worried that the Titanomachy had ranged this far onto the edges of the world, and he changed his course to avoid the storm. He rode fast, his horse uncomplaining, and he came unexpectedly upon a maze of tall misshapen cliffs above dry riverbeds, and there he saw a light on top of the cliffs.

It was a single unwavering light, like a lantern hung out as a signal to travellers. And though the Stranger was wary of the Escapement's traps, nevertheless he traversed the narrow paths that led up to the cliffs, until at last he came to a cave.

An ordinary oil lamp did indeed hang outside of the cave, on a stave driven into the ground. The Stranger dismounted from his horse and drew his pistol and both he and the horse entered the cave.

"Be not afraid, stranger. Come in peace."

The voice was rough, as though its speaker was not much used to speech. The walls of the cave were covered in moss. It was warm and dry, and a small fire burned cleanly farther back. A heap of dry wood was stacked neatly nearby.

As for the speaker, he stood by the fire, dressed in a simple robe and leaning on a staff. His beard was long but kempt. His eyes were deep and keen. He carried no weapon that the Stranger could see. The Stranger settled his horse near the entrance and advanced to the fire.

"Here," the hermit said. He went to the horse and patted him, and the horse snorted. The hermit brought out two small, wizened apples and fed them to the horse, who munched contentedly.

Outside, the storm seemed set to sweep over the canyon. Ankhs and crosses flashed like fireflies and the Stranger heard the tread of giant feet, and shivered. He had had enough of the machinations of Colossi and pupae.

"You have come from afar," the hermit said.

"Yes."

"From that other place."

"Yes," the Stranger said, surprised. It was seldom that such matters were discussed so openly on the Escapement.

"You carry a great burden."

"You seem very perceptive, hermit."

The hermit shrugged. "You travel alone to the edges of the world, stranger. Make the inference."

The Stranger was forced to smile. "That seems fair. I am travelling to the Mountains of Darkness, to seek the Ur-shanabi."

"The Plant of Heartbeat. Yes. I have heard that it flowers in the dark. But stranger, no traveller who crosses the twelve double hours of the night ever returns."

"You know much of what lies beyond?"

"It is said that, beyond the Great Salt Lakes, the land is populated by herds of lions, and wild scorpion men. But whether that is true or not, I could not tell you. You must pay the ferryman to cross the waters. Beyond lies the tunnel."

"I have a map," the Stranger said. Perhaps he felt a little defensive. "From Jefferson & Norvell, Medici, of Jericho."

"I heard Jericho has fallen."

"You hear much, here in the wilderness?"

"I hear the loons cry, and the earth tremble when the wild Harlequinade passes," the hermit said, complacently. "And they tell me that the old general who ruled over Hole is vanquished once again into the Doinklands, there to take on a new shape and form."

"You seem remarkably well informed, hermit."

Outside, the storm intensified. The hermit nodded, as though listening to something only he could hear. He pulled back his hood, and the Stranger took a step back when he saw the living shapes that moved over the hermit's skin. The hermit disrobed, with quick, assured gestures, and stood there naked in the light of the flames.

The hermit's entire body was covered in tattooed shapes, in bright inks of balloon-yellow and clown nose–red, mime-white and reptile-green. And as the Stranger watched, they *moved*, and he saw the intricate detailed mechanism of it, like tiny cogwheels moving in the exposed escapement of a clock.

The mountains of the Grand and Petit Philippe were there, and the Big Rock Candy Mountains. He could see the River Nikulin as it flowed into the lake, and the ruins of Jericho, where stone statues as tall as cliffs now stood in awful silence. As he watched, a fist rose from the dirt of the Doldrums, and something awful and rancid resembling a clown shambled back into being with a cleaver in its hand. On the plains of the Thickening he could see men and women in wagons heading north and east and south and west, fleeing the Tita-nomachy, but many of them were not people at all but merely people-shaped, and shadows animated them. He knew then that the war was eternal, that it was within himself just as it was external to it. Shadow battles stone; the lizard scuttles from the glare of the sun. So it is said on the Escapement, though what it means, he never really understood till then. He saw the Conjurer ride far and small, a black dot with white gloves in a wide expanse of desert, with a merciless sun beat-ing down. The bones of great creatures lay in the sand, and the Conjurer's horse traversed the ribcage of some fallen giant. Ahead of him was a circus's Big Top, several days' ride still away. And he knew then that the Conjurer, for reasons of his own, was at last returning home.

He saw Temperanza and the Kid ride out in the Doinklands. They hunted a vigilante group of *chasseurs de clown* who were a day ahead of them, but they seemed to be closing the gap. Temperanza was laughing, her single eye twinkling in the sun-light. The Kid looked carefree and comfortable, riding beside her, a rifle slung over his shoulder. The Stranger realised, with some surprise, that they seemed happy.

The Escapement was inked into the parchment of the hermit's skin. Or perhaps the hermit was himself the clock in which the Escapement ticked and moved. The Stranger found himself hypnotised by the constant shifting of the land on the hermit's skin. Then he saw himself, riding away from the cliffs and the dry riverbeds of that confluence. The storm had passed and the Titanomachy moved on. In its wake the rider found the debris of the war: a rock turned into a gaping mouth, with red, swollen gums; a golden tree, with fruiting reading glasses; here and there, half-buried in the ground, the skeletons of fish which played lovely, haunting music when the wind passed through them.

The Stranger rode towards the west, through sunrise and through sunset, until he came at last to the shores of the Great Salt Lakes. All was quiet, and the air was filled with the calming smell of bromide, and no waves lapped upon the shores.

In due course he came to the place where the ferryman waited.

When the Stranger awoke the hermit was gone, and sunlight streamed in through the cave entrance. In the ring of stones the fire was dead, though the embers were still warm. He saddled the horse and set out, away from the canyon. The storm had passed harmlessly in the night. The air felt clear and fresh.

He made good progress riding all throughout that day. Yet by nightfall he came unexpectedly upon a maze of tall misshapen cliffs above dry riverbeds. He thought it must have been a tributary in some long vanished time.

The Stranger traversed the narrow paths that led up to the cliffs, until at last he came to a cave.

A burning torch was driven into the ground outside the cave.

"Be not afraid, stranger. Come in peace."

He went into the cave cautiously. The hermit stood by the small fire, warming his hands.

"I hope this isn't going to keep recurring," the Stranger said.

"The road to the Ur-shanabi is seldom linear," the hermit said.

"Please," the Stranger said. "I need to find it."

"Why?" the hermit said.

And so the Stranger told him. He found many of the words confusing, the concepts hard. It was like dredging up an impossible memory, carried for too long within himself. And yet he told him of the child, how when he was born he emerged from the womb like a miner covered in coal, how he'd cut the umbilical cord and then removed his shirt and held the little person to his chest, skin to skin, giving him warmth, sharing his heartbeat.

"I'd sit every night with him and give him comfort and wait with him until he fell asleep," he said. "And I would do it till the end of time, if only time would let me."

The hermit listened him out in silence. Then he said, "Time is the medium through which we travel, stranger. But our journeys start, and so they end." He looked at the Stranger with compassion. "That first step must have a corresponding last."

"All I seek is medicine!"

"All you seek is escape," the hermit said. He removed his robe then, and the Stranger saw that the hermit's body was made of many shards of mirror. As the Stranger watched they reflected at him the many places of the Escapement, so that he saw the sun set over the snow-capped Maskelyne range and the Copper Fields below, and he saw the acrobats soar high above the Fratellini plains, and a storm of glowing ichthys fish as it burst over the Doldrums. And he saw farther still, to the far end of a hospital corridor, where a man in a janitor's uniform held a mop in his hands.

"And escape is futile," the hermit said. There was infinite regret in his voice.

The man had gone to the bathroom again. When he opened the door he saw the janitor on the far end of the corridor. He stood and stared. A lake of water had spilled over the parquet floor. It separated him from his destination. The janitor came walking towards him, his shoes stepping in the water, plop, plop, plop. The man tensed, with his hands by his sides. It was nighttime, there was a darkness behind the window. The janitor stopped. He stared back at the man. The moment lengthened.

The man took a step, and then another. His feet landed in the water. The janitor did not move out of his way. The man said, Excuse me.

The janitor did not reply.

Excuse me! the man said, a little sharply. There was a plant growing in a flowerpot on the far side of the corridor, by the dark window. Let me pass.

The janitor did not reply. Perhaps he didn't understand. His mop was stationed at an angle. The man was trapped unless the janitor moved aside.

Please, the man said, helplessly. I must pass.

To pass the water you must pay the toll.

Excuse me?

He looked again but the janitor had gone. The man pressed on. His feet trod in the water, then he was through the puddle and on the other side. He pressed on. The corridor length-ened. All light was gone. The man walked on. He walked and walked. At last he reached the potted plant.

He reached to pluck it, but all his fingers touched was cheap plastic.

When the Stranger awoke the hermit was gone, and sunlight streamed in through the cave entrance. He saddled the horse and set out, away from the canyon. It was a muggy day, and they made slow progress, over rocks that cast long shadows, and the horse's hooves scattered dreaming lizards, who fled from the glare of the sun.

As night fell, the Stranger and his horse came unexpectedly upon a maze of tall misshapen cliffs above dry riverbeds. A sole point of light shone high overhead. The Stranger and his horse climbed the steep and narrow roads until they reached the entrance to a cave.

A cabochon hanging from a metal pole driven into the ground cast bright yellow light.

"Gather round, gather round, boys and girls, here come the clowns!"

The Stranger stepped into the cave. The hermit stood in the centre of the ring, wearing a red tailcoat and a top hat. In his hand he held a whip which he swished through the air.

"Step right up, step right up, see the moving statues and the shadow puppeteers, see the one-eyed lady and the man who makes ducats disappear, marvel at the Stranger as he meanders on his way—"

"We *really* have to stop meeting like this," the Stranger said.

The ringmaster shrugged. "The road to the Plant of Heartbeat is long and filled with pain. Uncertainty is certain. Tiny forms in huge, empty spaces."

"This is just another maze," the Stranger said. "Just another snare in the Escapement."

He drew his gun and put it to the ringmaster's head.

"I want out," he said.

"This way to the Egress," the ringmaster said.

He gestured. Around them the cave expanded, disappeared. The Stranger saw the aerialists high above, leaping nimbly. He smelled popcorn and cotton candy and sweat. There were people in the stands all around the ring, cheering. A ballyhoo swept the stage. A charivari of clowns rushed onto the ring and began jumping into the air on giant trampolines.

"You can't shoot me," the ringmaster said, but gently. The Stranger turned and looked and he saw that the ringmaster now bore the Stranger's own face. He stared at his own reflection.

"Let me out," he whispered.

"Just follow the signs," his self said.

The Stranger squeezed the trigger. The water pistol jerked in his hand as a weak stream of water hit the ringmaster's face. His face ran down with paint. The people in the stands cheered. The Stranger threw the useless pistol on the ground. An arrow sign, lit by coloured cabochons, pointed deeper into the cave. He followed the sign. THIS WAY TO THE EGRESS.

The noise of the crowds receded behind him. He passed the tigers' cages. He passed the backyard of the circus called the G-Top, where a group of grafters and gauchos and joeys were drinking and playing cards. He passed a grease joint. He came to the Midway. It was surrounded by sucker netting. He passed through, passed rubbermen and spec girls, ropers and web girls, until he came at last to the concessions stand.

There was a body of water beyond the ticket booth. It stretched out to the horizon, until it met an all-consuming darkness. A hand-painted arrow sign pointed beyond the booth, and the Stranger was not surprised to see it said, THIS WAY TO THE EGRESS.

"I'd like a ticket, please."

"Then you must pay the price," the ticket seller said.

"What is the price?" the Stranger said.

"Something precious."

The Stranger pulled a handful of ducats from his pocket and the ticket seller laughed. The Stranger dropped the ducats to the ground. A small boat, he saw, bobbed on the water, waiting.

"What is the price?"

"What is the most precious thing you have?"

The Stranger thought about a day in early spring. They had been to the park. The sun shone down and green parakeets laughed in the high branches of the trees. They found a log and sat down with their backs against it, their faces to the sun. And the boy came up to him, unexpectedly, and put his arms around his neck and gave him a wet noisy kiss on the cheek. He said, I love you, Dad. It was the first time he'd ever said it.

"No," the Stranger said. "Not that. Anything but that. Please."

The ticket seller did not answer. The moment lengthened.

The Stranger reached deep within himself and plucked out a bit of his heart.

TWELVE:
THE PLANT OF HEARTBEAT

ON THE SHORES of the Great Salt Lakes the ferryman waited.

The Stranger kept having the discomforting feeling that he'd forgotten something. But since he couldn't remember what it was, he thought that it couldn't have been that important.

The air smelled of bromide and the sun hung in the sky. No fish frolicked in that dead sea and no waves disturbed its shores, and when the ferryman's oars sank into the water they pushed hard against the heavy salt.

As they journeyed across the Great Salt Lakes the sun traversed the half globe of the sky, from one horizon to the other. From high above, the Great Salt Lakes seemed infinite, and only a tiny black dot moved across the surface of the water.

But from the point of view of the Stranger the lake was merely a lake, the boat large enough if uncomfortable, and his purpose clear.

As for the old ferryman, he spoke not a word, but pushed the boat ever onwards, with the Stranger dozing in the hold, and the sun traversing the sky until it leaned to kiss the far horizon. The mountains rose above the Great Salt Lakes. With nightfall the ferry docked on the far side of the lake and the Stranger disembarked.

The ferryman watched him go.

The Stranger traversed the plains below the mountains. He made camp for the night in the foothills of Mashu. He lit a fire with fragile driftwood, crusted in salt. When he slept, he drifted to that other place, where the man was sitting vigil by the boy's bedside. The life support machines never wavered in their function. The soft sounds they made were like footsteps in the night. When the Stranger woke he did not know whether it was daytime or night, for such distinctions no longer mattered.

He climbed the mountain. At times there was an easy path to follow. At others, he made his way by hand and foot, seeking small fissures in the rock, grabbing for a hold on ancient roots and branches. The trees that grew on the side of Mashu were large and tangled, like giants of old, with mottled bark and a knotted mass of fibres. Tiny lizards scuttled in the undergrowth and heavy stones stood guard over the mountain paths, like so many sown dragon's teeth.

The Stranger climbed Mashu. Onwards and onwards he climbed, a tiny figure against that huge indifferent mass. Onwards he crawled. The sky overhead was a panorama of swirling orange and reds, an eternal sunset.

At last the Stranger reached a plateau below the peak. Here vast and trunkless legs of stone stood guard over a dark entrance.

The Stranger approached cautiously and his shadow walked beside him. Standing at the tunnel mouth were three mimes wearing masks. The masks were bone-white. One mask smiled. One mask cried. And one mask was entirely blank.

The mimes blocked the Stranger's way.

He said, "Please. I wish to pass through."

The mimes shrugged, wordlessly.

The Stranger said, "I seek the Plant of Heartbeat."

The mimes mimed sorrow, rubbing their eyes with their fists. The laughing one mimed counting ducats.

The Stranger said, "I have paid the ferryman."

The crying one pointed wordlessly behind the Stranger and shook his finger no, then pointed at the tunnel mouth.

The Stranger turned and looked one last time on the Escapement, for he knew now that to pass beyond it meant forsaking it forever.

Then he turned back and nodded.

The mimes parted for the Stranger.

The Stranger passed into the tunnel mouth.

The Mountains of Darkness lie beyond the known world, on the edge of wakefulness and dream. The man saw them now, as he sat in the room. He had sat in that room for a very long time and was destined to sit just a little while longer. On the bed the boy did not stir. His breathing was shallow and ragged. The man bit on his lip so hard that he drew blood, the better to stifle the scream that was building inside. The clock on the wall was a big round clock. It ticked and it ticked and it ticked.

Although they are called the Mountains of Darkness, and no man alive had ever mapped them, the Stranger realised that he *could* see, in some fashion, when he emerged at last out of the tunnel.

He had travelled the full twelve hours of the night.

A soft silvery glow emanated from the earth itself, and from the curious things that grew there. He saw small, delicate rocks, like fine jeweller's eggs, and shrubs that grew down the rock face like spun sugar. A cool breeze caressed his face. Tiny grey birds chittered overhead.

The Stranger came to a great big tree growing out of the fertile ground by a shallow brook. Small fruit hung from the branches of the tree, but try as he might he could not reach to pluck them. He did not know the name of the tree, though had Jefferson & Norvell, Medici, of Asclepius Gardens been there, they might have been able to furnish him with the scientific name of that genus, which is the *Arbor vitae.*

Flowers grew all about the Mountains of Darkness. They grew on the slopes and in the nooks and crannies of the mountain face and under rocks and trees and by the silent, silver streams, and some were the deep dark of space, and some were white as clay, and some were grey, and all were very pretty: but none was the Ur-shanabi. Their perfume scented the clear air and would have lifted the weariest traveller's heart, but not the Stranger's, for the clock on the wall tick-tocked, tick-tocked. He began searching, in quiet desperation.

A black bird startled him, erupting suddenly over his head,

cawing and beating its wings, but then it, too, flew away, and the Stranger was alone.

In the room the doctors came and went. On the wall clock the minute hand ticked slowly. Sir? Sir? somebody said.

Then: Give him a moment.

It was when he had lost all hope that he saw it. Far away, on the tallest peak! There grew the Ur-shanabi. It alone had colour in that silver-grey world. Red and yellow it burned, like a tiny flame, struggling against great winds. The Stranger hurried. He traversed steep mountain paths and narrow valleys, crossed rivers where tiny silver fish leaped into the air as he swam. He held on to roots protruding out of the ground, found footholds in the smallest faults of rocks. At last he reached the last and tallest mountain and he began to climb. Time lost all meaning. The tiny flame called out to him. Slowly and alone he struggled, climbing. A tiny figure crawling like an ant upon that great dark slope.

When he came to the top, the plant wasn't there.

The little figure on the bed was so still. Wan sunlight streamed in through the window. Soft footsteps in the hall. Was the clock on the wall still ticking? Had it fallen silent? We are all but clowns in this circus called Life. Gather round, gather round, come and watch the show! Father and son walk spellbound through the Midway, see the bright lights of the fair. Smell the cheap hot dogs, the spun-sugar blobs, hear the pitchmen's cries!

At last you come to the Big Top, your hands sticky with sweets. Sawdust on the floor, the lights are bright and bathe your face in yellows, reds and blues. Your little heart lifts in your chest.

Here come the clowns!

The canvas parts to let you in. The seats are full. The bally-hoo sweeps across the ring. The crowd cheers. Here come the clowns!

Do you ever think back to a time when you were truly hap-py? For just one moment, the world is stilled, and everything is filled with infinite possibilities.

If only you could take that moment and distil its essence, preserve it—not forever, but just long enough.

Below the mountain, the Stranger came upon a small calm lake, where shrubs grew along the banks. On the other side of the lake he saw a pair of eyes watching him and, startled, he took a step back.

The face that stared at the Stranger from the bushes on the other side of the lake was pale white and serious. The child's eyes were large and solemn, the mouth an exaggerated stroke of red, the nose a conical red protrusion. The child looked into the Stranger's eyes, with that strangely melancholic expression that is unique to clowns.

The Stranger half-expected him to flee, but instead the boy emerged from his hiding place and stood, and the Stranger saw that he held a bright red balloon in his hand. As the Stranger watched, the child came to the banks of the lake and prodded the water experimentally with his foot. Seemingly satisfied, he took one step, and then another, until he stood on the surface of the water.

Then he seemed to wait. The Stranger felt himself drawn to the bank. He tried the water. To his surprise the water felt elastic. He pressed one foot and then another, and the water held him. The child began to step across the water, lightly, and the Stranger did likewise, and in this manner they traversed the lake from opposite sides until they met in the middle.

The air was so fresh and still and birds sang in the trees and the silver light glowed softly all around them.

The little clown smiled, and it broke the Stranger's heart. There was so much trust in the little child's eyes. The child held the red balloon and passed it mutely to the Stranger.

The Stranger held the string and the balloon bobbed gently in the air. His eyes were wet and it was hard to see clearly.

He let go of the balloon and it rose into the sky.

He felt so happy, suddenly and overwhelmingly happy, though he could not articulate why. But "why" is a question only children, who do not know any better, still ask.

He stood there with the child and they watched the balloon drift farther and farther away, growing ever smaller against the endless sky, until it finally vanished from sight.

AFTERWORD

THE ESCAPEMENT owes a debt to a great many varying influences. The basic plot was very loosely inspired by the Hebrew fairy tale "The Heart of the Golden Flower," created by Z. Ariel in 1930. It, in turn, is based—to some extent at least—on similar stories in Russian fairy tales and in Hans Christian Andersen.

Similarly, I have borrowed from the ancient story of Gilgamesh at several points, and very loosely for some of the structure. The Ur-Shanabi was the ferryman of the dead in Mesopotamian mythology. The Plant of Heartbeat is found in of the Epic of Gilgamesh, while events recounted in Chapter Twelve are somewhat modified from what transpires in Tablet Nine of the story.

The Mountains of Darkness come from stories in the Jewish Talmud about the adventures of Alexander the Great. The mountains are covered in eternal dark, representing the end of the known world.

The Colossi in this book were inspired in equal parts by Percy Bysshe Shelley's poem "Ozymandias" (1818) and by

Czech artist František Kupka's 1903 expressionist painting *The Black Idol (Resistance)*. Where the pupae umbrarum come from, however, I do not rightly know.

I owe a particular debt to Michael Ende's 1984 surrealist collection, *The Mirror in the Mirror: A Labyrinth*, and to Dr Seuss's *Oh, the Places You'll Go!* (1990). Other obvious influences include Sergio Leone's *The Good, the Bad and the Ugly* (1966), the artwork of Salvador Dalí, the work of Shirley Jackson (Chapter Ten), and Tony Collingwood's wonderful animated movie *Rarg* (1998), from which I borrowed the pink flamingos in Chapter Eight.

Some of the terminology I've bent to my own uses in this novel, such as "thickening," "vastation," and "revel," is borrowed from John Clute's magnificent *The Darkening Garden* (2006), as are many of his ideas in that book on the nature of the fantastic.

In Greek mythology, the Titanomachy was the war between the Titans and the Olympian Gods.

Several figures from the Major Arcana of the Tarot appear in this book, including Temperance, The Lovers, The Hierophant, Justice, The Devil, and The Hermit.

Pogo the Clown (Chapter Three) was better known in life as John Wayne Gacy, a notorious serial killer and children's entertainer who was executed in 1994. The Bloody Benders (Chapter Nine) were a Kansas family who preyed on unwary travellers in the 1870s, much as described here.

The Styx (here, Sticks) is in Greek mythology the river that separates the world of the living from the Underworld. Similarly, Lethe is the river in Greek mythology whose water gives the gift of forgetting.

"Jefferson & Norvell" are perhaps better known as Laurel

and Hardy. The scene in Chapter Five of the Kid hanging from the clock tower is inspired by the famous scene in Harold Lloyd's *Safety Last* (1923).

Various clowns, magicians and circus folk lend their names to places and features on the Escapement, including Bobo, Emmett Kelly, Nevil Maskelyne, the Fratellinis, and many others. The Big Rock Candy Mountain comes from the classic 1928 Harry McClintock song.

Many of my books begin years earlier with a short story. In this case, "High Noon in Clown Town," published in *Postscripts #9*, edited by Peter Crowther and Nick Gevers, to whom my thanks, as always.

Internationally renowned author Lavie Tidhar grew up on a kibbutz in Israel and has lived all over the world, including South Africa, Vanuatu, Laos and the UK.

Tidhar won the 2012 World Fantasy Award for his novel *Osama*, a complex tale about the war on terror. That same year, he also won a British Fantasy Award for Best Novella and a British Science Fiction Award for Best Nonfiction. These were followed by the Jerwood Fiction Uncovered Prize–winning and Premio Roma nominee *A Man Lies Dreaming*. Tidhar has, further, been compared to Philip K. Dick by the *Guardian*, and to Kurt Vonnegut by *Locus*.

Tidhar's breakout novel, *Central Station*, received the John W. Campbell Memorial Award and the Neukom Literary Arts Award; it was nominated for the Arthur C. Clarke and Locus awards. It has been translated into ten languages. His next novel, *Unholy Land*, was shortlisted for the Locus, Campbell, Sidewise and Dragon awards, and was on best-of-the-year lists from *NPR Books*, *Library Journal*, and *Publishers Weekly*.

Tidhar's first middle-reader novel, *Candy*, was published by Scholastic UK in 2018. His full-length graphic novel with Paul McCaffrey, *Adler*, was published in 2020. He is also a columnist for the *Washington Post*.

Lavie Tidhar currently lives in London.